THE POWERS
OF THE MIND

THE POWERS OF THE MIND

RONALD J. FISCHER

ARCHWAY
PUBLISHING

Archway Publishing books may be ordered through booksellers or by contacting:

Archway Publishing
1663 Liberty Drive
Bloomington, IN 47403
www.archwaypublishing.com
1 (888) 242-5904

ISBN: 978-1-4808-1807-1 (sc)
ISBN: 978-1-4808-1808-8 (hc)
ISBN: 978-1-4808-1809-5 (e)

Library of Congress Control Number: 2015908610

Print information available on the last page.

Archway Publishing rev. date: 6/5/2015

Oh brave new world
that has such people in it!

—William Shakespeare, *The Tempest*

C H A P T E R 1

STEVEN THOMAS

S teven Thomas, age twenty-seven, was a very bright guy who loved to play tennis. He'd skipped grades in high school, getting his bachelor of science degree in electrical engineering, BSEE, at age nineteen and his MSEE at twenty. He was offered an assistantship to teach math, so he went back and got a joint MA in math and computer science while teaching. He got that at age twenty-two.

After a year, he became somewhat disenchanted with teaching and looked around for another job. He got a job offer from the Boeing Company to work in their space program so he took it. He enjoyed the work, but after two years he got greedy and changed jobs several times to make more money. The jobs, however, turned out to be boring, so he decided to go back to teaching. The summers off would give him more time to play tennis, and San Jose, California, had perfect weather for that. He found out that community colleges paid better than four-year colleges, so he ended up teaching math at San Jose City College under the condition that he also teach Basic Electric Circuits and Computer Programming. While working he always played tennis in his spare time. He eventually joined the United States Tennis Association (USTA) and the Association of Tennis Professionals (ATP) and became ranked, reaching a world rank of 187.

Steve was a game freak. He started playing chess in high school and continued into college. He also picked up contract bridge in college and later played a little duplicate bridge. A Japanese guy in college taught him how to play a game called Go, which was very popular in Japan. He read one book on it and played awhile but did not play it well. It was a difficult game to learn. Then a few of his bridge buddies started playing backgammon, so he picked up that. It was a good gambling game, and he made some money playing. It was a good application of the theory of probability.

Steve thought a lot about the state of the world and society. The world was a mess. Even the United States wasn't that good. Unemployment was considered high. The middle class seemed to be doing worse while the rich got richer. Europe and Canada had much better health care systems. It seemed that quite a few people used illegal drugs. In college he had tried marijuana. It was a great high! What was the harm in that? Some people were in prison for smoking a joint. Drugs should be legalized, he thought. Even the *Economist* magazine said it was the lesser of evils. What could he do? Nothing much, just work and play tennis.

One day Steven and his friend Paul Kist had just finished an invigorating round of tennis. They were both members of the local racket club. Paul was internationally ranked in the triple digits as well, and they practiced together often. They both played the pro circuit occasionally but never made any real money. Paul was a computer programmer at Lockheed in Sunnyvale.

"That was fun, Steve. You made some nice shots."

"Thanks. You made a few good ones yourself. How about a beer at my place?"

"Good idea. We can discuss women and sex." Paul nudged Steve with an elbow and laughed.

Steve biked back home, a distance of two miles, and Paul took his car.

Steve pumped the pedals of his bike hard to try to beat Paul to his place, but he got there just after Paul did. Steve unlocked the door, and they entered together. Steve handed Paul a can of Henry's, and they sat down to chat.

"By the way, Paul, how is your job holding up? I hear programmers are getting to be a dime a dozen."

"Programmers, yes. Good programmers, no. We just hired a couple of new guys right out of school. They are the pits. I think I'm considered one of the best programmers the company has, so I'm pretty secure. Of course, your security is the tops. Nobody who teaches and gets tenure will ever get canned."

"Yeah, it's pretty secure but sometimes pretty boring. Trying to teach calculus to students who are floundering in algebra is not fun."

"Hey, Steve, who is that chick I saw you with the other day down at the coffee shop? She looks pretty good."

"Yeah, Susan. She's pretty neat. Besides being good-looking, she's pretty intelligent. She majored in biology at UC Berkley. She teaches at San Francisco City College. It's funny, though—she doesn't seem to be that interested in biology. I like to watch the *Nature* series on TV, and we sometimes discuss it. We also talk about some TV programs, a movie, or some current events."

"Any sex?"

"No, not yet. I'm waiting for a signal from her. I think she's the marrying type, so maybe sex before marriage is out."

"So you think you might get hitched?"

"I'm not considering it. It's a huge decision. How about you? Who's the latest?"

"Yeah, Karen. She's almost great."

"Why almost?"

"Well, she works for a publishing company. She helps the publisher decide whether a book should be accepted for publication."

"Sounds like a pretty neat job. So explain the almost."

"Well, she wants to be a writer. She's written a couple of short stories and tried to get them published, but they were rejected. Of course, she didn't submit them to the company she works for. So, anyway, she seems a bit depressed about it. She is not really interested in settling down. Mainly wants a career."

"Does that upset you? I didn't think you were interested in getting married. Are you?"

"Maybe eventually. I'm enjoying single life too much right now, and sex with her is great. If she became interested in marriage, I might consider it. She'd have to get over this writing obsession, however. I think that someday I'd like to settle down and have a family."

"Interesting. Good luck with her. Well, I'm getting a bit hungry, so let's call it a day."

"Hey, Steve, how about playing this weekend?"

"I think I'm available. I'll give you a call."

"Okay, see you later."

C H A P T E R 2

A BUZZING IN HIS HEAD

Wednesday, May 30, 2018

Steve awoke with a strange buzzing in his head. It wasn't a hangover—he'd had hardly anything to drink the night before—and was like nothing he had ever experienced before. The previous day he had played several sets of tennis with his friend George Marks. It had been fairly strenuous. Could that be it? He didn't think so. He hoped he wasn't having a stroke or getting some kind of disease.

He had recently bought a new condominium and was in the process of fixing it up to his satisfaction. He decided to buy a fluorescent lamp for his new home office. He had been to the hardware store several times and was on somewhat friendly terms with the owner, Bert.

"Hello, Bert. How are you?"

"I'm fine. What's going on?"

"I need a fluorescent light for my new home office."

Bert led Steve to the lighting section. "Here, this is a great brand."

"Okay, I'll take it."

Steve bought the new lamp and several sets of bulbs. When he got home, he decided to test it first thing, in his true skeptical fashion. He found to his philosophical delight but his practical disgust that it didn't work. He double-checked it with new bulbs, but it appeared that the lamp itself was bad. Annoyed, he took it back to the hardware store.

Bert said, "Hey, you were just here a little while ago. Did you forget something?"

"Sorry to say this, but this light doesn't work. I checked it with several sets of bulbs, and it's the light itself."

"Gee, that's too bad. I've never had this brand fail before. I'll get you a brand new one."

When Steve got home and tested the replacement, however, he was frustrated to discover it didn't work either, even with another set of bulbs.

This highly unlikely event prompted him to draw a bottle of beer from the fridge and sit down to think things over. He felt he was being tested by some kind of god. Of course, that was nonsense. *Why would God, if there is a god, have anything to do with me?* After finishing his brew he got in the car and headed back to Bert's store. This time he was greeted by a slightly puzzled expression.

"What the hell is it this time?" Bert asked.

"You'll never believe this, Bert, but this one's bad, too."

"You'll have to prove that to me, since after you left I tested the first one, and it worked."

"What? That can't be. I checked the first one with several bulbs, so it had to be the lamp. Okay, let's check this one."

After they inserted bulbs and turned it on, the lamp did not light. Bert tried another set of bulbs. It still didn't work.

"There you go, Bert, I was right!"

Bert gave a puzzled frown. "Then why did the first one work when you say it didn't?"

Steve liked Bert; he had a true scientific nature. So how, Steve wondered, did he end up working in a hardware store?

Steve replied, "Let's test the first one again."

"That sounds like a good idea," Bert said with a smile. He then walked to the back room to get the first lamp. Steve could tell from his haste and style that Bert was sure it would work and just wanted to see Steve's face when he proved it.

At this time, a strange thought entered Steve's head. Bert was reliable. If he said it worked, it must have worked. But Steve had checked and double-checked, and it had not worked. Perhaps the law of the excluded middle in logic was about to be violated. Perhaps something could both be and not be at the same time after all. It was an interesting idea but just too fanciful to be true.

When Bert arrived with the lamp Steve felt the euphoria of a child with a new toy even before the box was opened. He could hardly wait for the test. Bert plugged the first lamp in, and, voilà! It didn't work.

"I was right, Bert," Steve stated with emphasis. "It doesn't work!"

Bert stared at Steve and looked aghast. Steve thought Bert was probably as upset with his enthusiasm as he was about being proved wrong. "But it did work after you left," he said rather sadly. "I know that."

Steve said, "I believe you, Bert, and I'm as puzzled as you are. Bert, did you know that we have witnessed something highly unlikely, like rolling two double sixes in backgammon?"

Bert's response surprised Steve. "I play backgammon too," he said with a spurt of enthusiasm. "I never would have taken it up if I hadn't run across this book in the library by a guy named Macgrill or something like that."

Steve said, "You read that book? I read it too some time ago. What a surprise! Bert, you amaze me! We'll have to play sometime."

"Oh, you'll probably walk all over me, what with your college education and all," he declared.

"You never know, Bert. Backgammon is a very forgiving game. By the way, do you play for money, and do you use the doubling cube?"

"Yes to both. It wouldn't be a game without the cube, but I play for small stakes."

Steve said, "You play the right way. Did you know that it's a favorite game in the Middle East? I played with a Turkish guy once, and he didn't use the cube and would not play for money. Anyway, right now I need a new lamp."

"You're right," he said, "but this third one we test before you leave."

"Right on, Bert, go to it!"

Bert dug out a third lamp and plugged it in, and it didn't work either. A test of a fourth lamp yielded the same result. Bert said, "The whole goddamned batch can't be bad." When their gazes met, Steve was pretty sure they were both thinking the same thing.

"Then why did the one that you brought back light after you left?"

Steve grinned ecstatically at their combined genius and noticed that Bert was also grinning.

"There's only one thing true about when all these non-lighting lamps don't light," Bert said with heightened enthusiasm. "Do you know what that is?"

Steve frowned and thought for a few seconds. "Yep—my presence."

"Right on, Steve! I really can't believe it, but the facts are staring us in the face."

"So what do we do now?"

"The only logical thing," Bert declared, "is eliminate you and see what happens!"

Steve's eyes opened wide in surprise at this announcement. *Does Bert want to kill me? No, that's not what he meant. He meant eliminate my presence, not me.* He stared at Bert for what felt like an infinite time.

Bert leaned over and said in a low voice, "Well, what do you say?"

Steve wondered, his mind was awhirl with ideas,

whether the beer had gone to his head because he'd drunk it on an empty stomach. Was Bert an alien from another planet? Had he been transported to another dimension? What was going on here anyway? No matter how unusual this was, though, it was a still a game of logic, he thought. *So play it*, he told himself. *Ignore any semblance to reality, and just use logic.*

"It's simple to find out if it's me. I'll just vacate, and you test again."

"That seems to be the only alternative."

"All right, how far do I have to go?"

Bert shrugged. "There's no way of knowing."

"My car is down the block a little ways. I'll go there and shut the doors. Is five minutes enough to test the four lamps?"

Bert said, "More than enough."

"Okay, I'll see you shortly, Bert."

Out of the corner of his eye Steve could see Bert's child-like enthusiasm for what was going on. It was like he had waited all his life to apply the logic that was in him but had never had the chance before. This was his experiment, and he was looking forward to conducting it.

As Steve headed for his car he thought, *Can this really be happening to me? Was that beer one hundred percent alcohol? Is God punishing me for my disbelief? Is he giving me another chance by showing me his power? Am I crazy? Is this a dream?*

He got in the car and closed the windows. Then he remembered, and at the same time felt, the buzzing in his head. It was still there, faint but the same as before. Could there possibly be a connection between this buzzing and this dream that he was experiencing?

Then he slunk down a little in the seat so the metal parts of the car could stop the possible rays of control, the ones his brain might be emitting, from leaving the car. A minute later, a woman pulled up behind him and walked past him on the sidewalk. She gave him a funny look, walked over to the driver's side of the car, and, since the windows were rolled up, shouted, "Are you okay?"

"Fine," he yelled back. "I'm doing an experiment." He then gave her the *V* for victory symbol, thinking, *What must I look like to her, slouching here on a hot day with the windows rolled up?*

While he waited his allotted five minutes, all sorts of ideas went through his brain. He wondered what was it like to go insane. Unbelievable things would probably go through one's head. As a teacher of math at the local college, he had the pleasure of teaching symbolic logic and the displeasure of realizing only about half of the students understood it despite his valiant efforts. Yet here he was putting it to the test in a most bizarre way.

His five minutes were up. He left the car almost in fear of the results of this experiment.

"Yo, Bert," he said, trying to sound casual. "What have you found?"

"As I logically expected but don't believe, it's you! They all test good."

Steve's eyes widened, and he shook his head. At this

point he felt that either he was in the midst of a nightmare or he was indeed insane. How could this be? Had he finally cracked under the strain of five years of teaching math and logic? He had to leave to be alone to contemplate all this. He was at a loss for words and just stared at Bert. Then, unable to think of anything else he could do, he put up his hand to wave good-bye and said, "I'll see you later, Bert."

"Wait, don't leave yet. Let's test them again while you're here," he said.

Steve said, "Great idea. Why didn't I think of that?"

With the dedication of a true scientist, Bert tested them all again, and none of them worked. "It's definitely you!" he said. They stared at each other. "There must be some kind of rays coming from you. Do you feel unusual in any way?"

Steve then recalled the buzzing in his head. "In fact I do. There's a strange buzzing in my brain, which I've never had before. Something like a bee buzzing."

"That's interesting. Maybe there's a connection. Here's my cell phone number—call me if you want to talk." Bert handed Steve a scrap of paper with a phone number scribbled on it. Steve stuffed it in his breast pocket and staggered toward the door.

Bert said, "Don't forget your lamp. Since you paid for it, it's yours. Maybe you can figure out what's going on."

Steve took it. The drive home was unreal. Luckily, it was short. When he got home he slid into bed, hoping somehow that this was all a dream and when he awoke all would be normal.

C H A P T E R 3

PHYSICAL CONTROL

He lay in bed for awhile and thought about this unique set of circumstances. It seemed that something in his brain was able to affect the external world. How could that be? What should he do? And why would it affect something as silly as a lamp? He dozed off and dreamt he'd been found out and had reporters hounding him, asking all sorts of questions like could he control anything else. He couldn't get away from them. He woke with a start at little after 8 p.m.

He got up and went over to the lamp. The buzzing in his head was still there, but it had changed slightly. It was more pleasant and varied in intensity. As he sat there and listened to it, he discovered it was controllable. He could turn it up or down. Then, to his surprise, he figured out how to turn it off. He then found that he could turn it off and on repeatedly. Then he got a brilliant idea: he would turn it off and see if the lamp worked. Lo and behold, the light worked when he turned the buzzing off.

So I can control it, he thought. *Wait, let me turn the buzzer on to see if the light fails.* He turned the buzzing on, and not quite to his surprise the light failed. He turned it off, and the light worked.

This situation amazed him. He could turn the light on and off with his brain. Where did he get this power? He decided to turn in, thinking that if this were a dream it would be gone when he woke up the next day. He really hoped that it would be gone. He flossed and brushed his teeth and hit the sack. By the time he fell asleep, it was 11:30.

Thursday, May 31, 2018

Thursday morning he woke around 9:30, surprised that he'd slept so long. There was still a slight buzz in his head, but it was milder, actually somehow soothing. He turned it off.

He normally postponed breakfast as late as possible and basically had only two meals a day. He went to the kitchen to fix himself a bowl of old-fashioned oatmeal. Unlike his college days, when he ate lots of junk food, now he tried to eat whole grains, fruit, and vegetables for health reasons. He got out the oatmeal, some strawberries and raisins, and a box of Grape-Nuts, which he usually added to the oatmeal. After adding water to the oatmeal he put it in the microwave for the usual two minutes and opened the utensil drawer to get a knife to cut the strawberries.

The knife popped out of the drawer and flew into his hand.

At exactly the same time he heard a slight beep in his head, but for some reason he felt that he had caused the beep. He laid the knife on the counter and tried to do it again. As before, it popped into his hand. He tried with other silverware and could move them all.

Did it mean that he could exercise mental control over objects, that he had what mystics called telekinesis? He'd never believed in telekinesis, but now it appeared to be a real power—and one that *he* had. Why?

He decided to experiment further. He tried retrieving other utensils from the drawer without touching them and was able to do so with his mental power. He saw a dish in the drainer about ten feet away. He pointed to it, and floated it over to his hand. He tried it with dishes, books, pots, and pans. He could move them all! He could even control the speed that they moved. Could he lift something heavy? He tried picking up the chair. It seemed a little more difficult, but he actually lifted it a couple of inches off the floor.

He couldn't understand this at all. He had to sit down and think. "Let me be one hundred percent logical," he said out loud, as though talking to one of his students. "I know this is happening. What can be the cause? Some supernatural force?" No, there was nothing supernatural. It had to be natural. Was there a god who was giving him this power? It depended what you meant by God. He didn't believe in the God that was part of most religions. If God was a force—an *it,* not a *he* or *she*—then he could accept it. After all, the big bang must have had a cause.

Then he thought about Bert at the hardware store. Bert already knew there was something strange about him. *What if he tells others about me?* Steve had to contact him and tell him to keep it confidential. Somehow Steve believed he could confide in him. But should he tell Bert about his newfound power? Since Bert knew about the lamp, he might as well tell him the rest. He had to call him.

He dug out the scrap of paper Bert had given him and dialed the number. After they'd exchanged greetings, he said, "Bert, I have some important news, but first I have to ask you a question."

"Go ahead," Bert replied.

"Have you told anyone about my strange powers regarding the lamp?"

"Not a soul," he replied.

"Thank God!" Steve said. "I have to talk to you as soon as possible. I have something to show you that you won't believe."

"After yesterday, I'm ready to believe just about anything," Bert replied. "I happen to be off work today, so I can come over to your place, or you can come here to mine."

Steve thought for a few seconds. Perhaps it would be better at Bert's place. He could then see if these powers worked somewhere other than at his home.

"I think your place would be better. What is your address?"

"It's 308 Jeffries Lane. Do you want directions, or do you want to use the Web?"

"I'll find it. What time?"

"Any time, I'm home all day."

"Good. I'll be right over."

He drove over to Bert's place. It was at the very end of a lane. Somehow it seemed to be the right kind of place for Bert. Steve had always thought of him as a somewhat secluded person. He got out of his car, walked over to the front door, and knocked.

Bert opened the door. "Come on in, Steve."

"Hi, Bert," he said as he followed Bert into the living room. "What's new?"

Bert smiled. "I should ask you that. You're the one who called me. What's the latest?"

"Bert, I have to tell you, no, show you, something, but you have to promise me never to tell anyone else about it."

"Since I kept your secret so far you can be assured I will keep it a deep, dark secret," Bert said.

Steve looked around for something to make move. Through an archway he could see the kitchen and spotted the dish drainer with a few dishes and utensils in it.

"Watch," he said. He then mentally picked out a spoon, pointed to it, moved it through the air, and caught it in his hand.

Bert's eyes widened, and his head shot forward. He just stared at Steve and shook his head. Then he said, "I don't believe that! Do it again."

Steve pointed to a cup on the drainer; it also flew to his hand. He handed it and the spoon to Bert.

Bert looked down at the items in his hand, shook his head again, and stared at Steve like he was an alien. "That's totally amazing. This has a name, you know. It's called telekinesis—something I never believed in until right now."

"I know the term, and I've never believed in it either. Sometimes I think I'm dreaming. What should I do about it?"

"I don't know. I suppose there's no way to find out why you have it. So the lamp was just the beginning. That was a strange beginning."

Bert stared at the cup and shook his head again. Then he said, "I guess you should just try and use it somehow. However, I wouldn't tell anyone else about it—not a soul! If reporters find out, you'll be hounded to death. You might even be called Satan by some people and get yourself killed. I would suggest doing something useful with it. Tell me, do you have to point to something to make it move?"

"I don't know. Up to now I've been pointing to the objects. Let me try it without pointing."

He picked out a larger bowl in the dish rack. Without pointing to it, he moved it into his hand.

"I guess not," he said.

Bert said, "Maybe you can make money with it."

"Make money? I never thought of that. How?"

"Do you play any sports? In particular, are you good at any?"

"Why, yes. I play tennis. I'm actually ranked 187 in the world, but that isn't high enough to make any money."

"There you go! If you can control the ball, you can get

to the top. You'd have to be very careful, though. You'd have to make sure nothing unusual is noticed."

"Right. Actually, all top players have pretty much the same ability. A double-digit player often beats a single-digit player, but then again I'm a triple-digit player."

"It doesn't matter," said Bert. "You can rise up to the top—just not too fast. You should practice your skills to see how it works in detail and make sure your shots are disguised."

"Right. I have a few buddies that I play with. I can try it on them. Lots of people practice by hitting the ball against a wall, so I think I'll practice on a wall first."

"I've just had a thought. One thing you should do is test your powers for speed and strength. For example, can you knock a bird on the wing down? And just how heavy a thing can you lift? Another thing is distance. How far away can something be and still be reached by your powers?"

Steve was surprised at Bert's questions. It was like he was becoming Steve's manager or something. Steve realized Bert was right, though; he should not take anything for granted.

"You're right, Bert. I'll do some testing. You got any other bright ideas?"

"Not for now, but I'm interested in just what you can do. Keep me posted."

"Thanks, Bert. I'll be in touch. See you later."

CHAPTER 4

THE TENNIS PLAYERS

Sam Finch and Henry Thomson were good buddies. They'd met in high school and discovered they both were interested in tennis. They were in the same math class when the teacher brought up the parabola. "All objects flying through the air take a parabolic arc," he'd said, "that is, in the absence of air resistance. Since there is always air resistance, the curve will not exactly be a parabola. Let's take a tennis ball." The teacher gave them the initial velocity and the angle of ascent and asked, "Now where will this ball land?" They'd learned how to solve that math problem.

After class Hank said, "Say, Sam, have you ever thought about playing tennis?"

"Funny you should ask," Sam said. "I just watched the finals of a tournament on TV. It was a great match. We have a couple of tennis rackets in the garage. Do you want to try it?"

"Why not?" Hank said. "I'm kind of fed up with basketball, and my dad won't let me play football. He considers it too dangerous."

"Mine, too," Sam said. "He used to play tennis, and I guess he used to be pretty good. He had some kind of ranking in the old days. Once, when I was around twelve, he took me out to the court, and we hit the ball around for awhile. I guess I didn't do so well, and we gave it up. I got the impression he thought I wouldn't be very good, but he never really gave me a chance. We only played that once. He was pretty busy with his job."

"Why don't we give it a try. What do we have to lose?"

So Sam and Hank took up tennis. After floundering around for awhile they found that they could actually have a nice rally.

"There must be books on the game," Hank said.

Sam said, "I remember seeing a book on our living room bookshelf. I'll get it, and we can bone up on the game."

The book was called *Tennis Techniques Illustrated*, and both eventually read it. They spent the entire summer playing tennis and enjoyed it immensely. They even found a local tennis group and started to play with other men. One guy Sam met was a good player. He agreed to have a game and was surprised that Sam actually beat him. "You play very well—you're a natural. How long have you been playing?"

"I started this year."

"That's rather amazing. Is your friend pretty good also?"

"Yes, I think we're about the same level."

"Well, keep at it. You may make the pro ranks."

Sam went back and told Hank the story. "He said we might become pros." And five years later they did just that. They joined the USTA and got ranked. After a short time they found that their ranks were both in the double digits!

CHAPTER 5

MEETING BECKY

Bert was right. He must test his powers in lots of ways: strength, speed, distance, and what else? He should to go out to a remote spot and experiment. He also wanted to practice against a wall to see how much he could control the ball.

He decided on the wall first. The club had a few walls, but he thought it might be safer to try a public court. He didn't want anyone in the club to see him making the ball do strange things. He knew of a court at a park down the street that had a wall, but it was late, and he was tired. He would try the wall tomorrow. He took a nice hot shower and turned in.

In bed he thought about his life at this point. He really could not believe it. He thought about God again. He thought about aliens. What could all this mean? He dozed off and fell into a deep sleep.

He dreamt of his girlfriend, Susan. She was playing

tennis with him, which was pretty weird since she didn't play tennis. He hit her a weird shot. She said, "How did you do that?"

He said, "Do what?"

"Make the ball move like that."

Then they were in bed together, but he could not do the obvious. Then Bert showed up and tried to explain the meaning of sex. All in all it was a very confusing dream.

The next morning, Friday, he got up late, around 11:30, probably because of his mental state, which was very confused. He ate his usual bowl of oatmeal with fruit. He decided not to go out to the public courts until later. They were usually busy in the morning and not very busy in the afternoon when most people considered it too hot to play. He decided to spend a little time looking into telekinesis online, wondering if anyone else claimed to have it. Wikipedia basically considered it superstition, which was what he expected. A few guys on the web claimed to demonstrate moving things mentally, but they were probably hoaxes.

Around 2 p.m. he picked up his tennis stuff and headed out to the public court. It was within walking distance. On the way he had to walk through the local park. No one was around, so maybe he could try a few experiments to see what he could do. He spotted a blue jay sitting on a branch. When it started to fly away, he grabbed it with the force in midair. He thought it looked surprised. He moved it backward. It struggled to go forward. He let it go.

Then he noticed an oak tree nearby and wondered if

he could break off one of its branches. He picked a rather large one and bent it up. It broke with ease, and he was kind of ashamed of himself for doing it.

He walked for a little while and stopped. He was alone, so he tried another test. He grabbed a small rock and threw it straight up in the air as high as he could. When it started to fall, he pointed to it and slowed it to a stop. He made it go backward, then forward, and then sideways. He wondered whether he could stop it if it were going very fast. With the force he pushed it very high, almost beyond visibility, and then let it go. It came hurtling down. When it was about six feet above him, he stopped it quickly. He tried a few more tosses. He found that he could create sort of a wall that the rock could not penetrate, kind of a force field like gravity or a magnetic field. He was amazed!

What about lifting things? In a parking lot nearby were several cars. Seeing no one around, he went to the back of one of them and lifted the back end. He could lift it easily. How about the whole car? He slid the force field under the car and lifted it with ease. He really could not believe it—he could lift a whole car. He looked up to the heavens and said, "God, what do you have planned for me?"

Steve then decided to head over to the court. When he arrived, he was happy to see no one around. He got out a ball and started to hit it against the wall. He found that he could do amazing things: make it curve up, down, and sideways; make it go very fast; and make it go very slowly.

There was a mark on the wall about one square inch in diameter. He tried to hit it. Out of ten shots, he hit it directly ten times. He found he could stop it in midair just like the rock. He was amazed beyond belief. He should have been happy, but he wasn't. He was still confused about how and why he had these powers.

Then another person entered the courts, a young woman, kind of good-looking. She glanced his way and started hitting the ball against the wall about two courts away. She seemed to have pretty good control. He decided to hit on his wall without using the force. They both hit for about five minutes. Then he noticed that she'd stopped hitting and was staring at him, like she was studying him. It was like she recognized him or something.   Then she said, "Hey, do you want to rally?"

"Sure, why not?"

She came over to his court. Then she stopped and stared at him again for a few seconds. Then she acted a little embarrassed.

He said, "You act like you recognize me. Do you?"

She stared at him strangely and then said, "You look slightly familiar, but I don't really recognize you from any-place I can remember."

At this point Steve thought, *Boy, this babe is a doll! She looks like my ideal woman! Pretty face, perfect body, slim and trim, long black hair. I should ask her out.*

She grabbed a few balls out of her bag and said, "I've got some pretty good balls."

"That's fine, since mine are kind of old."

They started to rally. She had great form and made excellent shots. She was very athletic. He was very impressed. In addition to her looks, her tennis form was great.

Then she said, "Say, do want to play a set?"

"At the risk of being humiliated, let's try one. By the way, my name is Steve Thomas. What's yours?"

"Oh, mine is Rebecca Jones, Becky for short. Nice to meet you. You hit the ball very well. I don't think you'll be humiliated. Let me hit a few practice serves."

She did, and her serves were superb. He wondered if she was ranked.

She said, "Okay, first one in."

It was really a fun set. She played very well, almost like a pro. He won it 6-4 without using the force. The next set was close, but he won it 8-6.

At the end of the second set she said, "Hey, that was great. I have to go, but we should play again."

"Yes, we should. You play very well. Are you ranked?"

"Me, ranked? No, are you?"

He kind of wished he hadn't asked. Now he had to tell her that he was ranked.

"I am, but not high enough to make any money."

"What's your rank?"

"ATP 187."

"That's the world tennis organization, right? Well, that impressive enough. So you think I should play in tournaments and try and get ranked?"

"Definitely."

"I play mainly for exercise, and time is a factor."

"Oh? What do you do?"

"I'm a computer consultant. I have to do a bit of traveling. What do you do?"

He was a bit ashamed to say, "I teach mostly math at the city college."

"What do you mean 'mostly'?"

"I have two double-E degrees and teach a basic electric circuits course and also a programming course."

"That's impressive."

"I'd say yours is more impressive."

"Not really. I've been away from the math details for some time. In fact I miss them. Say, do want to go for a cup of coffee?"

Was this beautiful babe actually asking him to get together? Under the circumstances, with this crazy power he had, he decided he should say no. Personal involvement would be a bad idea at the present time.

"I can't make it this time. Why don't we exchange phone numbers for a later date."

"Great, here's my card."

Her card displayed only her name, phone number, and email address.

Steve gave her his college card. He jotted down his home phone and email on the back.

She said, "Okay, great. I hope we can get together *very* soon."

He liked the way she said *very*. He wanted to kiss her right then, but he just stared and said, "Yes, very soon!"

She gave him a very seductive smile and paused, staring at him.

Finally he said, "Well, until next time. Bye for now."

He waited for her to turn and walk away, but she just stood there looking at him, so he turned, walked over to his bag, and picked it up. When he looked over his shoulder at her, she was still standing there like a statue.

He said, "You seem deep in thought. What are you thinking?"

She said, "Do you believe in *love at first sight?*"

His eyebrows rose in surprise. She was obviously making a pass at him. He dropped his bag, walked over to her, and stood close. She stared at his eyes intently.

He said, "Before today, no, but right now, yes." She inched a bit closer to him. He put his arms around her waist and pulled her slowly closer. She didn't resist, so he kissed her. She put her arms around his neck, and they engaged in a prolonged kiss.

Then she said, "Well, I guess we know where we each stand. How about a date?"

"Definitely. How about lunch or dinner sometime? I'll call you to confirm."

"Good, I'll wait with bated breath!"

She turned and walked away, but not too fast, as though she wanted him to study her. He admired her slightly swaying hip movement. God, what a doll! He couldn't believe she was turned on by him. He considered himself fairly good-looking but not great. Susan said he was cute but not handsome. What about him turned her on? He grabbed his bag and started walking back home. He thought about what she looked like: black hair, beautiful face and smile, nice figure. *And*, considering her job, she was obviously intelligent. He couldn't believe his good fortune.

Now he had to think about Susan. He'd never actually committed himself to anything, so maybe he would just not call her for awhile. Boy, did he have a lot to think about.

When he got home he grabbed a beer from the fridge and sat down with a few almonds. He thought about Becky. It suddenly came to him that there was something strange about the encounter, like it was planned from the start. It seemed she recognized him from somewhere. A girl like that could have just about any man she wanted. Why him?

Unable to figure it out, he decided to think about supper instead. Also, he should call Bert to let him know the latest. Then again, maybe he should first try his powers against an actual opponent.

C H A P T E R 6

THE FIRST ATTEMPT

9:00 a.m. Monday, June 4

Steve thought about who he should play against on his first attempt at controlling the ball on the tennis court. Mike Gipson came to mind. A little bit better a player than Steve, his rating was 160 or so. For some reason he didn't seem to be very bright, so he might not detect anything if the ball acted a little strangely. He gave Mike a call, and they made arrangements to play later in the afternoon.

They were both members of the same club, which had a racket ball court and eight tennis courts.

Steve was happy that Mike could play. Now to think about how he would try to control the ball. One obvious trick would be to nick the net to make the ball drop in just on the other side of the net. He remembered how the number-one player, Bruce Clark, had ended a match that way once. That had been pure luck. Net cords were pretty rare, though, so Steve couldn't use that trick too often. The simplest idea would be to just increase the speed of the ball. Not too much of course. Too fast would make it very obvious that something was up. Another trick would be to make a lob drop in close to the back line when his opponent was at the net. Also, the shot should not look like it was going out and then curve back in.

Steve decided to have a couple of eggs, whole wheat toast, and coffee for breakfast. While eating he contemplated again the strange set of affairs that surrounded his life. He couldn't believe it was really happening. He wondered if anyone else had such powers. He concluded that there must be someone. How could he be the only one? Telekinesis was something that was talked about, but no one had actually proved that it existed. So why did he have it?

He thought momentarily about saying a prayer and asking God what was going on but gave that idea up immediately. He had been brought up in a Christian home, since his stepmother was a born-again Christian. His father had never said anything about religion; in fact, he seemed to not have an opinion about anything. Steve's mother had died when he was very young, about seven months old. He'd often wondered what she believed. At one point—he couldn't actually remember when—he'd realized that the whole idea of religion was completely stupid.

Time for the match rolled around. He carried his tennis bag out to his car, got in, and drove over to the club.

In the main lobby he notice a few players sipping coffee or Coke. One was Hank Williams. Steve said, "Hi, Hank, how you doing?"

"I'm okay. How are you?"

"Fine. Mike Gipson and I are going to play a few sets. I haven't played him in a while."

"Do you think you've got a chance to beat him?"

"I'm an underdog, but you never know."

"Yeah, you're right. Good luck!"

"Thanks, I'll probably need it."

Just then Mike walked in. "Hi, Steve. Are you ready?"

"As ready as I'll ever be. Let's go."

They checked on court availability. Most players played early, so several were available. They walked out to court three and started to rally. Mike was in his usual good form, and they rallied normally. Steve tried accelerating the ball on a few shots. One shot picked up a little too much speed.

"Hey, where did you get that shot?" Mike asked.

"I don't know, just a lucky one. Must have hit the sweet spot on my racket."

"I guess so. I hope you don't hit it too often."

They each practiced a few serves as usual. Mike had a very good serve. Steve's wasn't too bad, but it wasn't as fast as Mike's.

"Go ahead and serve," Mike said.

"Okay. First one in."

For the first four games Steve played normally. He was behind three to one. Then he decided to try to put a little telekinetic speed on the ball. He also placed his serves in an awkward spot to Mike's backhand. Once he tried a net cord, just ticking the net and dropping it in close. It worked. Then he eased up and lost the next two points. Then, using his powers, he hit two aces. He eased up again and won the last point naturally.

"Great serving," Mike said as they changed sides.

Steve played normally until he needed to exercise his telekinetic powers, being careful to disguise his shots. He ended up winning the first set 6-4. He was a little worried about being detected, so he didn't use his powers in the second set and lost it 6-2. In the third set he turned on his power when he needed it and won 6-3.

Mike said, "Your game is improving. Let's play again soon."

"Sure. How about a coffee in the club lounge?"

"I don't have the time right now. I'll call you."

"Okay. See you next time."

Walking back to his car, he wondered again if he were dreaming. When he got home he gave Bert a call.

Bert answered. "Hello?"

"Hi, Bert. This is Steve."

"Hi, Steve. What's the latest news?"

"I took your advice and tried out my powers. I caught a bird in the air. I broke a thick tree branch easily. I was actually able to lift a car. Then I went to the wall on a public court and hit against it for awhile. It was amazing what I could do with the ball. My control was amazing. Also, I just played my first match. I won against a player with a slightly better rating than I. He probably would have beaten me except for my telekinetic tricks."

"Say no more on the phone. Come on over, and we'll talk."

"Okay, I'll be right over."

Steve thought about the fact that Bert didn't want to talk on the phone. Maybe he was worried that it could be bugged. He guessed that could happen, but it didn't seem very likely. Then again, maybe it was better to be safe than sorry. He should keep his powers very, very secret.

A bit hungry, he grabbed an apple, took a bite, and headed out the door with it. He arrived at Bert's place and knocked.

"Come on in—the door's open."

Steve walked in. "Hey, Bert."

"So, the first test was a success. Do you think your opponent might have detected anything?"

"No, I don't think so. A least he didn't say anything out of the ordinary."

"It seems like you've tested things pretty well, but you didn't try distance. How far away can something be and still be reached by your power?"

Bert was right. He should not take anything for granted. He should try his power in every way possible. He would try distance at his earliest opportunity.

Bert said, "I recently found out about something interesting. There's a high school basketball player in the news because he suddenly became very accurate. His percentage was in the nineties, and everyone was asking him how he suddenly became so good. He said it was probably just luck, but that percentage is way beyond luck. The average player makes around fifty percent of his shots. Hardly anybody sinks above sixty-five percent. For the last few weeks he seems to have cooled off, but he still plays quite a bit better than anyone else on his team. His cooling off may be on purpose to keep it a secret. I don't know if there's anything to it, but I'm going to keep tabs on him to see what happens next. I don't know what the chances are, but it may be that you're not alone. Why should you be the only one with such powers? If you have it, I think there's a good chance others do, too."

"I also thought about that. Why only me? What's this guy's name?"

"He goes by the name of Skip Hodges—his first name is actually Daniel. They call him Skip because he skips class a lot. He doesn't seem too smart. In fact he flunked one year and may not graduate."

"I guess the thing to do is to just keep tabs on him."

"Right. By the way, have you eaten? I cooked up some beef stew. Do you want any?"

"I just had an apple on the way over here, but I'm still hungry. I'll take you up on your invitation," Steve replied.

Once dinner was on the table and they'd started eating, he told Bert about Becky. "It was amazing," he said after telling Bert all about the encounter. "I couldn't believe the whole thing."

"That's rather strange," Bert said. "Maybe a little too strange."

"What do you mean?"

"Well, the way I look at all this is that someone or something else must be involved, someone who may be using you. You have to be very careful. With her you should proceed with extreme caution. What's her name?"

"Rebecca Jones, but she goes by Becky."

"Aren't you going with another girl?"

"Yeah, her name is Susan. We've only had three or four dates. She's very nice and pretty but nothing like Becky. So what's my next step?"

"My advice is don't get involved too deeply with Becky. Take it slow. Don't let her seduce you. Also, go out in the woods somewhere and check your powers completely. I'm really curious about distance. Can you move something one mile away? Check it all out. Meanwhile, I'm going to keep tabs on this guy Skip Hodges."

After dinner Steve headed for home. He was deep in thought about his strange powers and Bert's comments. As he walked from his car to his place, he noticed a few birds flying over. Could he grab two of them at the same time? Nobody was around, so he reached up with both hands and successfully grabbed them both. He brought them within a few feet of his head and then let them go.

One test done; next up, testing for distance and power.

CHAPTER 7

THE CLIMB TO FAME

Steve picked a USTA National event in San Diego starting Monday, June 11, and registered online. The tournament lasted two weeks, and he won it. It lowered his rank to 158. He won ten thousand dollars and decided to check for another tournament. He found one starting in a few days in Portland. He signed up and then flew there directly from San Diego.

When he arrived, he found housing for players was free. The director looked at him and said, "Steve Thomas ... you just won the San Diego event, right? Congratulations!"

"Thanks. To be honest with you, I was kind of surprised."

"Good luck in this one!"

"Thanks, I hope I don't need it."

"Well, you'll get a bye on the first round. You start tomorrow at 3:00 p.m."

This one lasted another two weeks, and again he won

it with the help of his powers. This time the cash prize was twelve thousand dollars. His final opponent, Sam Finch, said to him, "Where did you get that serve? Your placement was amazing! I think you hit the back service line about fifteen times."

"I've been working on it lately."

"Well, good job. I hope to see you in the next one."

Sam seemed to be a stickler for details. Maybe he should concentrate on being extra careful with the force. So far, though, everything was going according to plan. He checked his new rank. It was 132! Progress was being made! He had been gone about four weeks, so he decided to take a break and flew home to San Jose.

7:00 p.m., Friday, July 20.

When he walked into his condo he noticed three calls on his answering machine. He listened to the first one, which had been left Sunday morning at 10 a.m., two weeks ago.

"Hi, this is Becky. I thought I'd hear from you by now. I hope you haven't forgotten me, the loser in our tennis match. Please call me."

The next message was from Bert. "Hi, Steve. How is everything going? I think you may be away playing in a few tourneys. Let me know the results. I have a bit of news about our friend Skip. Let's get together."

The third was from Susan. "Hi, Steve. This is Susan. I haven't heard from you in quite a while, and I'm getting the impression you're losing interest in me ... and, well, actually I've started seeing someone else who seems rather nice. Anyway, please let me know what's going on with you. Bye."

Hmm, three messages. Who should he call back first? He couldn't resist calling Becky. He didn't want to lose that gorgeous dish. He dug out her card, called, and got a message. *You have reached the phone of Becky Jones. Please leave a message.*

That was a nice, brief message, a sign of intelligence. He hated idiotic messages like *Hello, I may be in the bathroom, eating dinner, or on another line. Please call back or leave your number so I can call you back.*

Steve wondered if she was traveling for her job. He left his message. "Hi, Becky, this is Steve. No, I haven't forgotten you. I just came back from two USTA tournaments, one in San Diego and one in Portland. To my surprise I won both. I can now afford to take you out to a nice restaurant! Call me, or I'll try you again later."

Next he phoned Bert.

He answered. "Hello?"

"Hi, Bert. This is Steve. I just got back from two USTA tournaments. I won them both. No one seemed to notice anything."

"Great! So everything's proceeding according to plan. Come on over, and we'll chat."

"Okay, but I have to get a bite to eat first. I'll see you in about an hour."

"Right. See you then."

Steve wondered if he should call Susan. To be polite he decided to call her. He got a recording.

"Hi, Sue, this is Steve. I'm sorry I forgot to call you to tell you I'd be out of town for awhile. I played in a couple of tennis tournaments and happened to win them both. Anyway, regarding our relationship, I'm not really ready for anything serious, so I think maybe we should quit dating for the time being. We can get together for a chat from time to time. Good luck in the future."

CHAPTER 8

MORE NEWS FROM BERT

After a snack of some pickled herring, cheese, and crackers, Steve headed over to Bert's place.

Bert opened the door and said, "Hello, champ."

"Hi, Bert. How are you?"

"I'm fine. So you're on your way to the top. That's great. Keep it up. How about a beer?"

"Great, I need one."

Bert opened two bottles and handed one to Steve. "So what's the latest with Becky?"

"She called while I was gone and left a message. I returned her call and got a recording, so I left *her* a message. One interesting piece of news is that Susan also called, wondering why I hadn't called her. I should've told her I was going to be out of town for awhile, but I forgot. Anyway, she thinks I'm no longer interested in her and started dating around, which is fine with me since I met Becky. I called her back and sort of called our relationship off."

"I see. As I mentioned before, be careful with Becky."

"So what's the latest with Skip Hodges?"

"Well, the news is that statisticians have looked at his record and decided that it can't be luck. The odds against it are too great. They tried to get in touch with him, but he won't talk to anyone. There's lots of idiotic speculation about how he's doing it. Some say magnets. Some say it's a trick ball with a motor inside. Some say he's an alien."

"Wow! That *is* news! So you think he has *the* power?"

"My guess is yes. All that other stuff is obviously nonsense. I guess the only thing to do is wait and see what happens next. I'm willing to bet he'll stop shooting so many baskets and let things cool off."

"I think you may be right. We'll see. Say, Bert, are you interested in a game of backgammon?"

"Sure, let me get the set out. How much do you want to play for?"

"Is one dollar a point too much for you?"

"I'm more used to quarters."

"Okay, quarters it is."

They played for a couple of hours, Bert winning about two dollars.

"Hey, great game, Bert. You play pretty well."

"There's a fair amount of luck in the game of backgammon. You'll probably win next time."

They decided to call it a night, and Steve left. When he got home it was about 10:30. About fifteen minutes later the phone rang. It was Becky.

"Hi, Steve. This is Becky."

"Oh, hi, Becky. I guess you got my message."

"Yes, congratulations on the wins. I knew you were good. I have some bad news. I have to be out of the country for about six months, but I want to stay in touch. Since we shared email addresses we can communicate that way. Maybe we should exchange addresses too."

"Wow, sorry to hear that. Where will you be?"

"Germany for one. Maybe other places."

Steve told her that he had a condominium. They exchanged addresses.

She continued, "I need to say one other thing. I guess you know that I'm very attracted to you, and I want you to know I am not interested in anyone else. Are you seeing anyone?"

"Well, yes, I was but not any longer. I only dated her for about a month. We had a slight misunderstanding about my month out of town. She took my absence of phone calls as a symbol of lack of interest, so she started dating someone else. I guess I could apologize and continue to see her, but after I met you I decided to let her go her own way. Can we get together one time before you leave?"

"I'm glad to hear that. Yes, I want to see you too very much, but I leave Sunday. Will tomorrow work?"

"Sure. I have a nice restaurant picked out for dinner."

"Actually, I'd like to spend the whole day with you so we can get to know each other better. How about a hike with dinner afterward?"

"That sounds good. I know of a couple of great places to hike. Have you ever been to Alum Rock Park?"

"Yes, I have, and I love it."

"Okay, when do you want to leave?"

"I have to do some packing in the morning, so how about one o'clock?"

He got her address and then said, "Okay, I'll pick you up at your place then."

"Good, I'll see you then. Bye."

"Bye, Becky."

That was an interesting turn of events, Steve thought. He was not taking Bert's advice. He couldn't forget that kiss on their first meeting.

Steve had often thought about the best way to get to know someone. At one point in the past he'd even made up a list of questions to ask. Religion was tops on the list. Then came interests and educational background. Did they have degrees? In what field? Then political stance. Republican, Democrat, or what? He would try very hard to get to know her and to avoid anything physical. He decided to hit the sack early in preparation for tomorrow.

CHAPTER 9

THE HIKE

Saturday morning Steve got up at ten o'clock and made a nice breakfast of orange juice, eggs over medium, whole wheat toast, and coffee. He had that breakfast twice a week, with oatmeal topped with fruit the other five days. He looked up Becky's address on Google Maps and arrived right on time. Her house was in a high-class neighborhood, and he guessed it would probably sell for over a million bucks. He rang the bell, and when she opened the door, she already had a day pack slung across one shoulder and a baseball cap on her head.

"Hello, Becky. How are you?"

"Great, and you?"

He thought about approaching her for a kiss but felt that maybe this wasn't the right time.

"Superb! I see you've got good hiking shoes on and look like you're ready for an invigorating walk."

"Right. *Be prepared* is the Girl Scout motto, not just the Boy Scouts'."

"Okay, let's go."

They got in Steve's car and started off.

Steve said, "You live in a classy neighborhood. Your job must pay well."

"Yes, I have a great job. It pays well, and there's never a dull moment. The trouble is it's time-consuming. I envy you, having the summers off."

"Yeah, that's one of the benefits of teaching."

"So we only have one day, and I want to know everything about you. Tell me your life story."

"My life story? That's a tall order. Well, let's see. You already know what I do for a living. I've always been a game freak. In addition to tennis I've played squash and racquetball, but I prefer tennis of course. I learned to play chess in high school and continue to play. I used to play in tournaments but now just play online. I played bridge for a while and also played an oriental game called Go, or Igo. For some reason it has two names. I also did a little gambling playing poker and backgammon. Right now I play only chess online."

"I played a little chess in college. My grandfather played. He gave me a book once. I think it was called *How to Be a Winner at Chess* by Reinhart or Rein something."

"That's the first chess book I ever read! I believe the author is Reinfeld."

"Yes, Reinfeld, I think that's it. So do you do any reading?"

"Yes, I occasionally read a novel. I used to like science

fiction. I read quite a bit of Dean Koontz. Have you heard of him?"

"Yes, I love the way he writes."

"Interesting we have that in common. I try to read some of the classics like *Great Expectations*. I really enjoyed *Huck Finn*. How about you? What else do you read?"

"Unfortunately not much except technical manuals. I'm really busy at work. In school I read Shakespeare. I also read some of Mark Twain's stuff. I agree that *Huckleberry Finn* was great! So, are you a religious person?"

"Absolutely not. I'm pretty much an agnostic. There may be some superpower out there, but I don't know how anyone can know anything about it. How about you?"

"I'm very glad to hear that. I pretty much agree. I used to call myself a pantheist—you know, *the universe is God* sort of thing. But now I'm basically an agnostic like you. That's another thing in common!"

"What was your major in college?"

"Computer science. I was torn between it and math, but I decided that computer science was more practical. I enjoyed it so much I went for my master's degree and got it in one more year."

"That's interesting. I knew you were not dumb."

"Thanks. Does intelligence count as having things in common?"

"Sure, why not. It's pretty important."

They arrived at the end of Alum Rock Drive, and Steve parked. Steve realized that she'd asked him some of the same question he would have asked her. Interesting!

Steve said, "Before we leave, I have a question for you. You seem to be very attracted to me. I've never considered myself great-looking, but you're beautiful and intelligent and could have your pick of any guy. Why me?"

"I don't really consider myself super great-looking. Not like these models with the long legs and great boobs. But, as to your question, I don't really have an answer. I've thought about it a lot, and I don't know why. It's like you're some kind of magnet, and your magnetic field has attacked my brain. When I first saw you, I knew you were it! You are pretty good-looking, lean, athletic, and intelligent, but there's something more I can't put my finger on. You must have some power of which I am not aware. Maybe you can tell me what it is?"

Steve, wide-eyed and speechless, stared at her in disbelief. Was his new power detectable to her? It seemed that it might be. He was tempted to tell her the whole telekinetic story, but, no, not a good idea.

He finally said, "No, I have no idea, though if I ever find out I'll let you know. Let's head out. I like the south rim trail. It's nice and shady. I hope it's not too steep for you. Then again, you seem to be in good shape, so it shouldn't be a problem."

"Yes, that's my favorite trail too. You know, it's rather amazing how much we have in common."

"Yes, it is. Does that seem to be part of the mystery of your attraction to me?"

"Yes, I think so. I almost feel like I'm dreaming. I hope I don't wake up!"

It was a nice, cool day, even cooler in the shade. They headed out and hiked without saying much to each other. He was wondering about her strange attraction to him. He recalled that kiss on the courts that gave him weak knees.

Suddenly she said, "What are you thinking about?"

"I'm thinking about you and how we met."

"What did you think of me doing what I did?"

"Honestly, I didn't know what to think. I thought that you might be a bit crazy, but crazy and smart, and a good tennis player. As I said, I was surprised that you were attracted to me."

"I was as surprised as you were. Like it was beyond my control. I know I'm not bad-looking, but, as I said, I've never considered myself super-great. Some men are turned off because they consider me too athletic. I've had quite a few dates, but none of them turned me on like you did. I had the impression you weren't really interested in me since you continued to hit against the wall. I was hoping you would ask me to rally, but you didn't so I asked you. Then at the end of our match when you walked away I was afraid that you'd never call, so I had to do something to not lose you. So I said something stupid and asked if you believed in love at first sight. I don't even know how that popped into my brain. But it obviously worked, and I'm very happy about it."

"Hey, you're giving yourself away. You should be playing hard to get." Steve once again wondered if his powers were somehow detectable to her.

"Yes, I know. I'm playing a stupid game, but I can't help it."

"I have to ask you something else. Most woman wear earrings. You don't wear them or any other kind of jewelry."

"No, I never cared for earrings. I hate the idea of poking holes in my body, even my ears. I never cared for necklaces or bracelets either. I even take my watch off at home. Would you prefer me to wear them?"

"Absolutely not! I think they're stupid. I'm really glad you don't wear any. And I take my watch off at home also."

"You do? Another thing in common!"

"You know, some men do something equally stupid."

"Really, what's that?"

"They grow mustaches. I've never understood why."

"But you have a short beard. Is that different?"

"Yes, I have a short beard for a reason—I hate to shave. One day I got fed up with shaving, so I just decided to let it grow. When it gets a little too long I trim it back severely. I have a shaver that I set to a quarter inch. What do you think of it?"

"I like it. It's nice and short, just the right length. Guys with long beards turn me off, and I agree that mustaches seem rather stupid."

"Another thing I like about you is your lack of makeup. Wearing lipstick is stupid, and false eyelashes even worse. I never understood why some women pull out their eyebrows and paint on false ones. It's a sign of pure stupidity!"

She smiled. "I'm really glad to hear that. I hate makeup, and I'm glad you don't like it either."

He wondered what they could talk about while hiking. Eventually he said, "One thing I think about a lot is evolution. Do you believe in it?"

"I do, but there are times when I can't imagine how it can take place. However, I can't think of any alternative."

"Neither can I. The sheer variety of living things is proof enough. I can't imagine God creating thirty thousand species of beetles, for example. Why would he? Humans are definitely unique, however. We're the only species that has language."

"Yes, I agree, but there are other species unique in other ways. Think of the elephant. It uses its nose as a hand! How unique is that? And what about the kangaroos. They use their legs like a spring. I often wonder how spiders survive. They're so fragile, and their main characteristic is patience. Then there's that web."

"Wow, I can tell you've thought a lot about it. Did you ever study biology?"

"Only in high school. How about you?"

"No, I took the usual physics, chemistry, and math. I learned a lot about biology by watching *Nature* and *Nova* on TV."

"Yes, I watch those programs also."

He was happy to have brought the subject up. He was learning a lot about her. He wondered about her interest in politics.

He asked, "Do you have any political leanings? Left or right?"

"I tend to be a little on the left. Republicans are so far

to the right that they're off the scale. You might call them Libertarians. How about you?"

"I might be a little more to the left than you are. I believe in free health care for all and a higher minimum wage."

"I do, too. I also think the judges in the Supreme Court should have term limits. Why should they be different than members of Congress or the president?"

"I never thought of that, but you're right."

He was very pleased he'd brought up things to discuss, and he was amazed at her knowledge and beliefs. They were so much like his.

IN LOVE WITH BECKY

A s they headed for the car after the hike, Steve said, "Are you hungry?"

"Yes! Where to?"

"Have you ever eaten at the Bold Knight?"

"Yes, some time ago. I recall that they had great prime rib."

"Right. Are you in the mood for that?"

"Definitely!"

They arrived at the Bold Knight and were able to get a table without a wait. Steve normally did not drink wine, but he thought she might. He said, "Would you be interested in a glass of wine to start?"

"Are you trying to liquor me up to seduce me?"

"Definitely. Would it work?"

"No comment."

He smiled. "Red or white?"

"Actually, I prefer ice water. Is that okay with you?"

"Sure. I like beer, but when I eat out I also have ice water. I've never understood why they charge three dollars or more for a sixty-cent beer. I think I read once that restaurants make more money on alcohol then food."

She smiled and said, "I like beer also. I know most women don't, so I guess I'm an oddball in that regard."

She selected Italian dressing for the salad, as did he. She said, "Another thing that we have in common! Then again, Italian is a rather popular dressing, so maybe it shouldn't count."

While eating he noticed her use of salt. "I see you like salt."

"As do *you*, I noticed. I know a lot of people consider salt bad for you, but that's somewhat of a myth. It's only bad if you have high blood pressure, which I don't. I love salt."

"Wow, that's another thing in common! And it counts, since a lot of people don't use much salt."

After the main dish he said, "Care for dessert?"

"No, thanks, but if you want any go ahead."

"No, I usually skip it. Is that another thing in common? Maybe it shouldn't count either, but I'm going to start a list."

She smiled. *What a gorgeous smile*, he thought.

"Yes, I can't quite believe it." She then said, "Shall we make like a spring tree and leave?"

He laughed. "I like that one. My favorite is *Let's make like a shepherd and get the flock out of here*."

She laughed. "Hey, that's a great one. I'll have to re-member it."

They finished up, he paid the bill, and they walked out to the car. He drove her back to her place and got out.

He went around to open her door, but she had already opened it and got out. He walked her to her door. She opened it, turned around, and stared at him rather stiffly. He stared back at her, feeling a bit awkward.

She said, "Aren't you going to kiss me goodnight?"

He leaned over to kiss her, and she laughed, grabbed him, and pulled him through the door.

She said, "You're not leaving for awhile!"

"I was hoping you would say that."

They went inside, and he noticed the quality of her place. She had top-looking furniture and a few high-qual-ity paintings on the walls. He noticed a famous Escher, another of Einstein, and much to his surprise one of Euler.

"You must know something about Euler," he said.

"You recognize him. Then again, being a mathemati-cian you must know all about him."

"Yes, he was an amazing guy. Made some great discoveries."

"I know. I had to write an essay about a scientist in college. I chose him. Care for a little more ice water?"

"Yes, I'm a bit thirsty after that meal."

They sat there sipping the water and stared at each other for at least ten seconds.

He said, "At the count of three let's each say the one word we're thinking. Ready? One, two, three!"

They both said, "*You!*"

She said, "Well, that settles that," and moved next to him. He put his hand against the back of her neck and pulled her lips to his. They were delicious. He reached down, inched up her skirt, and slid his hand along her thigh.

She didn't resist and said, "Looks like you're trying to seduce me."

"No, it's the other way around of course, and you're succeeding!"

"I don't think you've seen my bedroom."

He thought, *Oh God, here we go!* "You're right, but I'd love to."

She led the way, and he followed. In the bedroom she stood very close and started to unbutton his shirt. After about four buttons she said, "The sheets feel great, but you have to be nude to really appreciate them. I'll be right back."

She turned and disappeared into the bathroom, and he promptly undressed himself and crawled into the bed. The sheets did feel great. The lights dimmed, and he felt her slide into the bed. They made passionate love. When it was over they just stared at each other.

He said, "I have never felt this way before. I do believe I'm in love."

"Not as in love as I am."

"Yes, more than you."

"No, less."

"Hey, I wonder is there's a test for it. On a scale of one to ten I'm an eleven. What are you?"

"I'm a twelve!"

"Oops, I miscalculated. I'm a thirteen."

"Let's call it a tie at fourteen."

He said, "Fair enough." They both laughed. They kissed again and repeated the act. After that he felt his eyelids getting heavier.

She said, "You look like you're getting sleepy. Maybe too much wine. Oops, I mean water."

"Actually it's probably the food. It's been an invigorating day." They both gradually drifted off to sleep.

The next morning when he awoke she wasn't there. He checked the time; it was 9:30. He called, "Becky?"

From the kitchen she said, "I'm here. How about a little breakfast? What would you like?"

"Whatever you're having. Let's start with coffee."

"Okay, how about coffee, eggs over medium, and whole wheat toast?"

Steve opened his mouth in surprise. "How did you know? That's exactly what I have for Sunday breakfast."

"That's what I have too! Rather amazing!"

"My God, I can't believe it." He got up, dressed, and came to at the table. A cup of black coffee was at his place. Next to it was sugar, a package of Stevia, and cream.

"I didn't know if you drink it black or not."

"Believe it or not, I drink it with Stevia and cream. You obviously use Stevia also."

"Yes. How many things in common is that—at least four?"

"No, it's more. I'm definitely going to make a list."

He sat down to a delicious-looking plate of eggs and toast. Was this girl an angel straight from heaven? Actually, maybe this was heaven.

He said, "You're way too much. When did you leave heaven?"

"The day we met. I saw you from up there and couldn't resist so decided to come to earth and sin like Eve, except it was much better than eating an apple. Do you think I'll go to hell for my sin?"

"If you do, I'm going with you." They laughed.

After they finished breakfast, he said, "You know, I feel stupid. Something has occurred to me which I should have thought about before."

She looked puzzled. "What's that?"

"Pregnancy."

"No problem. Everything is under control."

"I just felt I was obligated to mention it. It was actually stupid of me not to say anything last night, but the whole thing kind of caught me by surprise."

"I was wondering if you would say anything, and I'm glad you did. Let me ask you something—do you think I'm a nymphomaniac?"

"I'm not sure. If you are, you're a very intelligent one. Actually, if what you say about your feelings for me is true, you aren't one. If men can chase women, then women can chase men too, right?"

"Good thought. Actually, around you I *am* a nympho. Anyway, I have to be at the airport at noon. Can you give me a ride?"

"No, actually I have a tennis match at noon."

She looked surprised and puzzled, but when he started grinning she smiled, obviously realizing it was a joke.

"Did you think I would actually say no after yesterday?"

"No, but you shocked me for a second. I'm packed, so let's start out."

As he drove to the airport he thought about her and the amazing number of things they had in common. He also thought about how good she looked in her gray slacks and light blue blouse. He was glad she wasn't wearing a miniskirt, but he wondered how she would look in one.

"You know, I really do believe you were sent directly from heaven."

She said, "Yes, I do think the gods definitely had something to do with our meeting."

He pulled up in the drop-off zone and said. "Have a nice trip. I won't say 'don't forget to write' like they do in the movies, but I hope you won't forget to email."

"The way I feel right now, it will be like once an hour."

He smiled. "Okay, see you whenever." They engaged in a prolonged kiss until an airport employee came and grabbed her bags and they had to say good-bye.

Steve felt on top of the world. He felt like he was the luckiest guy in the world. Then he thought about his powers. He wondered again if there was a connection between them and her feelings toward him. Then there were the things they had in common. There must be some kind of spiritual connection. It was just too much of a coincidence. There had to be something supernatural going on, but what? Then what about this guy Skip? Had he just fallen in love too? Steve laughed. The whole thing was just too absurd. This must be a dream—a wet dream!

C H A P T E R   1 1

WHO IS BERT?

Steve got home and gave Bert a ring. "Hi, Bert. What's going on?"

"Nothing really new."

"Hey, I was wondering if you wanted try another game of backgammon?"

"Good idea. My place or yours?"

"Since you've never been over here, why not mine."

"Okay, what's your address?"

Steve gave him the address and said, "How about this evening around 7:30?"

"That's fine. See you then."

After Steve hung up he wondered what was next in the tennis world. He thought about taking a year off from teaching to play in all the major tournaments. Would they give him a sabbatical? It would be without pay of course. He decided to look into it, but for now he was a bit tired from the day before. Maybe he'd had a little too much food or sex. He lay down on his bed and took a nice nap. He woke up around five, went out for fast food, and killed some time online until it was time for Bert to arrive. He then checked his email. No news was good news. He continued to browse the web for a while.

At 7:30 the doorbell rang, and Steve answered it.

"Hi, Bert. Come on in. Care for a drink? I have soft drinks, beer, wine, or whatever."

"I'll have a glass of ice water if you have it."

"No problem."

Steve poured two glasses of ice water and got out the backgammon set.

"You know what, Bert? I don't even know your last name. Also do you have an email address?"

"That's funny—I guess it's never come up," Bert said. "My last name is Barnes, and I'll write down my email address for you." He pulled out a small notebook, wrote his email down, tore out the page, and handed it to Steve.

"Bert, I'm thinking on playing the tournament circuits for the next year. I'm going to ask for a sabbatical leave. If I get it, I'll be out of town, but we can communicate via email or phone if necessary."

Bert grinned and leaned back in his chair. He took a sip of his drink and said, "What are you going to give them for a reason, superpowers?" He chuckled. "Just joking, of course. But what are you going to say?"

"I don't quite know. Maybe I'll just say *Personal Reasons*. As I recall that's been done in the past."

They started playing backgammon for the same rate,

twenty-five cents a point. After an hour and a half Bert was ahead but by only a quarter.

Steve said, "How about a refill on the ice water?" Bert nodded, so Steve refilled the glasses.

"Say, Bert, I'd like to get know you better. What do you think about the state of the world?"

"The world? That's a tall order. I guess illegal drugs is one of our biggest problems. I agree with the *Economist* magazine. Legalizing everything is the lesser of evils! There's a law called the law of supply and demand. The attempt to make alcohol illegal in 1920 proved that law can't be overturned. It just added to the crime rate. But politicians are too stupid to realize it. Making it legal would solve the problem. It would eliminate gang violence, and it could be taxed like alcohol and cigarettes are taxed now. Warning labels would tell people the dangers. The government would save money on criminal enforcement and actually make money on taxes. Everything should be legalized, not just marijuana. Most people aren't stupid. A small number would get carried away and overdose as they do with alcohol today, but people like you and I would smoke a joint and relax just like we have a beer today. Sometimes I wonder how many politicians are profiting from the drug war. Anyway, what's another problem?"

"I agree with you one hundred percent. I smoked a joint or two in college. The first one was great, but the fun wore off. Maybe the first one I had was the strongest. Anyway, I only smoked three or four times after the first. Then I quit.

Of course, drug enforcement then picked up, and I didn't want to go to prison for smoking a joint."

Steve then thought about another topic. "Most people wouldn't agree with me, but another problem is religion, amplified by Muslim violence. They claim to be doing the will of God, but I'm waiting for the president or a congressperson to say 'let's ask them how they know anything about God'. Are you a religious person?"

Bert said, "No, I gave that up at the age of twelve."

"So how *would* you describe your views?"

"Well, I'm an atheist in the sense that I've never seen, heard, or sensed God in any way, and I have no evidence that God ever did anything, except maybe create all the diseases in the world that kill so many people. So why should I believe in him? I use the word *him*, but God could be a *her*. Actually it would be more accurate to call God an *it*, since sex is a property of living beings. I would think that a god would be way beyond sex. By the way, did you know that according to the Bible God had lots of sons?"

"No, I didn't. I thought he had only one, Jesus."

"Check out Genesis 6:2. He had sons who fell for the daughters of men. They went down to earth to marry them. Nothing was said about who the mother of his sons was, nor about the daughters of God. It seems he had only sons and no wife. Maybe God was a male chauvinist! I spent quite a bit of time studying the Bible. I found it superstitious nonsense. By the way, if Genesis 6 is true, then we may be descendents of God. Maybe that's how you got your power," he added with a laugh.

"Well, Bert, it's great to hear your views. What about health care?"

"It should be free for all. Just ask a politician if he believes in free public education. Even Republicans will say yes. Then ask them if free health care isn't equally important. How can a kid learn anything if he isn't healthy? Maybe the Democrats are too dumb to ask that question."

"I agree again. We seem to be of like minds. What kind of education did you have?"

"I started college. I majored in physics, but after two years I had to quit for financial reasons. I really enjoyed the math, physics, and chemistry. Calculus was great! But my father had a hardware store and needed help running it. When he died I took over. That's why I'm where I am today."

"You never married?"

"No, I couldn't find the right person. I wanted to find someone with a few brains, but since I didn't have a formal education, not many females were interested in me."

"One other question—the economy, which is in the pits. Unemployment has been high for some time. What do you think?"

"Well, wages for the lower and middle class have been dropping for years compared to the top few percent in the upper class, whose incomes are skyrocketing. There should be some kind of minimum wage, and it should be tied to inflation. I believe the Europeans adjust theirs every year. Why don't our leaders do that? Because they're too dumb! They don't seem to realize that the health of the economy depends on consumer spending. If you don't have any money you can't spend any. Simple deduction, right?"

"Bert, you keep hitting the nail on the head. If you run for president, I'll vote for you."

"No chance of that. I couldn't stand the environment."

"Well, Bert, it was great talking to you about all this. I'm going to head over to the college tomorrow and see about my leave."

Bert wished him good luck and thanked him for the conversation and backgammon. They said their good-byes, and he left.

Steve had enjoyed talking to Bert. He was a smart guy, just as he'd suspected all along.

Monday morning, July 23

Steve recalled the dean's name, Seth Aims. He'd almost forgot since he rarely got to talk to him. He called his office and made an appointment to talk to him. He told his secretary that it was rather important. Summer was kind of slow, so he got an appointment immediately.

Steve appeared at his office. He told the secretary who he was, and she said, "Oh, yes, go right in."

He went in and said, "Hello, Dr. Aims. Thank you for seeing me so soon."

"Hello, Steve, nice to see you. What's the problem?"

"No problem, really. It's just that I would like to take next year off, without pay of course."

"Oh, really, how come?"

"My reasons are kind of personal, and I would rather not talk about them."

"Well, I think I can understand. I've been in situations in the past where I needed time off. We'll miss you of course. You have had great student evaluations in the past. You've given me enough notice to find a replacement, so, yes, it can be arranged."

"Thank you very much. Is there any paperwork that I have to complete?"

"Yes, you have to write an official letter of request and have me sign it. I think we have standardized copies on file. Ask Judy, my secretary, and she'll give one to you."

Steve said thanks again and left his office. He asked Judy about the form, and she got one out immediately. It was short and sweet, and he signed it and gave it back to her. She made him a copy.

"Is that it, Judy?"

"Yes. You'll get a letter at your home confirming it."

"Okay, thank you very much. Bye for now."

"Good-bye, and good luck on your leave."

"Thanks again."

Steve was very surprised, and happy, about how little time the whole process took. When he got home he immediately went to the Web, found the USTA, and looked for tournaments. He found the pro circuit and was surprised at some of the prize money. Quite a few were for ten thousand bucks, but some were fifty thousand, and one, in Vancouver, Canada, was for one hundred thousand. Then he found one in Aptos, California, for the same amount.

Then he realized that was the total purse. He figured first place would be about a fourth or half of the total. He really didn't care much about the money; at this point the important thing was to improve his ranking. He felt quite confident that he would win, so he decided to hit the biggest ones first, since that would increase his ranking faster.

He went to the ATP site to check his ranking. There he was, ranked 132. He went down the pro circuit list and picked out four of the biggest and registered online. He then booked airline tickets to get to the Aptos tourney, which started on Thursday.

Even though he could call on his powers, he needed to practice a bit to get in top form. He called Paul Kist.

"Hey, Paul, how about some tennis?"

"Yeah, great. When do you want to play?"

"ASAP, since I'm going to try the pro circuit seriously this time."

"Really? You must think you're pretty good."

"I'm getting better. I'm now number 132 in the world."

"What? How did that happen?"

"I played in two biggies and won them both."

"Well, I'd like to take you on so can I see how I do against a pro. How about this evening at the club?"

"Okay, how about 7 p.m.?"

"Right, see you there."

Steve demolished Paul easily. He only used his powers on occasion when he needed them. He hit a net cord once and hit a few accurate lobs. He also sped up the ball on a few occasions and hit a few tough, un-returnable serves.

On Tuesday and Wednesday he played several of his other buddies and won as usual. He was very careful to make his shots look natural. By Wednesday around 3:00 he decided he'd had enough.

He had forgotten all about his email. He might have gotten one from Becky. He decided to check, and lo and behold there she was. It was dated Tuesday, 11 p.m. He opened it and read. "Hello, handsome. I have arrived. I miss you. What's going on? Have you met any beautiful babes yet? Remember, you're mine! Actually I should not say that since I really don't own you. Give me an email jingle."

Her email made him think more about her, her long, black, straight hair, her light brown skin, and her gorgeous smile. He wondered about her heritage. Asian? He didn't think so. Italian? Jones was not an Italian name. He'd have to ask her.

He hit *Reply.* "Hello, beautiful. I forgot my email for a day or so. I have not met any beautiful babes yet. I'm not looking. Have you met any handsome guys yet?

"Guess what! Since I did so well in the last two tournaments, I'm going to play the pro circuit for a few months. I applied for a leave of absence for a year without pay and got it. I'll bring my laptop so we can still communicate via email. I'm sure at least a few guys are after you. I'm not forgetting I'm yours. I'm curious about your job. Let me know exactly what you do. Bye for now."

CHAPTER 12

THE PRO CIRCUIT

Steve flew to Aptos, played in the tournament, and won. He used his powers sparingly. He made sure he won by close scores like 6-4 or 7-5 and occasionally lost a set. The last two matches required a bit more of his mystical powers but no one seemed to detect anything fishy. At the end of the tournament he accepted congratulations and twenty thousand dollars!

He checked his email from time to time and maintained communication with Becky. He won the next two tournaments with good money. He hadn't heard from Bert, so he sent him an email. Bert replied and informed him that Skip Hodges had dropped out of high school and started playing pro basketball. He was doing very well, making good money. He managed to keep his shooting percentage well above average but believable. When approached by the press he just said, "Well, I guess I'm just pretty good." Bert thought he was hiding his ability.

Steve kept tabs on his tennis rank. It was down to 119. In order to qualify for the big ones he would have to break 100. He got emails from Becky as usual. She finally told him what she did. "I'm what's called a Systems Integration Engineer. Computers play a big role. It's quite an interesting job, and it pays well. I can't tell you more."

Steve wondered whether she had some kind of security clearance. It was another intriguing thing about her.

It was September already, and Steve continued to play in the circuit. He had made well over one hundred thousand dollars. He played in three more big matches and was surprised that his rank was down to 76.

On December 1 he got an email from ATP. It read, "We noticed your rapid improvement in your rank and are impressed. You are hereby invited to play in the French Open Tennis tournament beginning Monday, May 6, next year. You will receive a formal invitation by mail. There is no entry fee. Housing will be provided. You must arrive by April 29, one week before play starts. We suggest you arrive at least a week earlier than that since we like players to see Paris and meet other players. Please reply if you are interested in playing."

He was ecstatic. The French Open! He could not believe it. He might be on TV. In fact, with the force on his side, he would be. He immediately replied and accepted. He wondered about the prize money. He checked. The total purse was 7.9 million Euros. How much was a Euro worth in dollars? He thought it was around a dollar. He didn't care. He decided to quit playing the pro circuit. Then again, maybe he should play in one more tournament to make it look like he needed the practice. He took the next flight home.

When he arrived he immediately picked up his mail from the post office and went back home. It was mostly junk—no bills, since he paid them all automatically online. There it was: a letter from the ATP, the same invitation with an application form and postpaid envelope. He filled it out, signed, and sealed it. He would post it tomorrow.

He immediately checked his email. Nothing from Becky or Bert. He started writing a new one to Becky. "Hey, beautiful, guess what. Due to my success on the circuit I have been invited to play in the French Open Tennis Tournament in Paris! It starts on May 6, but I have to arrive there by April 29. I will probably arrive a week or two before that. They provide housing. I know you are close to the end of your tour in Europe, so I may see you here before I go. Let me know what's up on your end. Steve." He hit *Send*. Then he sent Bert the same news.

He got a return email from Becky. "What? I can't believe it. That's an amazing piece of news. You must have been holding back when you played me. Unfortunately, I have to remain here a little longer than expected. I'd like to see you play in the French, but maybe I shouldn't since I don't want to distract you. Anyway, maybe you can come earlier and we can *visit* ha-ha. Right now I'm at the Grand Hyatt in Berlin, room 307. I'll let you know if there are any changes."

He hit *Reply*. "I'm as surprised as you are. I'll try to make it to Europe in early April. I can buzz over to Berlin and, as you say, we can *visit* :-)."

What next? Plane reservations! He decided on April 4. Then he had to find a partner to practice. He knew he really didn't really need to, but he should anyway. He couldn't let anybody find out that he'd won without practicing. Who would it be?

He decided to mix it up and play with a variety of people. He practiced with Paul, Mike, and a few others. He also played in one more tournament on the pro circuit. He won of course.

He kept up his emails with Becky and Bert. He told them both he was practicing for the big one.

Monday, April 1, 2019

He knew he was going to visit Becky in Berlin, but he thought he should check in at Paris first. He checked with ATP to find out if it was all right to arrive in early April. He also decided he would need a couple more rackets. He thought ahead to possible endorsements and decided to buy more popular brands than he usually did.

Once his plans were set he emailed Becky and told her he was leaving for Paris and that he would arrive in Berlin on the twelfth, which was a Friday. He asked her for the address of the hotel. She emailed back and gave him the address.

April 4 came, and he left. He arrived in Paris and got his housing at Roland-Garros that day. He met a few of the other players and practiced with them. He examined the schedule. The first round was the round of 128. He recognized a few of the top names, including the number-one player, Bruce Clark. According to the schedule, assuming Steve won all the previous matches, he would play Clark in the semifinals. He thought about his TK power, wondering how permanent it was and why he had it. He thought he would probably keep winning, but if the power deserted him he'd be on his own. So what—it would be an interesting experience in any case, and he still had Becky!

C H A P T E R 1 3

BERLIN

As planned, Steve flew to Berlin on the twelfth. He got a cab, arrived at the Grand Hyatt at 12:30, and called room 307. After several rings he got a recording that the guest was not available. He figured she was working. That was all right, since he had eaten hardly anything for breakfast and was hungry. He grabbed his suitcase, went over to the hotel restaurant, picked up an English-language newspaper, and ordered his usual breakfast: coffee, juice, eggs, and whole wheat toast. The news in Germany seemed to be very good: unemployment rate lower than the United States, an occasional murder, football results, which in the United States was called soccer, and mention of the French Open.

In the lobby he noted signs for a hop-on, hop-off bus tour. It was two and a half hours, but he could turn around any time. He decided to try it. He checked his bag at the hotel, and then he left.

It was fun. He hopped off occasionally to visit a store or two. He thought about buying something for Becky, but what? He couldn't decide, so he skipped it. He arrived back at the hotel at 5:00 p.m. He checked Becky's room, but there was still no answer. He knew that German beer was good, so he went down to the bar and ordered one. The fellow sitting next to him struck up a conversation in English.

"You are an American, right?"

"Yes, how did you know?"

"Your shoes give you away. My name is Alex. What's yours?"

"I'm Steve. Nice to meet you."

"You know what us Germans think of Americans?"

"I can guess, but you can tell me. What?"

"We think they are nuts!"

"That's what I thought. Some of us are nuts, but some are not. There's a major conflict between the Republicans and Democrats. The Democrats think the Republicans are nuts, and the Republicans think the Democrats are socialists or communists. I personally agree with your health care system. The one we have is almost as bad as nothing. By the way, I believe you have a minimum wage. What is it?"

"Well, I'm very glad to hear your opinion. Our minimum wage is fourteen Euros per hour. I think that's about seventeen US dollars. Your country does not seem to realize that higher wages are good for the economy. People who have money spend it! So what are you doing in Berlin?"

"I'm scheduled to play tennis in the French Open in Paris. I have some free time, so I thought I'd visit Berlin. I actually have a girlfriend who is working here."

"The French Open, wow! You must be a pretty good player."

"Well, not too bad. I'll find out soon enough. Hey, this is great beer. I think our beer is limited to about 3.2 percent alcohol. I think German beer is a bit higher."

"Yes, that's another way the US is behind the times. Our beer is 6 percent. What is your girlfriend's name?"

"Rebecca."

"Is her last name Jones?"

Steve's eyebrows raised, and he tilted his head in surprise. "Why, yes. Do you know her?"

"Yes, we work together on occasion. She is very bright, not to mention good looking. I asked her for a date once, but she told me she was engaged. I said, 'Where is the ring,' and she said she didn't like rings. She said they just get in the way. You must be her fiancé."

Steve lied. "Yes. By the way, what kind of work do you do?"

"I'm really not a liberty to talk about it. Does Rebecca ever talk about her job?"

Steve wondered if Alex and Becky both worked for the government and if Alex was trying to find out if Becky gave out any information about her job. "I guess we never really discussed it in detail. She just said something about computers. Well, I must be going. Nice talking to you."

"Yes, good luck in the tournament. I'll be watching it. What's your last name?"

"Thomas. What's yours?"

"Hahn. I hope to see you later."

"Yes, bye for now."

As he left the bar, he wondered again about what Becky did. Maybe it was top-secret, classified government work. Perhaps that was why she wouldn't talk much about her job.

It was quite a coincidence, bumping into a guy who worked with Becky. He would have to tell her. He didn't realize it was as late as 6:30. He went over to the hotel phone and dialed her number again, and this time she answered.

"You're finally back from work."

"Oh, Steve, it's great to hear your voice. I just arrived. I'm starved. Are you hungry?"

"Yes, I am."

"Good, I'll be right down."

She came down, and they headed for the hotel restaurant. She looked very professional in her business clothes but a bit tired.

"You look like you've been working hard."

"You don't know the half of it, but today's Friday so I have two days of rest. Did you sign up in Paris?"

"Yes, I went there first. I'm going back on the twenty-second, so we have some time."

"Well, we have this weekend, but unfortunately I'm back to work Monday."

They ordered a meal, and he ordered his second beer. She also ordered one. "German beer is great," he said.

"You're right. It beats American beer by a mile."

They finished eating and took the elevator up to her

room. It was 9:50. She turned around and put her arms around his neck. They kissed, and then she said, "I'm beat. I'm going to take a shower and turn in for the night. This room has two single beds, so you can have the other one. Is that okay with you?"

"Yes, that's fine. Two in a single bed is not too comfortable. I'll grab a shower and turn in also. Oh, I forgot to mention I bumped into someone in the bar who knows you. His name is Alex Hahn."

"Really, what a coincidence!"

"Yeah, we were talking about you, and he said he asked you for a date once and you told him you were engaged. Who's the lucky guy?"

She grinned. "You know who it is—it's you! Actually, I tell men I'm engaged to ward off the hounds. They all seem to be decent fellows though. Actually, I have more trouble with the women. They seem to be jealous of me even after I tell them I'm not interested in any of their men."

They both showered and turned in. He dreamt about the tournament. The ball wouldn't behave. He lost. Then he woke up. A dim light was on. Someone was touching him, and he knew who. He said, "Hello, my sweet!"

"Hello. I woke up early and remembered you were here."

"What time is it?"

"It's around five."

He caressed her beautiful body and kissed her. They made love and fell asleep in the same bed.

He awoke around 9 a.m. There she was cuddled asleep next to him. He studied her. She was beautiful as usual. She stirred.

He said, "Good morning. Are you rested?"

"Yes, well rested. Are you ready for breakfast?"

"Yes. The usual?"

"Yes." She smiled. "Coffee, eggs over medium, and whole wheat toast."

They got dressed and went down to breakfast. Afterward they took a walk around town.

They continued to walk and talk. He asked her some of the same questions he'd discussed with Bert and found that she had the same point of view as he and Bert. He was very glad to hear that. He wondered if she ever wanted to get married.

He said, "Do you like kids?"

She stopped and looked him in the face. "Is that a proposal?"

"Not yet." He smiled. "Answer the question."

"Of course. Babies are very cute. You want to know if I want to have any of my own, right? I have thought about that. I think I'd like to have yours. Do you want to have mine?"

"Marriage is a big step of course. I always worry that after being married for some years the infatuation wears off. Right now I am in love with you, but will I be in ten years? Will you?"

"Who knows? Let's just worry about the present."

"Yes, I agree."

She showed him around Berlin. He asked about her job, and she said she really couldn't talk about it. As he suspected, she was sworn to confidentiality.

They spent the day walking and chatting and getting to know each other better. They had supper and took in a movie and went back to her hotel. Upon returning she gave him a key card to the hotel room and said he could stay there. On Sunday, they did the same as Saturday, walking around Berlin and talking. Monday morning she awoke early and was gone before he woke up. He arose, ate breakfast, bought an English newspaper, and picked up a novel called *Walden Two*. He spent the weekdays walking around town and reading. He stayed that week and another weekend and then returned to Paris.

It was time to play tennis!

C H A P T E R 1 4

THE FRENCH OPEN

He spent the time before the tournament practicing with other players and got to know several fairly well. One day at a get-together he was introduced to Bruce Clark, who, if all went as he planned, would be his opponent in the semifinals. Bruce said hello but very little else. On another day he bumped into Sam Finch, the guy he'd beaten in the final match in the tournament in Portland.

Sam said, "Hey, I know you. I played you somewhere, but I forget where. You beat me, as I recall. You made some unbelievable shots. I guess you're still in it. I'd like you to meet my friend Henry Thomson."

"Hello, Henry." They shook hands.

Henry said, "Call me Hank. Hey, maybe we can find a fourth and play a little doubles."

Sam said, "I'm sure we can find someone. I'll look around. Let's meet here at two."

They agreed. Steve remembered that Sam had been kind of shocked at his great play and was a little worried about being detected. Two o'clock rolled around, and they showed up with a fourth player.

"Hi. My name is Boban Dokik. You can call me Bob."

Steve asked, "Hello, Bob. Where are you from?"

"Serbia. How about you?"

"California, in the United States."

"Wow, I get to play with three Americans! Let's go!"

They got a court and went out to rally. Steve decided to not to use the force since there was always a risk that it could be detected. They played three sets. Henry was his partner. Steve slipped and accidentally used the force on two shots. He was a good player without it, but it was so tempting. They won the first set and lost the next two.

"Great workout," Sam said. They celebrated over a beer and chatted about the tournament.

Finally, practice was over, and the tournament started. He was scheduled to play one match a day for the first three rounds. Steve knew he was considered an underdog to say the least.

In the first three rounds Steve won, qualifying him for the round of 16. Thanks to the force he was doing well. As always he was very careful to disguise his shots.

There was a day of rest before the critical and important fourth round, and he spent some of it emailing Becky.

"Hello, my Becky. Round three was mine! Now to the round of 16." He mentioned that he'd played doubles with a player from the states he had played before. He also kept Bert informed.

He won the round of 16, which was followed by another day of rest and then the quarterfinals. He was surprised to find he'd be playing Sam Finch. Since Sam was a bright guy, Steve was going to have to be very careful with his shots.

"Hi, Sam, nice meeting you again in this round." Sam nodded but didn't say much. Steve realized Sam was bent on winning.

Steve knew he could always win his serve, so all he had to do was win just one of his opponent's serves.

Steve won the first set 6-4. He decided not use the force in the next set and lost it 6-3 but by carefully putting some extra, magical force on his serves won the next two 6-4 and 7-5.

Sam congratulated him. "Good match, Steve." They shook hands. Steve noticed a slight expression of wonder on Sam's face, as though he could not quite believe what had happened.

C H A P T E R   1 5

SAM'S DOUBTS

am and Hank sat in the corner of the lounge, chatting about the match over a couple of beers. Sam spoke in a very animated manner and seemed very upset. He used his hands, pointing at Hank when he spoke. "I tell you there's something fishy about his game. It's not just talent. I don't know if you've ever noticed, but the ball normally slows down slightly after you hit it. That's physics. Wind resistance slows it down. On a few of *his* shots, the ball actually went faster! That's impossible." He waved his arms to simulate the ball slowing down. "Then on some other shots I hit him, the ball curved very slightly toward him. It was hardly noticeable, but it was there, I'm sure. How can anybody do that? It's impossible. I think he may be from outer space!"

Hank smiled. "Yeah, maybe he's an alien. No, I think you're imagining things. How can anybody do those things? Impossible! Tennis balls sometimes curve. You're probably just upset because you lost."

"No, no, I know what I saw. I'm going to try and get the videos of the games and study them. They might show something. Also I'm going to tape his semifinal match with Clark to see how he handles it."

"You shouldn't say tape anymore. It's all hard drives and DVDs now. Anyway, that's a good idea, but I don't think you'll find anything."

Steve was also having a beer in the lounge. He was very happy with the results until he saw Sam and Hank talking over a beer in the far corner. It seemed a very agitated conversation. He wondered if it had anything to do with himself. Had Sam noticed anything? Maybe, but what could it be? He had been very careful to disguise his shots and tried to hit as few winners with the force as possible. He knew, however, that he could not do it perfectly. There had to be differences from normal play. Maybe an experienced player could notice things. As he was worrying about this, his eyes met Sam's. Steve looked away quickly and decided to leave.

Sam noticed that Steve was looking over at them and that when their eyes met Steve quickly looked away. He said to Hank, "Look—he just glanced at us and turned away right away, and now he's leaving. He looked a little guilty. That confirms my suspicions!"

Hank said, "Maybe you're right. As you say, let's investigate further."

Steve went to his room and emailed Becky. "Guess what, I won my quarterfinal match. That means I'm in the money. $200,000 at least. Wish me luck in the semifinal."

He also emailed Bert with the news. Then he lay down on the bed and thought about the match. Could his shots be detected as unusual? If so, which shots? He thought about when he'd added speed to the ball. Maybe he was adding it too late. He should add it right off his racket. The fact that it picked up speed later could be noticeable. His serves were the least detectable. If he won all his service games, he couldn't lose the match. He decided to concentrate on them.

His laptop beeped, letting him know he'd got new email, so he got up to check it. It was from Becky. "Congratulations, handsome! I recorded your match and watched it when I got back here. I was a little worried when you lost the second set, but it was great that you pulled out of it. I'm going to record your semifinal against Clark. I wish I could be there to root for you. Anyway, I'll see it. I wish you luck, but I hope you won't need it. Watch out for the groupies. I love you, Becky."

He wished she were here also. He thought about love. What did it mean, anyway? Was he just infatuated with her? He knew he was infatuated, but he believed there was more to it. It was amazing how many things they had in common. What about marriage? Should he propose? Should he tell her about his powers? He really couldn't keep it a secret from her forever. What would she think? Would it change their relationship?

He was tired, so he lay back down on the bed and took a nap.

He slept for about an hour and was wakened by a beep from his laptop. Another email, this time from Bert. "Congrats on your win. I watched you on TV. Great match. You pulled it off. I could not detect anything odd. I'll watch you Friday."

Steve realized he'd lost track of what day it was and checked his computer; it was Wednesday, so tomorrow would be a day of rest before the semifinal. He thought about how long the match should be—three, four, or five sets? What about tiebreakers? He had to keep the use of the force to a minimum and be more careful. Since he was playing against the number-one ranked player, maybe it should be five sets. He decided to play it by ear.

Friday rolled around. He and Bruce entered the court. The coin toss gave Bruce the serve. Clark served two aces and won the first game. In the second game Steve also served two aces, the first by use of the force, the second naturally. He lost the next point but won the next two. He ended up winning the first set 7-5. He decided to win the second, so he turned the force on, mainly on his serves, and won it 6-4. He was ahead 2-0. He decided to play without the force in the third set and lost it 6-3. Should he win the fourth set? For some reason his ego turned on, and he decided he wanted to show the world that he was a great player. He won the set 6-2 and the match with a final score of 3-1. He and Bruce shook hands. "Great match," he said.

Steve was headed for the finals. He was congratulated

by lots of people, including two good-looking girls. He had beaten the number-one ranked player. He was almost a hero. He entered the lounge bar, where a large group was gathered. Many said, "Great match! Great last set, 6-2!"

Two girls cuddled up to him, one on each side. One asked if he was married. He said no, and she seemed pleased. The other asked him if he liked to dance. He decided to lie and said, "No, I don't know how," even though he liked to dance.

She said, "Oh, I can teach you. Let's go dancing tonight!"

He apologized. "Sorry, but I have to be in good shape for the final."

Steve retired to his room. For some reason he was not particularly happy about his win. In fact, he was a little depressed. After all, it really wasn't he who won. It was the force. He again wondered about the whole thing. What was the purpose of all this anyway? Regardless, though, he was in the finals and had to finish it. He got online to check his winnings so far: eight hundred thousand dollars.

He also looked up who his opponent would be in the final. It would be a tall Swedish guy named Alex Bergman. He was ranked seventh. He had climbed the ranks very fast and according to what Steve found out had a great first serve. He knew that lots of first serves were faults, though, and he could handle the second serve. He checked out Bergman's statistics in the tournament so far. One 3-0 win, two 3-1 wins, and three 3-2 wins. Obviously he wasn't perfect.

He thought about emailing Becky or Bert, but they would probably email him. He lay down on his bed and contemplated life so far. Maybe he was meant to do something besides win tennis tournaments with his power. What would that be? If the public knew about his power, what would they think? Maybe the evangelists would consider him Jesus. The Jews might consider him their savior. Some might consider him Satan and try to kill him. He would have to keep his power a secret for as long as possible.

After the finals he would have enough money to quit his job. Of course he shouldn't stop playing tournaments with the French. There was Wimbledon and the US Open. He'd never played on grass. He'd always thought that grass was stupid. It was a little more slippery than hard court or clay, and by the time the finals rolled around there wasn't much grass left on center court. He wondered if England would ever wise up.

Before going to sleep that night he checked his laptop and found an email from Becky. "I don't believe it. You won again! You're a superstar! I hope you don't ditch me. Luck in the final."

He had no email from Bert. He guessed Bert thought it was obvious he would win.

CHAPTER 16

THE FINAL

Sunday, May 19

Steve grabbed his stuff and went out to center court at the prescribed time. After a brief warm-up, practice serves, and the like, they started. Alex won the toss and would serve the first game. Steve decided not to use his power in the first set, and Bergman went on to win it on his great serve. Steve didn't worry, since he knew he could always win his own serves.

In the second set Steve won his serves with the force when necessary, broke his serve once, and won the set 6-3, so they were at one set each.

Bergman won the third set, and Steve the fourth. In the fifth set Steve won the first game with his serve and lost to Bergman's serve in the second game, won his serve in the third and lost to Bergman's aces in the fourth. The score was two games each.

In the next four games they alternated again, each winning his own serves. The score was four games each.

Steve won the ninth game on first serve aces. He was ahead 5-4.

In the tenth game Bergman did not serve a first-serve ace, and they had a long rally, Steve hitting a shot deep to his backhand, coming to the net, and putting Bergman's halfhearted lob away. He led 15-love. With good first serves Bergman won the next two points, but his serve did not come through on the next, and Steve was able to win it on a force-field lob. The score was 30 all. Bergman then got his first serve in, but Steve was able to get it back. Bergman then flubbed a shot, hitting it into the net. Steve had the advantage and match point! He planned not to use the force on the next point, but it wasn't even an option because Bergman double faulted to end the match. Steve won it 3-2. The crowd cheered; he was a hero!

He was almost ashamed to go through with the winning ceremony. Then he had to talk to the TV announcer. She asked him how he felt. He told her he felt great but he knew he was a bit lucky winning on a double fault.

After all the press nonsense he went to the main desk. They said they could send his check to his bank via direct deposit, so he made the proper arrangements. It was for 1.65 million dollars.

He knew Becky would be working the next week, so he asked if he could stay in his room another week. The manager said, "Of course. Anything you want—you're the big winner!"

He retired to his room. Winning on a double fault—was that luck or providence? He lay down and fell asleep. He woke up around 8 p.m. and was hungry. He decided on a good meal. He went down to the hotel restaurant and ordered a steak deluxe, salad, baked potato, sour cream, and of course a beer.

He came back to his room and noticed an email from Becky. "Wow, you did it. I don't believe it. Now you can have all the groupies, one at a time. Can I be one of them? Will you be coming back to Berlin? I hope so."

He hit *Reply*. "Yes, but I thought that since you are working next week I'd stay in Paris to see the sights. I'll head over there on Friday. I'm ignoring the groupies, they can't top you!"

He also got an email from Bert. "You won as I knew you would. When will you be back in town?"

He replied, "Probably in about two weeks. I'll call you."

He hung around Paris for the week, read his novel, and played chess online. On Thursday night he ate a late, light supper. Since it was his last night in Paris, he decided to take a stroll.

After a few blocks he noticed that he was not in a particularly nice part of town. Then he came across a bar with good music coming from it. He glanced in and saw people dancing, so he went in and ordered a beer. He got a seat in a remote corner and watched the good-looking girls dance. Then one came up to him and said in broken English, "Care to dance?"

He hadn't danced in a long time, so he said, "Sure."
They went out and did a swing dance. He enjoyed it.
After it was over, she came to his table. "That was fun.
What kind of work do you do?"

"I'm a math professor," he said.

"Oh, wow. I never understood maths. I didn't know
teachers of maths could dance so well."

A typical comment from the average idiot, Steve
thought. "I think that math and dancing are two unrelated
things. Some people can do both."

"Yes, I guess that is so," she said.

Then the French Open finals came up on the TV, and
there he was. He guessed he shouldn't have been surprised
that bars in Paris showed sports on their TVs just like bars
at home. They showed the double fault and the interview
at the end.

The girl looked at him and the TV, yelled something
in French and pointed to him. The crowd turned, looked,
and came over to congratulate him.

He was surprised at how many spoke English. "Thank
you, thank you," he said. They bought him another beer
and wanted a speech.

He said, "Well, when you win on a double fault, you
know you're lucky." He wasn't sure they understood, but
they laughed. He chatted for a while and then said he had
to leave. They waved him good-bye as he left the bar.

It was late, and he decided to head back to his room.
As he was walking down the rather dark street, he saw
another guy was coming toward him. He stopped about

twenty feet in front of Steve, pulled out a gun, and said something in French. Steve shrugged and put his hands out to indicate he didn't understand. Then in English the man said, "Give me your wallet and ..." He pointed to his wrist. Obviously he wanted Steve's money and his watch.

Steve stared at him, thinking to himself, *Can the force stop bullets?* He had little time to think. *What the hell—if I die and go to heaven, or somewhere else, I may find out about the force.* He threw the force field about ten feet in front of himself, turned, and started to run. He heard two shots but didn't feel a thing. He turned, looked back, and was astonished to see two bullets sitting in the air about six feet in front of him. The guy fired two more, and they joined the first two. What should he do? Without thinking it through, Steve turned the bullets around and sent them back to the shooter at top speed. They all hit him in the chest and knocked him flat. The guy didn't move.

Steve thought that someone would have heard the shots, but it seemed no one was around. He had to get out of there fast, but he thought he'd better not run since he might be considered the shooter. He turned around and walked as fast as he could away from the scene. He was amazed that the force could stop bullets!

Walking at top speed, he headed back to his room. When he got there he decided to email Bert. He told Bert what had happened. He then said he would visit Becky over weekend and might stay in Berlin for a week or so.

CHAPTER 17

BECKY IN BERLIN

Friday morning, May 24

S teve packed up his tennis stuff to send back to San Jose since he wouldn't need it for the rest of his trip. After breakfast he bought an English-language newspaper and glanced at the front page. The headline read *Parolee Shot with Own Bullets—Police Confused.* He sat down and read the article.

According the article the parolee was still alive but had refused to tell the police how he'd ended up with four bullets from his own gun embedded in his chest and stomach. It also mentioned that the bullets had only gone about two centimeters into the parolee's flesh.

Steve smiled, amused at this turn of events. He realized he was extremely lucky that nobody saw him do it. Steve wondered if the guy could identify him. It had been quite dark, so he was pretty sure his would-be mugger hadn't got a good look at his face, but he might have noticed Steve's clothing. Maybe he should get rid of the clothes he wore that night. He packed them up with his tennis stuff. The tournament manager arranged for the package to be sent home at no charge.

He boarded his flight for Berlin around 4 p.m. Friday. The flight was due to arrive around 5:30, which meant he might not have to wait long for Becky to get off work. By the time he'd got his bag, cleared customs, and caught a cab to her hotel, it was a little before six. He hoped she'd be there. He paid the fare, grabbed his bag, and thought about letting himself into her rooms. Rather than surprise her he decided to ring her room.

She answered. "Steven, my hero. You won it. Come on up."

When he got there, the door was open with her standing in it. "I wouldn't have believed it. Not that I didn't think you were good but not *that* good."

Steve said, "His double fault on the last point proves that luck played a factor."

She put her arms around his neck and lifted her feet up. He held her and swung her in a three-hundred-sixty-degree circle while they kissed a long one. "I think you're about to get lucky again," she said with a suggestive grin. She pulled him into the bedroom, and they made passionate love.

Afterward, Steve said, "Boy, it's nice to see you again. You look so great."

They got up and dressed. She said, "How about celebrating with a beer?"

"I'd like nothing better."

Her suite had kitchen facilities. She went to the kitchen and came back with a couple of bottles. They sat on the couch. He took a swig and said, "The first swallow is the best one!"

"You're right. So tell me about Paris. Did you meet any nice women?"

"Not one. Actually I stumbled in on a bar where they were dancing so I went in. I did dance with one girl, but that was the only contact I had with women. You were on my mind the whole time."

"I didn't know you danced. I do too. What dances do you know?"

"The jitterbug is my favorite. I know the cha-cha and obvious the slow dance. I also like rock-and-roll dances like the twist."

"Wow, I love the jitterbug. Hey, we'll have to go out and do it some time, maybe tomorrow night."

After finishing the beer he said, "Shall we go out to eat?"

"No, I have a surprise. My suite has cooking facilities, and I did a little cooking. I made my favorite Mexican dish. I hope you like Mexican food."

"I do. I never thought of you as a homebody knowing how to cook."

"I cook for myself often. That way you can make the food exactly the way you like it. Salads are almost always better at home than the ones you get in a restaurant."

She then said, "Would you like another beer with dinner? I'm just having ice water."

"I'll take the same."

While eating he asked, "So how's the job going?"

"Oh, it's going, but I'd rather not talk about it. So what are you going to do with all that money?"

"I haven't really given it a thought. I think I'm expected to play Wimbledon. Have you ever been in England?"

"Yes, I did some work there one time. It was cold and rainy, not my favorite place."

After they finished eating, she said, "The only thing I ever eat for dessert is ice cream, and I only eat that about once a week, but I'm in the mood for it today. Would you like some?"

"I'd love some. What flavors do you have?"

"I'm a vanilla freak. But I have pralines and cream and coffee."

"I'll try the coffee. Do you think it will keep me awake?"

She smiled. "No, but I will."

He laughed. "I'm looking forward to it."

They finished eating, chatted for awhile, and went to the bedroom.

"I'm grabbing a shower. Do you want one?"

"Yes, I could use one."

She went into the shower, and while undressing he contemplated telling her about the force field. No, not tonight. Maybe never. She came out of the shower, and he went in. When he finished, he toweled off and came out. She was standing there nude.

"I don't think we've ever really looked at one another completely nude, so I thought this might be a good time."

They looked at each other up and down. He said, "I think I have the best view."

"Well, mine is excellent."

They moved closer and stared at each other's face.

He said, "I love your face. It's perfect."

"I never thought it was perfect, but I love yours." They kissed and went to bed.

CHAPTER 18

BECKY SUSPECTS

Saturday morning.

As they were getting dressed, Becky said, "I have an idea what we can do today. There's a museum here in Berlin called the German Museum of Technology. Since you're an engineering-type person, I thought you might be interested in going."

"Hey, that sounds great. Let's go."

After breakfast they left for the museum. They spent the whole day there. He was amazed at all the planes, tanks, trains, and rocket engines, some from World War II. "Hey, this is great stuff. I'm glad we came."

"I'm really glad you like it."

They found a restaurant near the museum for dinner and then headed back to her hotel.

She said, "How about teaching me a little chess?"

He was surprised. "Chess, my favorite game. Okay, I assume you have a set."

"Yes, of course, since I don't want to play blindfolded. I hear that Koltanowski was one of the best at that."

"How did you find out about him?"

"I boned up on chess while you were in Paris. I even tried a few games online. I mostly lost."

"We can play a friendly game, sometimes called a teaching game. If you make a bad move we discuss it, and you can take it back. Of course if I make one you have to let me take it back, too."

"Hey, that's a great idea. It sounds like fun."

He said, "You may already know about a few key terms used in chess. They are *fork, pin, discovered check, double check*, and maybe a few others I can't think of right now."

"Oh, I think I know about a few. Can you show me examples?"

She got out the set, and they played. She played better than he expected but made a few mistakes, which he corrected. She actually won a game in which he corrected only one error. After awhile they got a little tired of playing, and he showed her some fancy checkmates. She loved the smothered mate.

She said, "That was really fun, and I learned a lot. By the way, did you hear about that crazy thing that happened in Paris, a guy getting hit with his own bullets? Nobody can figure it out."

"Yes, I read about it in the paper. Unbelievable. I can't imagine how it could have happened. It's a mystery."

She looked at him in a strange way and then glanced away, hesitating.

"What's that strange look for? You don't think that I had anything to do with that, do you?"

"No, of course not. But then there is this strange attraction I have for you, which I really don't understand. There seems to be some strange force acting on me. What day was that when you were dancing in the bar?"

Without thinking he said, "It was Thursday night." Then he realized that maybe he should have lied.

She said, "Do you know that was the same night as the shooting? Isn't that a coincidence?" She stared at him as though expecting a response.

"Yes, that's what it is, a coincidence. How could I have anything to do with that?"

"I don't know. But you have some kind of power over me. I know that. Who knows what other kind of power you have. Sorry I mentioned it, but you have to realize that there must be some kind of strange force involved in the shooting."

He was surprised at her using the word *force*. She was a very bright babe.

"Yes, but I don't know how you can think that I was involved. I'm as confused as you are. Maybe the authorities will figure something out."

She said, "It's midnight. Shall we turn in? My brain is saturated with chess and other things."

"Good idea." They went to bed and melted together as usual.

Sunday morning, May 26

She said, "I wonder if you know how much you turn me on. I can't believe last night."

"You turn me on more."

"Let's not start that again. You know, I have a great idea for today—tennis."

He was kind of surprised. "Why not? I know you want revenge. However, I shipped my rackets back home. Do you have a spare?"

"Of course. Yes, I'm going to try hard to beat you this time. Don't use your magic power."

His eyebrows rose, and his head jerked back in surprise. He looked at her for a few seconds and said, "What magic power?"

"Just joking. I thought if you can control my brain maybe you can control my body too, other than in bed of course."

They ate breakfast and headed out to a public court. A court was available. He of course would not use his force field. She started serving and served very well, winning the first set. He won the second set 6-3. In the third set she surprised him with a few really great shots, and she won it 6-4. They played a fourth and she played very well again. It was tied it up at 6-6. They played a tiebreaker, and he won it 7-5.

She said, "Well, you have just shown me how you won the French. Did you let me win the second set?"

"No, I didn't. I played my best. Your game is great. You could easily become a pro."

They went back to her hotel, dressed for dinner, and then went out to eat. After dinner they strolled over to a park. There were quite a few pigeons around.

She said, "A lot of stupid people feed the pigeons, even though they are not supposed to, so the birds hang around forever. I don't believe in feeding wildlife, do you?"

"Absolutely not. The definition of *wild* is that they're on their own. If you feed then they become tame, not wild. Hey, it's getting dark. Let's walk around town a bit."

After a few hours walking she said, "Hey, I know of a neat game store. Do you want to go take a look?"

He said, "Sure, why not. I'm really not in the market to buy anything, but it would be nice to look."

They took a walk down a rather narrow side street and came to the store.

"Oh, nuts, it's closed. Wow, it's 11:30. I didn't realize it was so late. Oh, well, we can look in the window."

In the window were some nice chess sets, a backgammon set, and even a Go set.

He pointed it out to her. "That's a Go set. I think I mentioned to you once that I played it for awhile."

"Yes, I remember. You'll have to teach me how to play."

"Okay, when we get back to San Jose I will. In one sense it's boring. You put these little stones on the board and try to surround the other guy. Chess is much more exciting."

They left and headed down the block. Down near the corner a van was parked. As they approached two guys got out. One had a gun. They said something in German.

Becky translated for him. "They want our money, your wallet, and my purse."

Steve thought, *I can't believe this—two muggings in one week?*

He said, "Well, they probably need the money more than we do. We might as well cooperate." He reached for his wallet.

They approached, and the first guy looked at Becky, said something, and moved toward her. It was clear to Steve that they were going to grab her and take her away.

She backed up a step. "I am not!"

He reached over and grabbed her arm while the second guy slid open the van's side door.

That was too much for Steve. He couldn't let that happen. He added a force field about eight inches deep to his right fist and at the same time used the field with his left hand to grab the gun. He swung his right hand, accelerating the field forward, and hit the guy squarely in his forehead. He heard a loud crack and the guy went down.

The second guy swore and pulled out a gun. Steve grabbed it with the field and used the same force field to punch him in the ribs. He heard another crack. The guy folded, unconscious.

Steve knew he had to get rid of the guns, so he tossed them down the street. The second guy groaned. What if this guy had other guns and came after them? He didn't want that to happen, so he hit his lower leg in sort of a force-field karate chop and felt the leg break.

Then he said, "Come on, let's get out of here."

Becky just stood there, staring at him. He grabbed her arm, and they started walking.

After walking about two blocks she stopped and said, "Who are you? What are you?"

"I'll explain later. We have to get out of here now."

They walked quickly together, though not fast enough to arouse suspicion. Steve's heart raced. He couldn't believe that his secret was out, but they were going to kidnap Becky. He had no choice. What else could he have done? He glanced over at her and thought he saw fear in her eyes. Was she now afraid of him?

They walked another several blocks. She stopped. "You have to tell me right now."

"Please don't be afraid of me. It's a long story. I'll explain everything in your hotel room."

He was afraid she'd protest, but she simply nodded and resumed walking. When they arrived in her hotel suite, he said, "Becky, I'm really sorry for what happened. I do have this strange power. Don't ask me why, because I don't know. It just suddenly appeared last year."

He told her the whole story from the florescent light bulbs onward. He told her that Bert was the only other person who knew about it, and that was because he had been involved in the discovery.

"So I was right. Why couldn't you tell me before?"

"I was afraid of what you'd think. Maybe you'd ditch me. I was never going to tell a soul. If I told anyone, I'd have to demonstrate it, and it's the kind of thing that wouldn't be kept secret for long. It would become news fast, and I'd be the center of attention. I wouldn't be left alone. What would happen to me then? I'd be a freak. Actually, I am a freak. Some people would think I was a god. Some would think I was the devil. Some people might try and kill me. They might put me in the zoo. It has to be kept a secret. Do you understand?"

"I understand. Part of me doesn't believe it. I feel like I'm having a nightmare. So you *are* the cause of the bullets in that guy's chest in Paris."

Boy, was she quick. "Yes, I stopped the bullets in midair and turned them around and accelerated them back to him. I shouldn't have done it, but I was so surprised at being able to stop bullets that I couldn't think of what else to do. I didn't realize it would become news. I shouldn't have made them go as fast as they, did but there was no time to think."

"And that's how you won the French Open?"

He stared at her for a few seconds and said, "Yes, I'm ashamed to admit it. It was Bert's idea to turn the power into money. I thought it was a good idea at the time. Why not? Nobody gets hurt, and I get rich. Before all this I was a reasonably happy guy. I really wish it all hadn't happened. The real question is why and how? Will I ever know?"

"Now I don't know what I should do. My boyfriend is a god. There has to be a connection to how I feel about you. It was unreal because you are unreal. So why am I involved? If there is a god controlling you, it's also controlling me. I feel that you're so far above me that I shouldn't go to bed with you."

"No, you are part of it. I really believed your feelings

originally and thought there must be a connection to my powers, but I had no idea what it could be. Somehow you were meant to be part of it. You *are* part of it and can't deny it. We were meant to be together, don't you see?"

"Yes, you're right." She smiled. "Am I a goddess? I really don't feel like one. I guess I'm going to tag along for the final event if there is one. By the way, according to your story you demonstrated your powers for Bert. I'd like you to give me one, too, right now!"

He stared at her for a few seconds and then looked around. "See that salt shaker over there? Keep an eye on it." He picked it up with the force and floated it over to his hand.

"My God! I can't believe it. This must be a dream. Anyway, I have to go to work tomorrow. Will I be able to function? I hope so. I guess it's time hit the sack."

"Wait. You can't tell a soul! Absolutely, positively no one! Do you understand?"

"I do. You can count on me to keep it a secret."

As they undressed for bed, he said, "You know, if you really don't want to engage in sex, it's okay with me. I'll understand."

"I've made love to a god in the past—why should I stop now?"

Steve smiled and then said, "You know, after today I think I've had it with Berlin. I think I'm going to head back to San Jose tomorrow."

"I understand. Since I'm working we wouldn't be able to spend a lot of time together anyway," she said. Then she shook her head and added, "It's amazing that you were attacked twice here in Europe."

"Yes, it is too much of a coincidence. Maybe its part of the plan of providence for me."

She looked at him strangely. "The plan of providence?"

"Well, you have to admit that what's happening to me is very unusual. Something must be behind it."

"You're right. I guess only time will tell."

"When will *you* be back in San Jose?"

"I never know from one day to the next. I'll say good-bye now since I'll probably leave before you wake up."

They kissed good-bye, dressed for bed, and turned in.

C H A P T E R   1   9

BACK TO SAN JOSE

Monday morning, May 27

When Steve awoke Becky had already gone to work. He managed to find a flight that was to leave at noon, so he dressed, packed, called a cab, and went to the airport. He picked up an English newspaper and ordered breakfast at the airport. An article on the second page read,

> *Gang member Albert Faust was found dead with a broken cranium, apparently struck with a blunt object. His friend Jon Spitz, found nearby, had two broken ribs and a broken leg. Guns were found on the street nearby, apparently belonging to the two of them. Faust and Spitz are wanted for kidnapping and murder. Police were*

*pleased, but they were confused as to what
happened and who disabled them.*

That was another interesting turn of events. He was
becoming a vigilante like the guy in the movie *Death Wish*.
His flight came up. He boarded and flew back to San
Jose. It was a long flight, fourteen hours. After landing he
grabbed a bit of supper at the airport. He finally arrived
home. It was late, but he decided to email Bert anyway. He
suggested they get together the following evening.

He was tired and went to bed. After a good night's
sleep he awoke at ten the next morning. He lay in bed and
thought about the crazy sequence of events of the last few
weeks. Getting attacked not once, but twice. The force
was more powerful than he imagined, stopping bullets in
midair! He could adjust it a variety of ways. It could be
a *hand* to control things or it could be a *force*. He could
accelerate it to increase its power. Now Becky knew about
it. He hoped she had the sense not to tell anyone. He was
sure she wouldn't. Even if she did, why would anyone believe her? She would have no evidence, just her word. She
would be considered crazy.

What was next? Should he continue with the big three
and play Wimbledon? He'd discuss things with Bert and,
of course, Becky.

He got up and thought about making breakfast but
realized there was nothing to eat since he'd emptied the
fridge before he left. He went to grocery store and bought
the usual: meat, eggs, whole wheat bread, milk, fruit, salad

stuff, and a six-pack of beer. He also picked up a news-paper. When he got back he made a delicious bowl of oatmeal with all the trimmings—strawberries, raisins, and bananas. He hadn't had one for a long time.

He read the paper. He thought he might find a story about his last encounter. There wasn't one, but he did find a story about his encounter in Paris. The police were still puzzled. The shooter had told them he'd fired at a guy and the bullets came right back at him. They'd asked him if he could identify the guy in any way, but all he could remember was that man had been wearing a light blue shirt and black pants. Steve was glad he had shipped his clothes back with his tennis stuff. The police speculated about a strong magnetic field turning the bullets around but couldn't understand how a person could carry a device that would create such a field. He knew that they would discover nothing. It would be one of life's unsolved problems.

He then thought of his mail, which he had put a hold on. He went by the post office to get it. It was mostly junk, but there was a notice from UPS about his package. He drove over to their address and picked it up.

He went back home and unpacked the package. Everything was there, including *the* clothes. He decided to check his email, since he hadn't done so while he was in Berlin with Becky. He had quite a few messages. One was from Paul Kist: "Hey, Steve. Congratulations on the big win. I feel like I'm no longer in your class. Anyway, if you want to hit a few let me know."

Another, dated about a week ago, was from the

president of the racket club, Kevin Adams, congratulating him and telling him they wanted to have a party for him to celebrate. A second email from Kevin was dated a week later. "Hey, Steve, I sent you an email awhile ago. Maybe you stayed in Paris for awhile. Anyway, let me know the best time for the party. You can't cop out!"

Steve hit *Reply*. "I did stay in Paris for a little while. Any time is okay with me."

He got an immediate reply scheduling the party for the coming Friday at 7:00. He replied accepting the time.

He read a few other emails from guys in the club congratulating him. Steve felt embarrassed about his big victory. He knew he didn't deserve it. What the hell; he should pretend it was he who did it. In a way it was, but he knew that in another way it wasn't.

Steve felt like he needed a little exercise, but he didn't want to play tennis. He thought of Montgomery Hill Park behind the college on the other side of town. Trails there were short but steep. He headed out for a stimulating walk. While hiking he wondered what he would tell Bert. He would tell him about the second attempt at his life and how he'd handled it. And of course he would have to tell him that Becky now knew the score. Steve knew Bert would be upset, but there was no choice in the matter.

He wondered whether Becky might have sent him an email. After the hike he headed home and checked. Sure enough there was one from her. "Hello, my sweet. Guess what, Friday will be my last day of work for awhile. They owe me lots of vacation time and I decided to take it. I will be back in San Jose this coming Saturday. Can you pick me up at the airport? I assume yes. Love, Becky."

He jotted down the flight details she'd added as a post-script and then hit *Reply*.

"Hey, that's great news! Of course I'll pick you up. I still love you." He thought about her and longed to see her.

It was time for supper, and he was hungry. He made up a nice salad. He got a steak out, put it in the broiler, and ate the salad while it was cooking. He also popped a bagel in the microwave. He opened a can of beer. He thought, *Salad, steak, bagel, and beer—what a great combination!*

He thought about his meeting with Bert tonight. He would have to fill him in on the details. He knew Bert would be unhappy. He finished eating, cleaned up, and headed over to Bert's place.

"Hi, champ, come on in." He entered, and they sat down in the kitchen. "How does it feel to be the winner of the French Open?"

"Well, you and I know it wasn't really me. It was this strange power that I have. I don't mind the money though."

"You said you had something to tell me that I wouldn't like. What is it?"

"Believe it or not I was attacked again. This time I was with Becky. There were these two guys. They wanted our money, and I was willing to give it to them since I didn't want to let Becky know anything about my powers. But then, in addition to our money, they were going to take her away. I found out later that they were kidnappers. I remember her saying something like 'I'm not going anywhere,' but this guy grabbed her by the arm. At that point I didn't have a choice, so I blew up and knocked the shit out of them. That was the first time I'd used my force fields to actually kill someone. I didn't really mean to do that."

"Force fields, that's an interesting term. You used it in your previous email. Reminds me of electric and magnetic fields in physics."

"Yes, I think that it's appropriate, don't you?"

"Definitely—it is exact. What happened next?"

"Anyway, I hit one squarely in the forehead. I heard a loud crack, and I found out later that I killed him. The other one pulled out a gun that I grabbed with the force. Then I hit him a good punch in the ribs and broke his leg to make sure he wouldn't pursue us. We were lucky there was no one else was around, so we bugged out without being detected. Becky saw the whole thing, and now she knows all about my powers. There was no way to avoid telling her. I told her the whole story from the very beginning, florescent lights and all. I swore her to secrecy. I'm sure she will keep it quiet."

"That's an interesting turn of events. I really would like to meet this woman. Is she coming back to town anytime?"

"Yes, she's arriving this coming Saturday. She's taking time off from her job. I don't know if I ever told you this, but she claims there's some kind of force causing her attraction to me. She says it's not natural, and since she found out the truth about my telekinetic powers she believes there's a connection."

"That's interesting. She may be right. Since we don't

know anything about the source, the force may be applying itself to her in a strange way. Hey, I'm using the term *the force* too. It's just like in *Star Wars*, but it's a different kind of force. All this stuff is boggling my mind. I need a drink. Care for a rum and coke?"

"Yeah, I need one too. Make it a double."

"I'm going to have a double too."

Bert mixed two drinks. They tasted good. For a while they just sat there thinking. Neither one spoke.

Bert finally said, "By the way, I've been thinking about Becky's last name, Jones. There was a famous British physicist named R. V. Jones. He worked on intelligence during World War II. It'd be pretty wild if she was related to him."

"Interesting. I'll ask her when I see her."

"You know, maybe you can use your powers to straighten out the world. It's a mess. For example, Hamas firing rockets on Israel. The Jews should have never left Gaza. Why don't you go over there and make believe you're Superman. They'd listen to you if you showed them a little power."

Steve laughed. "That would be an interesting experience, but I don't want any part of it. You got any other bright ideas?"

"Yeah, how about this one. Our calendar is crazy. Some months have thirty days, some have thirty-one, and of course February has twenty-eight or twenty-nine. I have a suggestion for a new calendar."

"Really? Tell me about it."

"We should have thirteen months of twenty-eight days

each so each month is identical. Thirteen times twenty-eight is three hundred sixty-four, so you have an extra day as a holiday per year. That could be treated like a kind of leap day or something. Of course on leap years you have two days off. With that calendar every month of the year would be the same. The date would be on the same day in every month, so for example if the seventh is a Friday in January the seventh will be a Friday in every month."

Steve thought about it for a few seconds. "You know, that's a great idea. I just thought of why it works."

"Really? Why?"

"Well, fifty-two, the number of weeks in a year, is divisible by thirteen."

"Hey, that's interesting. I guess only a mathematician would think of that. But it won't work. Do you know why?"

"No, why?"

"Because too many people consider thirteen an unlucky number, that's why. I wonder how many politicians consider thirteen unlucky."

Steve said, "I would guess a few. You're right, most people are superstitious. I read somewhere that sixty percent of the population believe in angels. Hey, how about a game of backgammon?"

"Good idea. Your glass is empty. How about a refill?"

"Okay, just one more, but make it a single, not a double."

They played for the rest of the evening. Steve ended up winning two dollars. "Looks like I had my revenge. You take too many doubles."

"Right, but for twenty-five cents a point why not take a chance?" They laughed.

Bert said, "Are you going to shoot for Wimbledon?"

"I think I should. If I don't people are going to ask why not."

"As I said before, I think you should consider doing something more significant that winning at tennis."

"Yeah, but what? All right, I'll think about it. I've had enough backgammon and booze for awhile, so I'll take off."

"Okay, it was a great evening, very informative. See you later."

Steve left and headed for home. He really liked Bert. He had a lot of good ideas. That calendar one was interesting.

Steve awoke at around 9. It was Wednesday. What should he do today? He decided to skip tennis for awhile. Time for breakfast, oatmeal as usual.

Maybe a nice hike would be good. He decided on Alum Rock Park. He remembered his hike there with Becky. When she arrived he would have to talk to her about Wimbledon. Should he play? Why not? She might be going back to work around that time. There was no reason why he shouldn't play. Still, he would wait and talk to her about it.

He headed out to Alum Rock for his hike. He parked and started out, the south rim trail as usual. As he hiked he thought about the beauty of the park, the twisted tree trunks, the switchback trails. He arrived at the top and took a look down below. Then he remembered something Bert said. *How about distance?* He thought this might be an interesting place to test it. There were a few people in the valley below. There were trees on the far hillside. How far away was that? He thought it might be about half a mile. He decided to try to make them move. He reached out with the force and shook a small pine tree. It was easy. What about strength at this distance? He picked a large pine and decided to chop the top half off. He double-checked to see if anyone might be looking in that direction. No one seemed to be so he applied the force and chopped it off with ease. Power at a distance did not seem to be a problem. He wondered if there was an upper limit to his power and to his distance. There must be, but how would he test that? He finished his hike and headed back home.

He was sweating. It was a warm day, and it would be nice to cool off somehow. He decided to take a dip in the condo complex's pool. He remembered the novel he had been reading, *Walden Two*. He hadn't read it since Berlin. He put on his bathing suit, grabbed the novel, and headed over to the pool. The water felt great. He got out, toweled off, sat down on a lounge in the shade, and started reading.

In the next few days Steve rallied with his friends Paul and Mike. He told them he would rather just practice shots than play sets. They agreed since they thought they would probably lose.

Friday night rolled around, and he went over to the club for his party. There was lots of beer, wine, and snacks. He got lots of congratulations. It was a great time.

The next day was Saturday. He headed up to the airport to pick up Becky. When she saw him she ran over and hugged him. They kissed.

She said, "You don't know how glad I am to see you."

"Not gladder than I am."

"I'm not getting into that sequence again."

They got her bags, put them in his car, and climbed in. He said, "Are you hungry?"

"Yes. How about the City Diner? It's kind of on the way to my place."

"Sure, that's one of my favorite places to eat."

"Wow, another thing we have in common."

They headed over to the diner and ordered. She said, "So what have you been doing this past week?"

"Nothing much. I filled in Bert about the details of our last encounter, and I told him about you, including the fact that you now know the score about my powers. He was a little alarmed, but he understood that it was unavoidable. He wants to meet you."

"I'd like to meet him too. He sounds like an interesting fellow. What else did you do?"

"I got several emails from friends congratulating me and one from the president of the racket club that I belong to. They had a party for me last night. During the week I got together with two of my friends, and we rallied, but we didn't play sets."

"Did you get any congratulations from females?"

"Don't tell me you're jealous."

"Of course I am. I know I don't own you, but I want to."

"You know you are number one, and there is no number two."

She smiled and hugged him. "I'm very happy to hear that. Of course my feelings are identical."

They finished eating, and he took her back to her house, unloaded her bags, and carried them in. "What have you got in these bags? They are quite heavy."

"Well, I knew I was going to be away for some time so I had to pack quite a bit of stuff. So what else did Bert say?"

"I kind of decided that I would play at Wimbledon, but he disagreed. He thought I should do something more important with my powers. What do you think about that?"

"I guess it's your decision. After Wimbledon is the US Open. Then there is next year. You can make it a career, right?"

"I guess I can, but I don't think I really don't want to. I think Bert is right. I should do something more useful."

"I do, too, but I can't think of what. Hey, why don't you be Superman? When you're Clark Kent I can be Lois Lane!"

"Very funny! Maybe me coming back as Jesus would be better. The trouble is I can't take everyone to heaven."

"Well, you and I know the world is an ungodly, pardon the expression, mess. Maybe you can straighten things out."

"Oh, yeah? You make it sound easy. What exactly would I do?"

"We have to sit down and work out the details. With the power you have you can get a large following. For example, you can become the president of the United States.

You can even become a dictator. Do you have any ideas as how the government should work and what you could do?"

"I have a few. Free health care for everyone. And did you know that the California community colleges used to have free tuition? But why not have free tuition for everyone everywhere? Students today have to borrow lots of money to get an education. That doesn't seem right since higher education is good for everyone. Of course, colleges would still have entrance tests as they do now. If you don't qualify you don't get in. I think that free tuition would overall be good for the economy. Another thing wrong with the world is the unequal distribution of income. In statistics they used to talk of quartiles, but now they use quintiles."

"Really? So which is better?"

"Quintiles are better because with quartiles the median was on the boundary between the second and third, but with quintiles it is in the middle of the third quintile. The first quintile is the very poor. The third, or middle, quintile is essentially the middle class. The median is in the middle of that class."

"Yes, I can see where quintiles are better."

"Anyway the income of the lower three quintiles is going down while the income of the fifth quintile is rising. Actually in the fifth quintile, the income of the super rich, the upper one or two percent, is a heavily weighting factor. Anyway, in general, income is becoming more and more unequal."

"So what can be done about that?"

"I don't know. One thing is to have a decent minimum wage. I think that, free health care, and free public education through college would help a lot."

She said, "Hey, this sounds a little like *Brave New World*. Did you ever read that book?"

"Yes, I think I read it in college. *The perfect society.* Everything is planned, and the drug Soma keeps people happy. But it didn't work, and I forgot the reason why. That reminds me that I'm reading this novel called *Walden Two*. It's about the ideal society."

"I read that some time ago. It was very idealistic. But, wow, you have a lot of good ideas."

They didn't speak for a few minutes. Then she said, "There's one thing I don't understand. To what extent can you protect yourself? You showed that you can stop bullets, but can you stop them if you don't know where they are coming from? For example, suppose someone tries to shoot you in the back? Can you put up a shield to protect yourself? And can you stop any bullet no matter how powerful the gun?"

"I don't know the answer to that. Furthermore I don't know how to test it. Maybe Bert has some idea how to do it. He wants to meet you, so let me call him, and we can get together, maybe tomorrow."

"Hey, I just thought. If you become president, you'll have lots of bodyguards and won't really need back protection."

"That's assuming one of my bodyguards doesn't try to kill me of course."

"Right, and he would be very famous if he did kill you."

"Seriously, though—become president? I don't think so. Becky, you seem to have spent some time thinking about my future. I'm surprised."

"I have. I feel like I'm part of you. If you have this strange power, you shouldn't be bothering with tennis. Think big! Use it for some good."

"You and Bert have given me food for thought. I really don't know what I should do now."

"Simple—formulate a plan. Let's talk to Bert tomorrow. By the way I'm a bit tired from my trip, so I'm really not in the mood for lovemaking."

"I understand. I have a lot to think about. I'll call Bert tomorrow and keep you posted."

"Okay, see you later."

They got up and walked over to her door. She opened it, and Steve started to leave.

She said, "Don't I get a kiss goodbye?"

"So you're not too tired for a kiss." They kissed, and it turned out to being a long one.

"I just changed my mind. You're not leaving for awhile."

"I remember you using those exact same words once before."

"I remember them, too."

Becky closed and locked the door. They each took a shower, went to bed, and made passionate love.

PLANNING FOR THE FUTURE

Sunday, June 2

He awoke around nine and glanced over at her. She was beautiful; in fact he could not think of anyone, including movie actresses, who was more beautiful than she. He remembered the phrase, *Beauty is in the eye of the beholder*, which might be true to some extent, but he thought that was not quite true. There was something absolute about true beauty. Then he thought that maybe the attraction she felt for him was a contagious disease and that he'd caught it. She stirred and opened her eyes.

"You're studying me," she said.

"Yes, and it's giving me much pleasure. Ready for breakfast?"

"Yes, but you know what? There is nothing to eat in the house since I emptied the fridge before I left."

"That's exactly what happened to me when I got back home—nothing in the fridge. Let's eat out."

"No, let's go shopping for food. We have never done that together."

"Okay with me."

They got dressed, and she got out a pencil and paper to make a list.

"Let's see ... milk, eggs, bread, orange juice, salad stuff, and meat for the future. I have plenty of coffee and beer of course. Can you think of anything else?"

"I like cream for my coffee."

"Oh, yes, I forgot that. That's what I use. I'll be darned, that's another thing we have in common. Some people use half and half, but I like cream. Did you ever make a list of things we have in common?"

"No, I haven't yet. It's on my list. That's funny, a list for my list. That reminds me, when I was growing up my family had a swimming pool in the back yard, and we had a plastic pool cover to warm the pool. When it was off we had to cover it with another cover. We called it the pool cover-cover. It was sort of a joke around the house."

"That's funny. By the way, you never told me anything about your family. Did you have any brothers or sisters?"

"Yes, one of each. My sister got married and moved to Massachusetts. My brother joined the marines, went to Iraq, and got killed."

"Oh, I'm so sorry about that."

"Yes, bad things happen. He was the oldest, and I was the youngest. I didn't know him very well. How about you?"

"I'm an only child, no brothers or sisters. I kind of wish I had one or two."

"I've wondered about your heritage. Your last name is Jones. Is that English?"

"My father was English, and my mother Italian. Her maiden name was Fermi."

"Oh, that's interesting. Enrico Fermi was a famous physicist. He worked on atomic physics and quantum theory. Was she related to him?"

She raised her eyebrows in surprise. "Believe it or not he was her uncle. She talked about him a lot."

"By the way, Bert mentioned a famous British physicist active in intelligence during the war. His name was R.V. Jones. Have you heard of him?"

She looked surprised again. "Yes—he was my grandfather."

"Wow, you're related to two famous people. Now I know where you got your brains."

"Yes, I guess that had something to do with it. Brains are to some extent inherited, but they can pop up anywhere."

They went to the supermarket and bought the items on the list. He offered to pay, and she said, "Sure, you're rich after the French." They came back, and she made breakfast. While she was cooking he called Bert.

"Bert said 7:30 tonight is fine. Is that okay with you?"

"Sure, I'm looking forward to it."

While they ate the usual breakfast of orange juice, eggs, whole wheat bread, and coffee they chatted.

She said, "Do you have any new ideas on planning for the future?"

"No, nothing more than we discussed earlier. Do you?"

She said, "If you're going to try and change things, the first step is to let your powers be known. How do you go about it? It should not be through the public, nor the press. I think you should contact the government. In fact it should be the president. You should prepare a very, very convincing demonstration."

"Are you serious about all this? I should contact the president? How would I go about that?"

"Well, you can't just call him up and make a date. You'll have to talk first to an underling and work your way up of course. I think there's a web site called The White House or something like that. Send them an email or call them."

"If I ever get to see him it has to be very convincing. Moving objects of course. And I could have Bert shoot a gun at me. He could shoot four bullets at me, and I could stop them and return them to him. Bert could hold out his hat, and I could drop them in it, for example. That would be very convincing."

She laughed.

He said, "I don't know what else I can do. Maybe lift something heavy. Did I ever tell you that I lifted a car once?"

"You did? No, you never told me. Wow, there seems to be no limit to the power."

"There must be, but as yet I don't know what it might be. Any ideas as to what we should do this afternoon? We could play tennis, chess, or whatever."

"I know what to do. You mentioned playing backgammon with Bert so I went and bought a backgammon set in Berlin and brought it back here. You can give me a lesson."

"Wow, I'm surprised. Okay, let's do it."

Steve explained the details, and she said it sounded fun. They played a few sample games for practice, not for money. He felt she had a pretty good idea of the game, so they played for one dollar a point. She made a few fundamental errors, and he won thirty dollars. She went for her wallet.

He said, "Forget it. That was a free lesson."

"Okay, but I'll be ready for you next time."

"In my opinion backgammon is the best gambling game."

"Better than poker?"

"Yes!"

"It's about supper time. How about if I broil a nice steak with a salad and rice. Care for a beer?"

"Definitely."

They opened the beers and toasted to the future. She prepared the meal, and after dinner they headed over to Bert's place.

They knocked, and Bert opened the door. "Come on in." They entered. "You must be Becky. Nice to meet you."

"And of course you're Bert I've heard a lot about you."

"All good I hope. I've heard good things about you too. You all sit down. How about a drink?"

Steve said, "I'm thirsty after that meal, so I'll just have some ice water. How about you, Becky?"

"I'll have the same. Bert, we, as you, have been thinking about Steve's future. I think he should do more than
win tennis tournaments with his remarkable powers. He
says you agree. What do you think he might do?"

"I believe I suggested something of that sort, that he
should go over to Israel, say, and straighten them out, but
he said no way. He seems to want to go to Wimbledon
next."

"He has a few ideas about straightening out the USA.
Why don't you tell him what you think, Steve?"

Steve said, "Bert and I discussed a lot of things before.
For example if the politicians had any sense they would
give free health care for everyone like there is in many
other countries. Also I believe in free college education for
all. Also the drugs that are now illegal should be free, and
prostitution should be legal. How is that for starters?"

Bert said, "Becky, I assume Steve's told you I'm in favor
of all of that. But, Steve, how in the hell would you use your
powers to change things?"

"Becky suggested that the first thing would be to contact the president somehow. If I could meet with him, and
a few others in Congress, say, and convince them of my
power, that would be the first step."

Bert said, "Right, and the next step would be for you to
be put in a position of power." Then he added, "Actually,
the first step is to determine if you're really serious about
all this."

"Well, it's a choice between that and me continuing
to win tennis tournaments. The latter is the simplest, of

course. The other is too risky. The government might consider me dangerous and try and lock me up."

Bert said, "Yeah, but you know they can't do that. They couldn't come anywhere near you."

"You forget they have the army and all their weapons. They could probably annihilate me."

"You have to convince them you're on their side. Then they'll welcome you with open arms."

"But then when I tell them about my plans, they might change their minds. I tell you what. I'm going to think about all this and let you know. In the meantime how about a game of backgammon? Say, did you know that three can play?"

Bert exclaimed, "Really? How does that work?"

"One person is said to be *in the box* playing against the other two. Each opponent has a doubling cube. When the box doubles he doubles all of his opponents. They can drop or accept independently. They can also independently double the guy in the box. He can drop or accept the double to that particular person. If the guy in the box loses, he loses the box and one of the other players becomes the box."

"Hey, that's fascinating! Becky, do you know how to play?"

"I've had one lesson from Steve, but I think I can handle myself. I'm willing to give it a try."

Bert said, "Good, then. Let's play. Since I have several backgammon sets I have two cubes. Twenty-five cents a point of course."

They set up the board and began playing.

They had a great time. Bert ended up winning $2.25, Becky lost $1.75, and Steve lost fifty cents. Bert said, "Becky, you did pretty good for a beginner. Maybe you should go to Vegas."

"No, thanks. Gambling is not my thing. It was fun though."

Steve said, "By the way, Bert, how close are you to retirement?"

"Well, I can sell the hardware store for a bundle. And since I have social security and a fairly large retirement fund, I can retire any time. But then what would I do? The hardware story keeps me busy."

"Hey, you could go back school and study physics."

"I have thought about that. College tuition is pretty steep, however."

"You can always just study on your own. I always wanted to know more about relativity. We could study together."

"Maybe. Anyway, Steve, the ball is in your court. Let us know your decision regarding solving the world's problems."

"I have a lot to think about. I'll let you know. See you later."

They left.

On the way to the car Steve said, "Becky, you've never seen my condo. We can go there for the night."

"Good idea. I'd like to see it."

They headed over to Steve's place. When they got there they went inside, and Becky smiled and said, "Hey, I don't have any nightclothes."

Steve grinned. "I like you just as you are in your birthday suit, but if you get cold you can use one of my tee shirts or a bath robe."

Steve thought again about the future. "So what do you think I should do, keep playing tennis or save the world?"

"Save the world. Why not? Somebody needs to do it. I think you were chosen for it. Why else would you have the power that you have? It must be part of a general plan by God or whoever or whatever is out there."

"You may be right. I'm going to sleep on it and decide tomorrow." They turned in for the night.

CHAPTER 21

SAM CATCHES ON

Sam Finch and Henry Thomson were sipping coffee at Sam's place. They had spent quite a bit of time looking at the TV records from the French Open.

Sam said, "I'm convinced that the ball just doesn't act naturally. Don't you agree?"

Hank said, "Yes, I'm convinced, but how can he do that?"

"I don't know, how but the evidence is there right in front of us. Maybe he has God on his side, or maybe he sold his soul to the devil. Then again there is something called telekinesis, which I have never believed in. The question is just what do we do about it?"

Sam refreshed the coffee. They stared at each other and their coffee cups.

Finally Sam said, "Well, we have several choices. We can go to the French director and show him the evidence, go to the press and expose him, or go to Steve himself and ask him to explain himself."

Hank thought about it for a few seconds and said, "Interesting choices. I think I prefer the last one. We should give him the benefit of the doubt."

They agreed and sat down to compose a letter to Steve.

When Steve and Becky arose Monday morning he decided to check his email. He was surprised to see one from Sam Finch. He opened it and read it.

"Hello, Steve. You may remember me. We played in two tournaments including the French. You beat me twice. However, I had the sneaking suspicion that there was something strange about your game, so Hank Thomson and I got a hold of the TV records of the French and studied them. We looked at your matches with me, the semifinal with Clark, and the finals with Bergman. We decided that you are doing something tricky with the ball. We have no idea how you did it, but our evidence is convincing. We thought about going to the director of the French, but we decided to give you a chance to explain. Please respond. Yours, Sam Finch."

"Oh my God. I've been discovered."

"What? What are you talking about?"

"One guy that I beat in the French was Sam Finch. Read this email."

Becky read the email. "So they found out that you were cheating, if you want to call it that. What do we do now?"

"We can't let them expose me. I have to let them in on it. What else can I do?"

"It looks like your decision was made up for you. It

would be stupid to continue playing tennis. Time to contact the president."

"Time to contact Sam Finch first. I wonder where he lives. I'll reply to his email right now."

Steve hit *Reply*. "Hello, Sam. Congratulations on your detective work. Yes, you discovered my secret. Rather than me trying to explain it, I think we should get together, and I can show you in person. Please, please, do not discuss it with anyone else. I live in San Jose, California. Where do you live? Yours, Steve."

He said, "How does that email look?"

After reading it she said, "It looks fine."

He hit *Send*.

He said, "It looks like my secret is getting out. I guess I'll have to give a demonstration for Sam and probably Hank. Then there's no reason why I shouldn't contact the president if possible. You said there's a website called the white house or something like that?"

"Yes, it's called *whitehouse.gov*. I think you can respond via email or call them on the phone. You'll probably get some low-ranking person, but what else can you do?"

"Okay, let's do it." Steve went to *whitehouse.gov* and clicked on the link that said "Email the White House."

"Okay, now what do I say?"

They discussed it and agreed on a message that he typed into the appropriate box on the form.

Dear Sir. I have something very important to explain. I would consider it of international importance. Unfortunately, if I told you about it you wouldn't believe me, so I have to show you. It is something that very few people should know about, so I would like to meet with someone of the utmost responsibility to demonstrate it and would ask that it be kept a secret. Thank you, Steven Thomas.

After they'd both reviewed it, he hit *Submit.* He got an almost immediate reply in his email.

Thank you for contacting the White House. Due to high volume we are unable to answer every email. We do, however, read every email and may respond if we feel that the issue is important. Thank you again.

She said, "The obvious canned reply."

"Well, that's that. It's time for breakfast. On most days I have oatmeal with fruit and of course coffee. Do you want to try it?"

"I'd love to. In fact I often have oatmeal and sometimes some other types of cereal like bran flakes, shredded wheat, or Grape-Nuts."

"Believe it or not, I sometimes have those same three. I try to eat high-fiber stuff."

"Wow. Add another one to your list. Oh, I forgot, you really don't have one. When I are you going to make one?"

"It's on my list." They both laughed.

Steve made breakfast, and they ate without saying much. After eating she said, "I'll clean up, which is what us women are supposed to do, right?"

"Wrong. The duties should be shared."

She smiled. "I knew you would say that, handsome. Give me a kiss."

Just then the computer beeped. It was an email from the White House. They read it together:

> *We have just reviewed your email and would like more information as to what you have to show us, but if, as you say, you can't tell us, we are willing to meet with you for a demonstration. Your information seems to come under the category of Intelligence, and as you said, of international importance, so we are asking that you meet with our CIA representative.*

The message went on to give the address and to say that a meeting had been scheduled for this coming Wednesday at 11:00 a.m. It asked that he reply to confirm the appointment.

He said, "Wow, that was fast. The CIA! I really don't want to talk to them."

"Looks like you have no choice. At least that seems to be pretty high up. I think if you impress them, the president will hear about it soon enough. I think you should accept."

"I guess you're right. It will be San Francisco on Wednesday. I can obviously make it." He hit *Reply* and agreed to the time.

He said, "I can't believe how fast we actually got an appointment. Maybe they are paranoid about terrorist threats. How do you think they'll react when I demonstrate my powers?"

"I have no idea. I'm a little worried about it."

"I am too. I don't think you should go. Just in case they get a little crazy, I don't want you to be involved."

"But I would really like to see their faces when you demonstrate."

"I know. I'll just tell you all about it. I insist that you don't go."

"Okay, whatever you say. I'm curious as to how you're going to demonstrate."

"Oh, just pick up a few things like a pen or book or whatever is lying around. Nothing violent of course."

It wasn't long before an email arrived from Sam. "Hello, Steve. Nice to know we were right. Hank and both I live in Monterey, not far from you. We can't make it this weekend, but how about the following Sunday? Give us your address and the best time. Sam."

Steve replied with his address and set the time at 2:00 p.m. He said, "Well, Becky, we are off to the races. I hope the horse doesn't buck too hard." She laughed.

"Gosh, I forgot to email Bert to keep him informed." Steve took care of that, and then they headed out to Becky's place so she could get some clothes and toiletries.

They spent Monday and Tuesday together and got to know each other better. They played a little tennis, chess, and backgammon. They took a hike at Alum Rock Park.

After breakfast Wednesday morning Steve said, "Let me take you home. I'll call you when I get back and fill you in on the details."

"Okay, good luck. Call me immediately."

"Yes, will do. Don't worry."

CHAPTER 22

THE CIA

Steve headed for San Francisco and found a paid parking lot near the CIA office. He walked over to the building, which had *Central Intelligence Agency* in big letters on the side. He entered the building and was confronted by a woman who asked what his business was. He told her, and she checked a list and said, "Okay, please enter."

Once he passed through the doorway, he was immediately confronted by two tall, husky gentlemen and a lady.

The woman said, "Welcome to the CIA headquarters. I'm sorry, but we have to check you for weapons. It's standard policy."

One of the guys frisked him. "Okay, you're clear. Susie here will take you to your appointment."

On the way out Susie said, "I'm sorry for that. I know they seemed impolite. It's unpleasant, but it's unavoidable."

He and Susie went through another doorway into a

lobby with elevators. They went up two floors, got out, and entered another room.

The room was large, containing about ten desks and about that many people. There were two aisles leading to back rooms. At the nearest desk was a woman, obviously the secretary for the room. Susie introduced him to her and said that he had an appointment. She looked down at a list and said, "Oh, yes, just go to room two down the left hall. You will be talking to Mr. Harper. He is one of the assistant vice presidents in charge of intelligence here in San Francisco."

Steve thought, *That's what I need, an 'assistant' vice president. I wonder how many there are.*

They went down the hall and entered another office. There sat a secretary with a door right behind her.

Susie said, "Hello, Maggie, this is Mr. Thomas here to speak with Mr. Harper."

Maggie said, "Oh, hello. Yes, we have been expecting you. Have a seat right here, and I will let Mr. Harper know you are here."

She entered the rear door. Steve sat down. He started to worry. There was too much security for his liking, but maybe he should have expected that. He wondered what an assistant vice president of the CIA did. She came out and said, "You can go in. Mr. Harper will see you now."

Steve entered Harper's office. He came over and offered his hand to shake. He was a wimpy-looking guy who seemed to have no confidence at all. With a very insincere smile he said, "Nice to meet you. Please sit down. This city is very crowded—did you find a place to park?"

"Yes, I parked in a paid lot."

"Your email sounded interesting. You don't seem to be carrying anything to show. What do you have to show me?"

Steve said, "It's something I don't want to show to just anyone. I'd like to show it to the person in your organization who is as high up as possible."

"Unfortunately you'll have to be satisfied with me at the present time. So what is it?"

Steve stared at the back wall and thought for a few seconds about what to do next. He decided he had no choice.

Harper said impatiently, "Well, what is it? You're wasting my time—let's have it!"

Steve turned his head and faced Harper. He looked around for an object to pick up. He saw a rather large paperweight in the shape of the world on Harper's desk. "Do you see that paperweight over there?"

Harper glanced at it. He turned back to face Steve and said, "Yes, I see it, so what?"

"Look at it again, and keep looking at it."

Harper turned and looked at it, and Steve picked it up with the force and moved it up to the ceiling and then to his hand. He then put it on the desk in front of Harper. Harper's eyes and mouth opened wide.

He said, "How did you do that?"

There was a coffee cup on Harper's desk. Steve said, "Look at that cup." While Harper was looking he picked it up and floated it over to his hand, looked into it, and said, "It's empty. No coffee for now." He then placed it in front of Harper.

Harper stared at it and then at Steve. He then grabbed the phone, dialed a few digits, and said, "Send them here right away."

Steve said, "What are you doing?"

Harper said, "You may be dangerous. I sent for security."

"What do you think I am going to do, kill you with a paperweight?"

Harper said nothing and just stared at Steve like he couldn't believe what had just happened. The two lugs who'd frisked him came in. Steve stood up and said, "What are you doing? What are you going to do, arrest me?"

Harper said, "Let's not call it an arrest. We just have to confine you for awhile. Take him away."

Steve said, "I'm sorry I can't let you do that."

Harper giggled, and the two guys laughed and moved toward Steve. With a sweep of his right hand he used the force to knock their feet out from under them. They fell in a heap on the floor. Harper glared at the two guys, seeming not to believe what he saw. The two guys got up, and each one pulled out gun. Steve grabbed the guns with the force and yanked them from their hands. The guns just hung in the air for a few seconds. Steve glanced around and noted the nearest wastebasket. He moved the guns above the waist can and dropped them in. The two lugs backed up against the wall, and all three of them stared in wonder at Steve. He thought Harper was about to cry.

"I came here to show you something useful, and you treat me like a criminal. What I want is to see your boss. No, not your boss, your boss's boss. In fact I want to see the top dog in this outfit."

Harper whined, "Yes, sir, right away. Please let me make a phone call."

"Go ahead." Steve thought, *He actually called me sir. I'm making progress.*

Harper turned to the two guys. "You two can leave."

One said, "Can we have our guns?"

Steve said, "No!" and they left, still looking rather astonished.

Harper talked shortly on the phone and then hung up. A few seconds later he got a return call. He answered it and said, "Yes, Rich, it's very urgent! Okay, I'll be right up."

Harper said, "Richard Edwards is in charge on the west coast. I have to speak with him before I introduce you. Please wait here."

Harper left, and Steve looked around. He noted the paperwork on Harper's desk. One was a chart showing helicopter surveillance; another paper had Steve's name and his appointment time. After about five minutes Harper returned.

Harper said, "We can go up to Dr. Edwards's office now."

Steve thought, *Dr. Edwards. Does this guy have a PhD?* When they went through Harper's outer office the workers were standing around talking to each other. When he appeared they all stopped talking and stared. Steve said,

"Good afternoon," and smiled. They just kept staring. They probably all knew of his trick of knocking down the thugs and taking their guns. He didn't want that to happen. His powers were becoming known. He didn't like it.

They took the elevator up two floors, got out, walked over to another door, and entered. They were greeted by a secretary and another guy who looked important.

He said, "Come in. My name is Tony Wallace. Dr. Edwards's office is right here." They all entered another door. Sitting at his desk was a professional-looking gentleman. He rose and said, "Steven Thomas, I believe. My name is Richard Edwards. Nice to meet you." He didn't offer to shake hands.

Once everyone was seated, he said, "I have just heard of your amazing ability, being able to move objects with your brain. Where did you get this ability?"

"One day it just happened. I may write a book on it some day. It's called telekinesis. Have you ever heard of it?"

"I have, but I never believed it was possible."

Steve said, "Neither did I until it happened to me."

Edwards said, "I would like to see a demonstration myself. Can you perform one for me?"

Steve thought he'd better make it convincing. He started by removing a pen from Edwards's pocket and floating it over to his own hand then and then laying it on the desk.

He said, "Look at the bookshelf," pointing to a bookshelf against one of the walls. Everyone looked. He picked out two large volumes and drew them out, turned them upside down, and put them back in.

Edwards frowned and said, "I'm convinced. I understand you defended yourself very well against our two security men. Is there a limit to your power?"

Steve said, "Why do you want to know?"

Edwards looked embarrassed. "Well, it just seems to be a natural question."

Steve thought about it. If he were going to institute some changes, he might have to use some power.

"My power seems to be quite strong, but I don't really know about any upper limit. As you already know I can disarm an attacker and probably kill one if necessary."

Edwards stared at Steve for a few seconds. A few beads of perspiration appeared on his forehead. "I see. So tell me, why did you come to us, and what do you want us to do?"

"I thought I might be of some use to our government. I really didn't know how to contact anyone, so I went to *whitehouse.gov* and said I wanted to show something to someone important who is in charge. I ended up here. I would really like to see the president."

"You mean the president of the United States?"

"Yes. Why not? I have a few ideas about changes that can be made. My power seems exceptional. Why shouldn't I use it?"

"Well, you have made your powers and your wishes quite clear. I will pass this information on to the higher ups. The president will definitely be informed about you and your powers. However, your wishes to meet with him personally may not be possible since you are in a position to do him harm. Perhaps you should write down the things you would like to see him about."

"Okay, I'll do that."

"I guess that will be enough for today. Tony will see you to the door."

"Okay, thank you for seeing me. By the way, on my way up here I passed through Mr. Harper's office, and several people stared at me like I had a disease. I think it advisable that they do not know my name and that they keep the incident a secret."

Edwards smiled. "You're right. We will take precautions to keep your identity a secret. Thank you for sharing your powers. It has been an amazing experience for us."

Tony said, "Okay, Steve, follow me." He led Steve out to the main corridor. Then, after looking to see if anyone else was around, he said, "I guess you know you have to be very careful. Some members of this organization may want to get rid of you. I don't know if they can, but they may try."

Steve was surprised that someone in this place would actually give him a warning. "Thank you for your concern, Tony. Perhaps we can keep in touch." Steve pulled out his card, jotted his home email and phone on the back, and gave it to Tony.

"Thanks, Steve. Here's my card. You can take the elevator down and leave from there."

"Okay, thanks again."

CHAPTER 23

WHO IS ROBBING THE BANKS?

Steve went to the parking lot to pick up his car, paid the parking fee, and left. On the way home he thought about the sequence of events. He was surprised that they'd tried to arrest him. He wondered what the CIA might do next. Would they try to kill him? The warning from Tony was interesting. He wondered it Tony was to be trusted. He could be faking friendship. He didn't think they would try anything, but he wasn't sure. He knew they could figure out where he lived. Would they search his place? He arrived home, parked and went into his condo. It was about 3:30. He thought about the experience in San Francisco and still couldn't quite believe it had happened.

He was tired, so he took his shoes off and lay down on the bed. In one minute he was asleep.

He dreamt that the CIA was after him. They had

bazookas. The marines joined them. He ran, but they caught up with him and fired. He woke with a start. It was 6:30.

He thought about the dream but then remembered the day's experience. He then emailed Bert, explaining the events of the day.

He smiled and called Becky. "Hi, Beck. I'm back. It was an interesting experience. I can come over, and we can talk if you like."

"Sure. Come on over. My parents used to call me Beck. I like it. It's an even better nickname than Becky. See you soon."

"Okay, bye."

Steve wondered again if the CIA would consider searching his place. They might do it. He remembered a Sherlock Holmes story where Holmes used tricks to find out if someone had paid him a visit, tricks like leaving pens, papers, and books in specific positions to see if they had been moved. He decided to try it just for kicks. He opened a desk drawer exactly one centimeter and another three centimeters and closed the others. He left his bedroom door ajar exactly five centimeters. He put some old math papers on his desk, placed a notepad on top of them, and used a protractor to rotate it exactly thirty degrees to the horizontal. If they wanted to see the papers they would have to move the notepad. Then he grabbed his laptop and left for Becky's place.

When he arrived he knocked. She opened the door and said, "Come in, handsome." He went in, and they sat down on the couch.

She said, "It's way after five—time for a beer?"

"Good idea. I can use one."

She went to the kitchen, fetched two bottles of beer, and said, "Okay, I'm ready for the news."

Steve explained the sequence of events to Becky. Then he said, "There was another guy there named Tony. He seemed to be an assistant to Edwards. He was selected to show me out and, when we were alone, told me to be careful since I may be in danger. He didn't seem like he really belonged in the group. We exchanged emails and phone numbers. He may turn out to be a valuable friend. Then again he could be faking it."

"That's interesting. It looks like you made progress and you had fun. This guy Tony seems interesting. Maybe he's a mole." Becky snickered.

"Yeah, maybe he works for the FBI." They both really laughed.

She said, "One thing I love about you is your sense of humor. The FBI. That's really funny."

"If you hadn't said 'mole,' I would never have thought of it." They laughed again.

"You know, another thing I love about you is your voice. Your students must love to hear your lectures."

"My voice? What's so great about that?"

"I don't know. It's kind of melodic."

"That's interesting. Nobody's ever mentioned my voice before. In fact I like yours also. Many women have high-pitched voices. Yours is lower and just perfect."

"Gee, thanks. Anyway, how about a salad, a steak, and a baked potato drenched in butter and sour cream?"

"That sounds great. Will you marry me?"

"Yes, but only after you speak to the president."

They laughed again. Becky started to make the salads. Steve's laptop beeped.

Steve looked. "It looks like a long email from Bert. I emailed him just before I left. I'll read it later."

"Okay. Here's a nice salad. Chow down!"

After the great meal she said, "Now let's look at Bert's email."

Steve read it. "Wow!" he said.

Then he looked at Becky and remembered he'd never told her about Hodges. He told her about Hodges and about Bert's theory that the basketball player might have the same kind of telekinesis power as Steve. Then he said, "And now Bert has some amazing news about him. Let me read the message to you."

Steve read aloud: "Hi, Steve. Thanks for the news. That's very interesting about Sam. How are you going to keep him quiet? Then again it seems the whole world is going to find out about you soon. I wonder if the French Open people would consider you a cheat. I doubt it. You played according to your own abilities.

"Anyway, have you been keeping up with the news? In the last several weeks three banks have been robbed in Brooklyn, Philadelphia, and Chicago. They are unique in that the doors and the safes were cut open with the same kind of tool, maybe a laser. The video cameras in the banks showed that there were always four guys and they all wore the same kind of mask, so it looks like the same gang committed the crimes. The banks were all hit around two am, and on two occasions a security guard was knocked unconscious with, it seems, identical blows to the same part of the head. One died. The cameras could not seem to identify any object that was used to knock them out. Since the banks were in three different states with similar modus operandi the FBI was called in.

"Now get this. Skip plays for the Brooklyn Tigers, and this team played basketball games in those three cities the same days those banks were hit! Now is that a coincidence or what? I guess you could consider the evidence circumstantial, but I personally believe the Skip had something to do with it. He may have powers similar to yours, and he is using them to rob banks! We can discuss further when we get together. Bye for now, Bert."

Becky said, "Wow, that's amazing!"

"I don't know. It could be a coincidence. Then again, adding to that the basketball percentage, it could very well be true. Maybe the FBI should be given a tip, and they can track him."

Steve replied to Bert's email, "Hi, Bert. That was rather amazing news. Maybe you should contact the FBI and suggest that Skip be followed. I'm not sure how you can do it. You don't want them to connect it to you. Maybe you can send an anonymous letter. See you soon, Steve."

SKIP HODGES, CHIEF SUSPECT

Steve asked Becky if she subscribed to a newspaper. She said no, she just caught the news on TV. She said, "We can catch the news around eleven o'clock. In the meantime you can give me another chess lesson. I want to eventually be able to compete with you."

She got out a chess set, and they played for the rest of the evening. At 11:00 they turned on the TV. The lead national story was that a Bank of America branch in Boston had been robbed and that the FBI thought it was perpetrated by the same group who'd robbed banks in the cities Bert had mentioned.

Steve said, "Wow, another bank robbery. I wonder where the Tigers were playing."

Later in the news came the sports. "The Brooklyn Tigers win again, 110 to 93, led by their chief scorer Skip Hodges, this time defeating the Boston Chiefs in Boston."

Steve said, "The same city again. Another coincidence?"

"I don't think it is. This guy has to be stopped. If he has your kind of powers, no one will be able to stop him. It might have to be you."

"I've often thought that there must be another person with the same powers I have. Why would I be the only one?"

"I've often thought that also. Why would you be unique?"

"If he has the same power, I wonder if there's any difference in powers between him and me. Anyway, first things first—we need proof. Somebody has to notify the FBI. Let's talk to Bert tomorrow."

"Okay, let's do that. I'm a little tired. Are you ready for bed?" He agreed, and they turned in.

The next day, Thursday, after breakfast, they called Bert on the phone. He answered and said he would rather not talk on the phone. He suggested they come over to his place that evening, 7:30 as usual. They agreed.

Steve said, "So, Becky, we have today to ourselves. What do you want to do?"

"There's always tennis, but I'm in the mood for a vigorous hike. How about you?"

"Sounds good. Have you ever been to Mission Peak? It will give you a good workout because it's pretty steep."

She had never been there, so they got ready to go. He said, "We should carry water and hats since there's essentially no shade up there."

They each got a day pack, water, and hats, and then they started out. After a good hike they went out for dinner and drove over to Bert's place.

Bert opened the door and said, "Hi, gang, come on in. Did you see the news about the bank robbery in Boston? The Tigers played there the same day!"

"Yes, we heard. Your theory looks very good." They went in and sat down at the kitchen table.

Bert immediately passed them each a piece of paper and said, "Here is my letter." It read,

Dear Sir:

I have what might be important information concerning the multiple bank robberies. The person who I believe may be involved is Skip Hodges, basketball player for the Brooklyn Tigers. As evidence for my belief you should note that his team, the Tigers, have played in the very city of the robberies on the very date of each of the robberies. I know that he is somewhat famous but, nonetheless, he should be checked. For reasons which I prefer not to explain at the present time, I prefer to remain anonymous.

Sincerely yours.

Bert said, "I went to the FBI web site. They had email addresses and phone numbers. Finally I found an address in Washington, DC. If I write I obviously won't put down my return address. I hope they don't ignore my letter."

Steve said, "This is an excellent letter. To be on the safe side you should mail it from the public post office, not your home. Also, wipe it for fingerprints."

Bert said, "Yes, I will. Okay that settles that. Now, how about some backgammon?"

They agreed and spent the remainder of the evening playing.

After a fun evening they left and headed home. Steve said, "Becky, I have to tell you something I did. I thought that the CIA might come to my place and search it, so I set up a few things to test it. I'd like to go home and check. If they visited me, maybe I should temporarily move in with you. My place may not be safe. I'll drop you back at your place first."

"I understand. What kinds of things did you do to check?"

"I left several desk drawers and my bedroom door ajar a specified distance. If they aren't at that distance when I return, I'll know I've been visited."

"Wow, that seems like a neat trick. I knew you were a smart guy. Will you marry me?"

"Yes, but not until I talk to the president." An old joke, but they still laughed a little.

Steve took her home and left for his place. When he arrived in the parking lot everything seemed normal. He went in and looked around. He looked at the desk drawers. One of them that should have been shut was open. He got out his ruler and measured the others. They had been moved. His bedroom door was wide open, and the notebook had been moved. He knew someone had been here. He went into his bedroom. One bureau drawer was ajar. He had an envelope on his closet shelf where he kept some spare cash. He checked it. The money was still there. There was no reason why they would rob him. They just wanted to know more about him. He phoned Becky.

"Hi, babe. Guess what? I've had visitors."

"Really? Anything stolen?"

"No, not even some cash I had in my closet. I guess they just want to know more about me."

"Do you think it's safe to stay there?"

"Probably, but you never know. I wonder if I should call Edwards and let him know that I know what they did. Then again I think I'll just play dumb."

"I think you're right. Anyway, if you want to live here for a while, it's okay with me."

"Thanks. I'll let you know."

Time passed, and the three of them, Steve, Becky, and Bert, all separately kept tabs on the news; in fact, they all watched the same channel on TV. A few days later one the news anchors announced, "Several CIA employees have reported that the main office in San Francisco was visited by a man having strange powers that may be considered telekinetic. Telekinesis is the ability to move objects through mental power alone and has never been scientifically verified. When asked who this person was, they said they did not know. They asked to remain anonymous since they were afraid of losing their jobs. We were at first skeptical, but more than one person gave the same report."

Steve thought, *Well, the cat's out of the bag. I hope nobody believes it.*

Becky called and said, "I guess you saw the news. At least it isn't the CIA officials who are talking. They seem to be keeping it quiet."

"Yes, but I may hear from them soon."

Steve also kept tabs on the Brooklyn Tigers. They were scheduled to play in Miami. Two more days went by, and then the news broadcast included an update on the bank robbery cases:

"In response to an anonymous tip, the FBI surprised four masked men attempting to rob the Bank of the East in Miami, Florida. Of the four one was apprehended, and one was killed in a gunfight. The other two got away. The FBI reports that one of the fleeing suspects was able to remove their guns from their hands and knock them down without touching them. He seemed to have telekinetic powers. They were unable to chase after them because both police cars were disabled with flat tires. An FBI spokesperson said, 'We know who he is.' When asked who, he said he could not say at the present time. This brings to mind our recent report about a visitor to the San Francisco CIA office who seemed to telekinetic powers. Was it the bank robber? If so, why would he visit the CIA? Calls to the CIA asking for more information have not been returned."

Steve called Bert. "Hey, Bert, did you see the news?

Your letter seemed to have worked. I hope they don't think it's connected to me, the CIA visitor."

"Yes, I'm surprised they actually read my letter. So now they know who's robbing the banks. They must have put a tail on him and followed him. The trouble is they didn't catch him. Maybe they never will. If anyone gets him, it'll probably have to be you!"

"My God, what do I do now? If I confront him, he may be powerful enough to kill me."

"Let's wait and see what happens. The FBI will definitely confront him. Since he's making so much money playing basketball, maybe he'll go straight. He'll have to change his identity of course. Maybe leave the US."

"Go straight? With that power, he probably won't. I guess the only thing we can do is wait. The CIA is obviously going to know about this, and they'll probably call me. I guess I can tell them what I know. I won't mention you, of course."

Bert said, "I have another piece of news. I'm going to retire. Friday will be my last day. I found a buyer for the hardware store and sold it for a nice price. It's put me in excellent financial shape. I can even go back to college and study physics!"

"Hey, that's good news. We can now spend more time playing backgammon."

"You're funny. You may not have much time for anything except chasing down Skip Hodges. Let me know if the CIA calls you."

"Okay, I will. Talk to you later."

Steve hung up. At least the FBI was on to Skip. He wondered if the CIA and the FBI would get together and compare notes. He decided to call Becky.

"Hello, my sweet. Have you heard the news lately?"

"Yes, I just did. The FBI didn't ignore Bert's letter, and I guess they know that Skip is the bank robber. What can they do now? We know they won't be able to catch him."

"Right. Bert thinks he may try to go straight. Since they know who he is, his basketball career is over. I think things are going to get worse. Oh, by the way, one other piece of news—Bert is retiring."

"Oh, that's great. I wonder why? Maybe it's all this stuff about Skip."

"Maybe, but I think he was about ready."

"If you say so. I don't think that Skip can go straight, except maybe straight to prison. But would a prison hold him? Anyway, do you want to come over here? I miss you."

"I miss you too, but I think that I may get a call from the CIA so I'm going to hang around here for a few days. I'm a bit nervous about the whole thing. I'll call you in a day or two."

"Okay, I'll be waiting."

C H A P T E R   2 5

THE CIA NEEDS HELP

2:00 p.m., Friday

The telephone rang; it was Edwards. "Hello, Steve. Are you aware of what's going on back east?"

"Yes, I'm following the news. It seems I am not alone with my powers."

"Yes, it seems so. I think we need your help to get this guy. Thanks to an anonymous tip we know who he is. Believe it or not, it is Skip Hodges, the professional basketball player. At least he didn't get the bank in Miami. He was making great money as a basketball player, so why would he bother to rob banks? We caught one of his henchman, and he turned out to be a Mafia gang member. Why he would fool around with the Mafia is anyone's guess. Anyway, we would like you to come out to Washington as soon as possible. Can you leave today?"

"Do you know where he is?"

"No, but we know the location of the Mafia headquarters in Miami, and he might not be far away from there."

"Okay, where do you want me to meet you?"

"No need for that. We have sent a plane, and you'll be taken to the right place. I am sending a man to your place to escort you to the San Jose Airport. He'll be with you on the trip back east. When can you be ready?"

"It won't take me long to pack. What is the name of my escort?"

"Tony Wallace. I think you may remember him. He's my chief assistant here."

"Yes, I remember him. When will he arrive?"

"He will be there within the hour."

"All right, I'll be ready."

Steve was glad to hear it was Tony who would accompany him. He felt that Tony was a trustworthy guy, but then again it might be a ruse. He hung up and called Becky. "Hi, Beck. Guess what, I'm wanted in Washington. I have to leave in about an hour on a private jet."

"I can't believe it. So they know about Skip and his powers, and they think you're their last hope, right?"

"Yes, something like that. Anyway we can stay in touch via email. I'll be thinking of you. Bye for now."

"Okay, good-bye. Stay safe!"

He hung up and started to pack. He wondered just what he could do. It seemed that Skip's powers were rather strong. He was able to break safes, knock people out, grab guns, and flatten tires. How could Steve get him? It would probably need to be some kind of a surprise attack.

In about a half hour there was a knock on the door. Steve walked to the door and said, "Who is it?"

"Tony Wallace from the CIA." Steve opened the door.

"Hello, Steve. I'm glad to see you again. Are you ready?"

Steve grabbed his bag, "Yes, let's go." They drove to the airport and boarded a plane. It was a small jet. They took off.

Steve said, "This is a nice plane. I've never flown on a private jet before. How long have you worked for the CIA?"

"About ten years."

"From your remarks in the past you seem to be suspicious of the organization."

"Yes, I am. Have you ever read the book *Confessions of an Economic Hit Man?*"

"No, but I remember hearing about it."

"It's about power and money. If it's felt that you are any kind of a threat, there could be an attempt to eliminate you. Be careful who you trust."

Steve thought it rather strange that this guy Tony would befriend him. Should he trust him?

"Who will we be talking to in Washington?"

"The president knows about both you and Skip. They know he is a crook, and they're not sure about you, mainly since you say you'd like to see some changes to be made. By the way, what would you like to see changed?" Tony was obviously feeling him out.

Steve told Tony what he would like to see changed in the country, including free health care for all Americans. Tony replied that he was in favor of it and said that since it worked in Europe and other countries like Canada, why not here? Steve was happy that Tony agreed. Steven then mentioned legalizing what were presently illegal drugs, citing the *Economist*'s position in favor of legalizing everything. Tony said, "I can understand that. Since we are the biggest customer of illegal drugs there is no way to stop it, so why bother? One thing you should note, though, is that there are organizations who profit from drug enforcement, like my group, the CIA. They might want to keep it illegal to keep them busy and hence in demand."

Tony then turned on what seemed to be a strange-looking TV set, saying, "I need to check the news."

"Former basketball star, bank robbery suspect, and alleged 'TK person' Skip Hodges has invaded a government office in Miami. He and a group of about twenty other men have taken over a main building. He then made a statement claiming he's an alien, the first of his race to arrive here on Earth with a mission of taking over the planet. He is holding the employees of the building hostage and demanding 200 million dollars to set them free. He has given the government forty-eight hours to comply. People in Miami are leaving en mass. Roads are clogged beyond comprehension. As yet we have no word from the White House."

Steve said, "Oh my God! Everybody now knows who he is. I wonder what his fans think. An alien? I doubt it. Maybe we should head for Miami. If I confront him with my powers, he might back down."

"You might be right. Let me contact Washington."

Tony got on a fancy radio phone and called. After some discussion he hung up.

"It's a go. We change course for Miami." He notified the pilot about the change in plans, and the plane banked to the right and straightened out on its new course.

On the way Tony said, "It is very important that as few people as possible recognize you, so we'll try to keep your identity a secret. When we land, we'd like you to wear these." He handed Steve a black, hooded sweatshirt, a black hat, and dark glasses. Steve was a bit surprised but agreed.

They finally landed in Miami. The plane taxied to a stop, and the doors opened.

Tony and Steve walked down the steps of the plane and onto the tarmac. A black SUV drove up to the plane, and three men got out. One fellow came up to him. "Hello, Steve. My name is Frank Dillon. I head up the FBI on the east coast. Please, gentlemen, come with us."

As they walked the few steps to the SUV, Steve noticed that the weather was cloudy with a definite chance of rain.

Once they were all in the SUV and the vehicle was moving, Dillon said, "We understand you have powers like this guy Skip. We find this whole thing beyond belief, but we hope you can help."

Steve replied, "I find it hard to believe myself. There must be some god-like power beyond it."

Dillon nodded. "Perhaps. Anyway, let's get to the problem at hand. Since most traffic is on its way out, we should be able to quickly make it over to where this idiot is holding up. We've tried establishing a dialogue with him, but he refuses to talk."

After about a half an hour they made it to the government office building. It was 12:25 a.m. eastern time. Police were everywhere. Reporters were kept back out of the way.

Dillon said, "The last time we spoke to him he appeared on that upper landing. He had a loudspeaker system, as do we. Let's try to contact him again."

Dillon spoke into the microphone and said, "Mr. Hodges, we have new information. We need to speak to you immediately." Nobody appeared. They waited five minutes, and Dillon repeated his message. Finally Skip came out. He was a lean, clean-shaven guy with a crew cut, and tall, which made sense for a basketball player, Steve thought.

Skip said, "Well, what is your information?"

Steve said, "Let me speak to him."

Steve took the mike and decided to use Hodges's real first name. "Hello, Daniel. I am an alien like you. In fact I am from your planet." Steve stopped and waited for Hodges's reaction.

Hodges just stared and seemed confused. He finally said, "No, you can't be."

Steve said, "Why not? If you can be here so can I."

"You can't have my powers, I know that."

"But I do have them. I can prove it."

"Oh, yeah? Let's see it."

Steve turned to Dillon. "I have to do some damage to the building. Is that okay?"

"Of course. Anything at all to get rid of that guy."

Above Hodges's head were three windows. Steve decided to use the force to crush them and pull them out so the glass would fall on Hodges.

As Steve reached out with the field, he could feel a force field in front of Hodges. He pressed against it. It seemed pretty strong. Hodges looked surprised. Fortunately, there was no field above his head. Steve reached up, pushed in the windows to dislodge them, and then yanked all three windows out, at same time saying, "Okay, get ready to duck."

The window frames and glass came tumbling down on Hodges, who ducked and tried to move out of the way. He looked shocked. He stared at Steve for a second and then immediately went inside.

Dillon said, "Hey, that was great. It looks like you scared the shit out of him. I wish I knew how you did it. What do we do now?"

What do we do now? Steve thought. *How am I supposed to know?*

Finally Steve said, "We wait. I don't think he'll give up. We have to wait and see."

After thirty minutes had passed, Dillon said, "I think we should try and contact him again. It's probably better if you talk."

Steve agreed and said, "Hello, Daniel. Are you convinced? Come on out, and let's talk."

They waited. He didn't show. They waited some more. Nothing.

Dillon said, "What's next?"

"I don't know. It's late and dark. I don't think we should go in. Let's wait until sunup and give it another try."

"I think you're right. You must be tired from that long trip. There's a bed in the van over there. Get some rest. We'll keep watch and wake you if we have to."

"Okay, I can use the rest. See you later."

Steve climbed into the van. He thought about contacting Becky but decided against it. He saw a nice, comfortable-looking bed. He took off his shoes, hat, hooded sweatshirt, and glasses. He lay down under a blanket and fell asleep immediately.

He awoke abruptly to the sound of gunfire. He rushed to put his shoes on and heard the roar of car engines. He ran out and saw several police cars with their front windows smashed. Three SUVs and another car roared out of the lower floor of the building, which housed a parking lot. Four policemen fired at the cars, but the bullets seemed to have no effect. Two police cars attempted to follow them but were immediately forced off the road. Steve knew it was the telekinetic force. The criminals couldn't be followed.

Dillon said, "It looks like, thanks to you, we scared the hell out of them. They can't get too far away. The state police have been notified and will give chase. Then again, with his power, they probably won't be able to do much."

Steve said, "Right, but hopefully you'll be able to keep track of his whereabouts."

Dillon, Steve, several FBI agents, and a bunch of policemen entered the building and found that several men inside had bruises. The woman had not been injured. All were alive and well.

Dillon said, "Thank God no one was hurt. What a relief! Mr. Thomas, we want to thank you for all this. We couldn't have done anything without you. At least we have him on the run. Unfortunately we may have to call on you again."

"Of course I will be available, but I'm not sure what I can do."

Just then Tony showed up. "Great job, Steve! You came through in the clutch. I'm sure you'll be getting a reward."

"Reward for what? We didn't catch him."

"No, but you saved lots of government employees and maybe 200 million bucks."

"Well, I guess I did something after all. I'll be very happy if we can get rid of him somehow."

Tony smiled. "You're right. Anyway, we should resume our trip to Washington."

Dillon called the airport from his cell phone.

Steve decided to email Becky with the news. "Hello, Beck. It looks like we scared Skip, but he managed to get away. I am flying up to Washington to meet with the top dogs. I'll be in touch."

Steve, Tony, and Dillon then climbed into the back of the black SUV and were driven back to the airport. They drove right up to the plane. The three of them entered plane and took seats.

Since he'd told Skip he was an alien, Steve wondered if they thought he really was one. He decided not to ask.

He then thought that the FBI or the CIA could probably get access to his emails and hence learn about Becky. He should have thought of that. He decided to not allow anyone access to his laptop.

During the flight, on a few occasions both Tony and Dillon glanced at him in a strange way.

Steve said, "I know what you're thinking. You're wondering if I'm an alien, right?"

Tony and Dillon stared at each other for a few seconds, and then Dillon turned to Steve and said, "Yes, since that's what you told Skip. Are you?"

"Absolutely not! I don't know how I or Skip got these powers, but I know that I'm one hundred percent human. There may be something supernatural about it, but I have no idea what it might be."

They seemed satisfied, but he thought they were not completely convinced.

CHAPTER 26

STEVE MEETS THE VICE PRESIDENT

They landed about noon. When they entered the airport a huge number of reporters were there asking questions. The FBI men surrounded Steve, but the reporters held up mikes and shouted questions. A couple of FBI men answered some of the questions. Steve was glad of the disguise. He was hustled into a limo that took them to a building Steve did not recognize.

Tony, Dillon, and Steve went to a large conference room. Coffee and cookies were available. Steve was given a seat at the head of the table. He was still wearing the hooded sweatshirt, hat, and glasses. Steve recognized the vice president, the speaker of the house, the Senate majority leader, and five or six others. He was surprised to see that Edwards from the west coast CIA office was there also.

Dillon spoke first. "It is very important that we try to keep the identity of this person as confidential as possible.

That's the reason for his attire. We will also use alias John Smith as his name."

Vice President Andrew Charles spoke and introduced the other members of the group. He then said to Steve, "We are all very happy to meet you and very thankful for what you have done. Everyone in the room has been told about your powers, but those of us who've not seen for ourselves are a little skeptical. Could you give us a brief demonstration?"

Steve had known that was coming. He looked around. In one corner of the room was a small table with a chair next to it. He said, "Watch that chair over there." They all looked. Using the force he picked up the chair, turned it upside down, and put it on the top of the table. They stared back at him in amazement and said nothing.

The vice president spoke. "That is astounding. How did you get this power?"

"I don't know. One day it suddenly appeared. I kind of wish it hadn't. I suspect that there's a reason, but I don't know what it is."

"You know there was a ten-million-dollar reward for catching the men who robbed those banks. We want you to have it."

"Since we haven't caught him yet, I don't think I should accept it."

"We also know that he threatened the lives of many people, and you saved us from dealing with their safety, so we insist. If you catch him, we'll give you another ten million. The money has already been deposited into your account."

Steve was at first surprised, but on second thought it was rather obvious the FBI could find out everything about him, including his bank account. "Well, thank you. You know that Hodges and I both have the telekinetic powers, but I have no idea whose, if either, is strongest, so I don't really know how much I can help. But if he shows up again I will be available of course."

"Mr. Smith, I want you to know that your name has been kept secret from almost everyone in this room. You may not have realized it, but you are probably the most famous person in the United States right now. Reporters will want to follow you everywhere, so we have called a press conference for you to help fend them off. It will be in the pressroom down the hall. I'll accompany you down there now. You should keep your current attire on and maybe pull down your hat a little to cover your face as much as possible."

The meeting ended. He and the vice president went down the hall to the pressroom. There was a stage and a person who Steve thought might be the president's press secretary. About twenty members of the press sat in front of the stage, and a number of TV cameras were set up in the back.

After he and Steve walked onto the stage, Vice President Charles said, "As I mentioned earlier, you have only ten minutes, and we will take one question at a time."

They started asking questions: how he got his power, when he got it, was it more powerful than Skip's, was he an alien, was Skip an alien, what was he going to do next, on and on. Finally it was over, and some rushed out to transmit their stories to their newspapers, magazines, and radio and TV stations. Others were busy talking on their cell phones.

When the room was empty of reporters, Vice President Charles said, "We have another request. We would like you give you a thorough physical exam. With your extraordinary powers, we would like to try and determine any possible scientific reason for them. Do you agree to such an examination?"

Steve stared at him for a few seconds. "Sure, I don't see why not. I'd like to learn more myself."

Steve was escorted to a medical center in the building. He was introduced to a doctor and two scientists, was given a physical exam, and took a variety of tests. He was asked to demonstrate his powers. They set up several instruments intended to measure any type of field emanating from him. They could not detect anything electromagnetic but did detect the physical force itself. They then thanked him for his cooperation.

Steve asked, "Have you found anything significant?"

One scientist said, "Nothing at all obvious. We're going to study the results of our measurements further. If we find anything, we'll let you know."

Steve left and encountered the vice president in the lobby. "Thank you for allowing us to examine you," Charles said. "This may seem silly to you, but we are a little worried about your safety. Lots of people, including reporters, may be able to figure out who you are and where you live. Somebody may even try to kill you. Therefore, we would like you to consider moving to a safer location. We have a specific gated community in mind. It is in Los Altos, not far from where you live now. Would you consider it?"

Steve thought about it. He wondered how anyone would know where he lived. He supposed the employees in the San Francisco office might find out who he was, and of course the CIA and FBI in DC knew, and they might have leaks.

He said, "You may be right, but how about let's see what happens in the next week or so. If things get bad, I'll call you."

"Okay. You should do it through the CIA. Just call Dr. Edwards, and he'll handle it. You are of course welcome to stay and visit the capital."

"Thank you, but under the circumstances, with my disguise and all, I think it best if I return immediately."

"I understand. Anthony Wallace can accompany you back to the airport, and you two can fly on our private jet back to San Jose."

Steve thought, *Who is Anthony Wallace? Oh, that's Tony.* "Thank you very much, Mr. Charles. It has been a fascinating experience."

"It was beyond fascinating. It was amazing—in fact, not believable!"

Steve and Tony left for the airport.

Tony said, "I'd offer to buy you a meal or a beer, but I think it's better if we just leave as soon as possible."

"Yes, you're right. Why risk anyone seeing me?"

He bought a newspaper before boarding. On the plane

he opened the newspaper. The front page read, SECOND TK PERSON CONFRONTS BANK ROBBER SKIP HODGES—HODGES ESCAPES, STILL AT LARGE.

He looked at Tony, who was doing some paperwork. Tony looked up and said, "I think we did pretty well in keeping your identity a secret."

"I hope so. Of course, the CIA and FBI know me, so it may not be long before it leaks out."

"Right. That's why the gated community idea is good. You should accept it."

"I probably will, but not just yet."

"You can't be too careful. Since practically everyone now knows what you're wearing, I'd like you to take off your sweatshirt and hat and wear this other jacket and hat. You can keep the glasses." The jacket was light blue and a different style. The hat was red.

When they landed in San Jose, there were no reporters or anyone suspicious around. Tony drove him back to his place. Everything looked normal. He got out of the car.

"Hey, Tony, care to come up for a beer?"

"Why not, since my task here is complete."

They went in. Again, everything looked normal. Steve got out a couple of cans of beer and opened a can of mixed nuts. They sat down in the kitchen.

Steve said, "I almost forgot how good that first swallow of beer is."

"Right you are! The second isn't bad either."

Steve pondered a moment and then decided to see how much Tony knew.

"Did you know that my apartment was searched once?"

Tony looked a little surprised and then said, "Yes, I knew that. How did you know?"

"I have a few little tricks to find things like that out."

"You're a pretty clever guy. Then again, being a math teacher, you can't be too dumb. Speaking of teaching, I assume that with all that money you now have, you're going to quit."

"I haven't even thought about that. I guess you're right. Why should I work when I don't have to? The next question is how am I going to spend my time? I'll have to think about that."

"I know one way—tracking down Skip Hodges!"

"You know, for a second I forgot all about him. That may take me the rest of my life."

They finished the beers, and Steve said, "Here—this jacket and hat are yours."

"No, they're yours. Keep them as a souvenir." They then said their good-byes.

After Tony left, Steve thought about Becky. He glanced at his watch and noted the time, 7:10. He called her on the phone.

"Hello, Beck. Guess who?"

"Oh, John, it's you."

"What? Who's John?"

"Why, John Smith, my new boyfriend. Isn't that you?"

He laughed. "You catch on fast. Do you want all the news in person or over the phone?"

"In person of course. Come on over."

Steve headed over to her place. He brought the newspaper. When he arrived she hugged him and kissed him madly.

"You don't know how much I missed you. How about a beer?"

"I just had one with Tony, but I'll take another." They sat down in the kitchen. She said, "I like your new jacket and hat. Where did you get them?"

"Presents from the CIA. Part of my disguise."

"So tell me the story. Don't leave anything out." He told her everything in detail, including the fact that Hodges wanted 200 million dollars, the gated-community offer, and the ten-million-dollar reward.

"My God, ten million? I guess you don't need me any more. You can have anything or anybody you want."

"Yes, but I only want you. You know what we can do? Get married and have a family."

"I don't know … you haven't talked to the president yet."

He shook his head at the old joke. "Don't you want to marry me?"

"You're not a normal person. You haven't caught Skip yet, and maybe you never will. Who knows what he'll do next. Under the circumstances I don't think I want to consider marriage."

"I guess you're right, but will you ever?"

"Maybe. But let's not think about it. Let's just enjoy each other right now. I see you have a copy of the newspaper. Have you read it?"

"Well, not everything. What did I miss?"

"The religious freaks think you were sent by God. They think Skip is Satan. They're trying hard to find you. They want to talk to you. Then there's the paranormal group. They always believed in telekinesis, and you are the proof. They want you to join them. They're looking for you too. This is what I mean by you aren't a normal person. You never will be. What I don't understand is me. How do I fit in? Why do I have this feeling about you? I feel like you trapped me and I can't get away, but I really don't want to get away. I love being trapped!"

"Becky, you're scaring me a little. I don't want you to feel trapped."

"Maybe trapped is the wrong word. It's just that even if I wanted to I couldn't stop loving you."

"Hey, let's stop thinking about all this. I haven't eaten supper, have you?"

"Actually when I got home today I was tired and took a nap, so I haven't eaten yet. Let's go out. How about the City Diner?"

"Great idea. Let's go."

They went to the diner, ordered, and ate. They didn't say much to each other for awhile. Then she said, "So what are they doing to find Skip?"

"They're looking. He obviously won't be playing basketball anymore. They're worried as to what he'll do next. I'm on call."

"What do you think he'll do next?"

"Well, he is involved with the Mafia-type people. Since he was interested in extorting money from the United States government, he may consider another country. Who knows?"

C H A P T E R   2 7

STEVE MEETS WITH SAM

He finished the last of his meal and leaned back in his chair. Becky smiled at him from across the table. "Penny for your thoughts," she said.

"Oh, I was just thinking about our crazy life up to now."

"I know," she said. "It has been more than insane."

Steve motioned for the waiter and paid when he came. "Come on—let's get out of here."

They walked hand in hand to the car and headed back to her place. They went in and sat down in the family room.

She said, "What game should we play for the rest of the evening?"

"I don't know. How about just chatting about the meaning of life?"

"That's a tall one. You start."

"Have you ever read any proofs of the existence of God?"

"I think so, but it's been a long time ago. Refresh my memory."

"The idea of God occurred to me because of this strange power that I have. I don't think it's related to God in the usual, religious sense, but there must be some kind of being behind it all."

"I thought the same thing, but there's no way to find out what it is or anything about it."

"One guy I knew said that the probability that everything that exists on Earth that is needed to support life is so small that there had to be a God. It couldn't happen by chance. As a simple example, did you know that when water freezes and turns to ice it expands a little and becomes less dense than water? That's why it floats. I don't think anything else does that. Anyway, he argued that if that were not true there would be no life on Earth, since water in lakes would not freeze from the top down. He gave quite a few more examples and actually gave the probability of life existing as one in ten to the power ninety-nine, which proves that there must be a god behind everything."

"So what did you say?"

"I said that he might be right that a lot of the laws of nature had to exist for us to have evolved and there might be some kind of force behind it which you might call God. But I said if some of those laws were not true and others were, the kind of life we have here might not exist but some other kind might. He didn't quite know how to respond to that."

"Hey, that was a good reply."

"One of my favorites is called the ontological proof. It goes like this. God by definition is the most perfect being, but if two beings are equal in all ways except that one exists and the other doesn't, then the one that exists is more perfect than the one that doesn't. Therefore God exists."

"Hey, I like that one. How do you refute it?"

"Do you agree that mathematics is the most perfect science?"

"Let's see. Physics, chemistry, and biology all require measurements, but measurements are never exact. In mathematics you don't really need measurement. Yes, I agree."

"Wow, I'm glad you noticed that. Now what is mathematics about? It's about numbers, points, lines, planes, et cetera. Do they exist? No, none of them physically exist. Numbers are ideas; they don't physically exist. A point has no dimensions, so it doesn't exist, and neither does a line, since it has only one dimension. A plane has two dimensions and zero thickness, so it doesn't exist either. They are all abstractions. None of them exist. Therefore the most perfect science is about things which do not exist. So the ontological argument is false. In fact, it proves the opposite. The most perfect being does *not* exist."

"Brilliant! Let's get married."

"Right after I talk to the president."

With a slight grin he shook his head frowning.

Then he remembered Sam and said, "By the way, Sam Finch is coming up Sunday. I have to figure out what to tell him. Maybe I should just be completely honest with him. Include him in the secret."

"I think you're right. Just be honest. The trouble is, he may want you to confess to the French Open people and have them take your money back."

"I know what I can do. I can offer him some money to keep him quiet."

"Sounds underhanded, sort of like a bribe. In fact it is a bribe. How much will you offer him?"

"Well, I think he would have earned about two hundred thousand dollars in the quarterfinals if he'd won. I think I'll offer him a hundred thousand. If he seems unsatisfied, I can bump it to two hundred. If worse comes to worst, I can kill him."

Becky's eyes popped open. She was shocked.

Steve said immediately, "I'm only joking of course."

"That's a very bad joke!"

"I know. I'm sorry I said it. Please forgive me. However, I think the money idea will work."

"I do too. Shall we turn in? I'm in the mood for love."

"My mood is your mood."

They went to bed.

The next morning they woke and ate breakfast.

She said, "You're not saying much today."

"I guess I'm thinking about my meeting with Sam."

"That's understandable. Good luck with it."

He eventually left and went back to his place.

Sunday

Steve put on a pot of coffee. He had plenty of beer and wine in the fridge. Sam and Hank showed up at the agreed time.

"Hello, guys. Come on in. Care for a drink—coffee, beer, wine?"

Sam said, "I think I'll have a beer."

Hank said, "Me, too."

After getting three beers out Steve said, "Let's get down to business. You're accusing me of manipulating the tennis ball, right?"

"Right. We have proof right here on this DVD if you want to see it."

"That won't be necessary. I have to tell you a story. Last year something happened to me that I can't explain. I got the ability to control objects with my mind. Don't ask my how it happened because I don't know. It just happened. Anyway I decided to use it to make money, in particular win tennis tournaments. I played the pro circuit and won. Then I was invited to the French, and, as you know, I won it."

Steve knew he would be asked to give a demo. He said, "Let me demonstrate. Look at that dish over there in the drain." They watched as he used the force to pick it up and move it to his hand. They just stared at him for a moment.

Then Sam said, "Do you happen to be John Smith?"

Somewhat surprised Steve said, "Yes, I am."

"Wow, so it was you who confronted the bank robber!"

"Yes, that was me, but I just scared him. He's still loose. Who knows what he'll do next."

Sam just stared at him. "Wow, I don't believe it."

Hank said, "Neither do I. How can you do that?"

Steve said, "Sometimes I don't believe it myself." He then thought about the *bribe*. This would be a good time to bring it up.

"Sam, I know I sort of cheated you out of a chance to win some money in the French, and I'd like to give you some money as compensation."

"I really didn't think at all about getting any money. Of course, I could use it—who can't? How much are we talking about?"

"How does one hundred thousand dollars sound?"

Sam's eyes widened, and his head moved back in surprise. "Wow, that's more than enough!" He looked at Hank. "What do you think, Hank?"

"I guess since you did all the work in figuring it out, it's fine with me."

Steve said, "I'll also give you, Hank, fifty thousand."

Hank grinned. "Thank you, Steve. I can use the money, of course."

Steve continued, "However, part of the deal is a guarantee that you tell absolutely no one about me. Absolutely means just that—your girlfriends, best friends, parents, everyone! Secrecy is important! If my real name gets in the news who knows what could happen. Secrecy is absolutely vital."

Sam said, "You can trust us. We will absolutely keep it a deep, dark secret."

Steve got his checkbook and wrote two checks. In the

memo part he wrote 'gift'. They thanked him profusely and left.

He made a note to call the bank tomorrow to tell them that two large checks would be cashed. He was glad that it worked out so smoothly and that it was over.

C H A P T E R 2 8

SKIP STRIKES AGAIN

He decided to call Becky. "Hello, sweet one, how are you doing?"

"I have a strange little headache, which is rare, but otherwise I'm okay. What's the latest?"

"I met with Sam and Hank. I gave Joe a hundred thousand and Hank fifty thousand and swore them to secrecy. Everything seemed to work out fine."

"Great. What's next?"

"I was going to ask you if you cared for a little tennis, but with your headache maybe you're not up to it."

"Yes, I think I'll just take a nap. I'll call you later."

After he hung up, he grew a little worried about Becky. Why had she used the word *strange*? He should have asked her, but he hadn't thought of it.

He went out, took a short walk for exercise, and bought a newspaper on the way back. He was surprised to see the headline LOS ANGELES BANK OF THE WEST

ROBBED: *Authorities Suspect Skip Hodges, East Coast TK Person*. He read the article; it said that authorities hadn't confirmed whether "the TK person, John Smith" would be called in.

Wow, Steve thought, *Skip is at it again.* He suspected he might get a phone call from the CIA or FBI, but what could he do?

He decided to take a little hike for exercise. When he got back, there was a phone message. "Hello, John. This is Richard Edwards from the CIA. You may have heard the news. Hodges is at it again, robbing banks, this time on the West Coast. We don't know what to do. We thought that you might have a few ideas. Let us know. Richard."

He realized they were sticking to his alias. He thought about the situation and called Edwards back. He got his secretary but was immediately transferred. "Hello, Richard. The only way to catch him is to try and find out which bank he will rob next. I would have to be there and catch him by surprise. The chances of that happening are not good."

Edwards agreed. He said, "We know where the Mafia headquarters is in LA. He may be there. If we can surprise him with you there, it might work."

"It's a long shot, but if you want to try it we can."

"Okay, we'll let you know."

Around nine o'clock Becky called. "Hi, Steve, I'm feeling better. That headache was kind of strange. It really wasn't much of a headache, just kind of a purring in my head. Do you want to come over?"

"Wait a minute, a purring in your head? Do you remember my story about the florescent lights? It started with a buzzing in my head. You called it a *purring*. Could you call it a buzzing?"

"No, it was more like a cat's purring."

"That's strange. I guess we'll just wait a see what happens. I guess you haven't heard the latest. Skip hit a bank in LA."

"Oh, no—he's still at it? What can you do?"

"Not much. Edwards from the CIA called me. He said they could try hitting the Mafia headquarters in LA because Skip might be there. It's a long shot, though. I suggested trying to figure out which bank he's going to hit next. I'm a bit tired, so let's skip getting together tonight. I'll call you tomorrow."

He hung up feeling a bit depressed. Why was all this happening to him? What had he done to deserve it? And this purring that Becky felt—was she going to get the power? He hoped not. He liked her just the way she was. His brain was awash with ideas. He turned in early.

The phone rang, and he woke with a start. He glanced at the clock. Twelve midnight. Who would call at this hour? Maybe it was Becky. He answered it.

It was Edwards. "Hi, John. I'm sorry to call this late, but we just had a hot tip. They may be going to hit a Chase bank in San Francisco early Tuesday morning. It will probably be around two am, like the others."

"How did you find that out?"

"We got an anonymous call. It was from the LA area. Of course, it could be a prank, but we can't ignore it. We think it may have been from a Mafia member who's unhappy with Skip for some reason and wants to get rid of him. We'd like you to come down and help us set up a trap." They agreed to meet in the CIA lobby, and Steve hung up.

That was an interesting turn of events. Here was his chance to put Skip away. He'd have to catch him by surprise, but how? Maybe the CIA had a plan. He wondered what happened to the FBI. Maybe they were working together. He turned over and went to sleep.

Monday morning

Steve woke up, ate breakfast, and checked the TV news. The robbery in LA was a featured story. He called Becky and got her answering machine. He told her about the possible bank robbery in San Francisco and that he was going down there to help.

Around three p.m. he went out to his car and drove to San Francisco. When he entered the CIA lobby, he looked around but didn't see Edwards. Another fellow in the lobby appeared to notice that he was confused and came up to him. "Are you looking for Edwards?"

"Yes."

He stared at him shortly in awe but eventually shook hands with him. "We're meeting in this room over here."

They went into a conference room. Edwards and Tony were there.

"Hello, John, have a seat."

A cute girl served coffee and cookies.

"Thank you," he said, "These oatmeal-raisins are my favorites." She grinned and did a flirting wiggle of her head.

Steve smiled back and thought about Becky.

Edwards said, "We have a plan. We're going to post two guys in the main vault. All of us will be wearing bulletproof clothing. We've studied the tapes from the other robberies—it takes Skip almost exactly five minutes to cut through the vault door. He doesn't carry a gun, but the other three are always heavily armed. This time when the bastards break in they'll be confronted. At the same time we'll hit them from behind. Timing is critical, since we don't want them to shoot too many shots at our guys in the vault. Of course, our guys can shoot back. They will be shooting at close range, so there is hardly any danger of them shooting us. We hope there will only be four of them as usual. We'll be waiting across the street from the bank. You, John, will be with us."

Edwards continued, "We hope you'll be able to surprise Hodges and disable him. I won't be there. Tony is in charge."

Steve asked, "Does anyone at the bank know about this?"

"Absolutely not. We'll inform the bank manager of our plan at closing time."

Steve thought it sounded like a good plan. They all studied the floor plans of the bank.

Around closing time they arrived at the bank, and

the bank manager was informed. The vault was opened, and two CIA men got in. They were supplied with water, snacks, and some padded chairs to relax on. Steve and the rest went across the street and waited.

A little before two a.m. Skip and his gang showed up. Steve immediately recognized the tall and lean former sports star with his clean-shaven face and crew-cut hair-style. They watched him use his power to slice open the front door lock. It looked so easy.

Tony said, "We wait four minutes, and then hit them! Steve, you should be in the lead since only you might be able to subdue Skip."

Four minutes went by. "Okay, let's go!" They crossed the street as quietly as possible and entered the building. The four robbers were in front of the vault, and it appeared that Skip had just cut open the lock. They opened the safe door and were confronted by the two guys in the vault. Gunshots were exchanged. One robber went down; Tony shouted, "Give it up! Put your guns down and hands up. You're under arrest!"

Another guy turned and started to fire but was mowed down by gunfire from Tony and a few others. Steve pushed the force out fast against Skip but hit a force coming from the opposite direction. Steve shoved back with more power. The two forces collided, and Skip was pushed up and back. His head hit a beam on the ceiling. He fell to the floor and didn't move. He was unconscious. Tony rushed up and handcuffed him.

Tony said, "It's all over—we got him."

Steve said, "You don't have him. When he wakes up he'll have the force. He'll just tear up the handcuffs and walk away. He may kill someone in the process. There's only one choice—you have to kill him."

Tony frowned and said, "We can't kill him. It's against the law."

"If you put him in jail, he won't stay there long. He'll break out with his force and walk away."

"We have to take that chance."

"All right—it's your funeral."

They picked Skip up. He was still unconscious. They discussed taking him in for medical care, but Steve said, "Do you want him to wake up?" They agreed that jail was the first priority. They arrived at the jail. Skip, still unconscious, was put behind bars. They discussed trying to revive him, but Steve voted no.

"You wake him up, and he might kill you with his power."

Edwards arrived and said, "You got him! Thank God! Great job, Steve—I mean John." They all shook his hand and congratulated him.

Steve didn't smile but just shook his head and said, "To be honest with you, I hope he never wakes up. If he does he may be out in a jiffy."

He thanked everyone and left. Then he thought that since several guys in the group obviously saw him, they could identify him. He wondered how long before the whole world knew his true identity.

He got home around five a.m. Tuesday morning. He went over to the fridge and opened a beer, sat down and thought

about the experience. He was surprised that it was the colli-
sion of the two forces that pushed Skip back, like a recoil. He
wondered how much damage had been done to Skip's brain.
He hoped a lot. Only time would tell. He turned in.

Steve opened his eyes and looked around. *What time is
it?* He glanced at the clock; it was 11:50. The phone rang.
"Hello, is this Mr. Thomas?"

"Yes, it is."

"This is the Wells Fargo bank. We are happy to inform
you that an additional ten million dollars has been deposited to your account. We would like you to come in next
week and discuss future plans for the money."

Wow, another ten million! "Okay, thank you, I'll call you."

They hadn't wasted any time and had actually done
what they said they would do: give him another ten million.
He hoped that they wouldn't regret it.

He fixed himself a nice cup of coffee, ate breakfast, and
checked the news at noon.

"News flash! Bank robber Skip Hodges has been
caught. The FBI got a tip that he would rob a Chase Bank
in San Francisco and set a trap to catch him. They were
aided by the other telekinetic person, John Smith. Hodges
is now in jail in San Francisco."

Steve thought, *Not for long.* He wondered how long
it would take him to break out. He thought about Becky
and phoned her. "Hello, handsome. I got your message. I'm
glad you're still alive. What happened?"

He told her what happened in detail.

"Wow, unbelievable! A successful operation. Congratulations. Come on over, and we'll celebrate."

"Okay, I'll be there shortly."

He drove over to her place. He was pretty sure it was not over and Skip would be out free again before long.

He parked, walked up to her door, and knocked. She opened the door, and he went in. They hugged.

"You're my hero again. How about a nice cup of coffee with Stevia and cream."

"I just had one with breakfast, but another sounds delightful."

They sat down and sipped the coffee. He said, "You know, of course, that it may not be over."

"I thought of that too. When he wakes up he may be able to break out of jail."

"Right. You may not like me for this, but I wanted them to kill him. They refused and said they couldn't because it was against the law."

Becky thought for a minute. "I guess they had to follow the law, but since the circumstances are extremely unusual killing him was the best thing to do."

"I'm glad you agree. I was worried that you wouldn't. I think there's a good chance they'll regret it, but I guess they had no choice."

"I have some bad news—I have to go back to work next Monday."

"Oh, no—Berlin again?"

"No, thank God. I'll be right here for awhile."

"Oh, great. You know, you can quit that job. I have

tons of money. Did I tell you that they gave me another ten million for catching him? They promised me they would, but I still couldn't believe it."

She stared at him for a few seconds and then looked away.

She looked back at him and then said, "You are unbelievable. Not only do you have superpowers, but you are rich."

"Right, and I really do want to marry you. What do you say?"

"Steve, I want to marry you, too. But I keep thinking that you're not really human. You're more like God."

"I know I have this ridiculous power, but I'm not God."

"You're not God, but you're halfway there. Let's see if Skip gets out. If he does, you'll be obligated to get him again. The next time he may get you."

"Yeah, you're right. Let's try and lead a normal life and forget about all this. By the way, what's with this purring in your head? Is it still there?"

"No, it went away after about fifteen minutes. It was kind of strange though."

"Hey, what happens if you get the power too? We can conquer the world together!"

She laughed. "Yeah, you can be Superman, and I can be Supergirl."

Steve smiled but then thought, *If she gets the power, that would change everything. What would she do then?*

He just stared for a few seconds and then said, "Okay. In the meantime how about some tennis?"

She agreed.

CHAPTER 29

THE JIG IS UP!

The next day Steve called Edwards to find out the status of Skip and was told that Skip was conscious but didn't seem able to get out of jail. They thought the blow might have made him lose his power.

Steve called Becky with the news. She sounded happy but unsure. She said, "Let see what happens after another week or two. Oh, and I told my boss at work that I'm thinking about leaving."

"Really? How come?"

"I'm kind of fed up with it. It's a lot of work and responsibility, and it's not exactly safe."

"You've never really told me what you actually do."

"I can't. I can tell you that I have a top-secret clearance, but that's all I can say."

"I see. Well, the decision is yours."

Over the next two weeks Steve and Becky spent time together and grew convinced that they belonged together.

Skip was still in prison and seemed to have lost his power. Steve read in the newspaper that Skip had been charged with bank robbery and murder and that a trial was planned.

Steve phoned Becky and told her the news.

"That's good news but not great news, since if his power comes back he may still get out."

2:00 p.m., Tuesday, August 6, 2019

The semester would start in about three weeks. Since he had lots of money, Steve decided he should resign his position at the college.

What should be his next step? He would like to talk to the US president to present his ideas, but that probably wouldn't accomplish much. Maybe he should just run for president himself. Why not?

He decided to write a letter of resignation to the college dean. Then his doorbell rang. He checked the peephole and saw a group of reporters and a few TV cameras outside. The jig was up! He opened the door, and one man stepped forward.

"Hello, my name is Carl Jenson from the *San Jose Mercury News*. We now know that your alias is John Smith, that you have telekinetic powers, and that you are the one who captured Skip Hodges. We also know that you were the winner of the French Open this year. Can you please do us the favor of an interview?"

Steve noticed that they were excessively polite. Maybe they were afraid that he would smash the cameras to smithereens. The cameras were rolling. More people were gathering around. A few cops were some distance in the background. Reporters had their notepads and pencils ready. What could he do? He stepped outside and closed the door. "It seems I don't have much choice in the matter. What do you want to know?"

"First did you use your powers to win the French Open?"

"Yes. Next question?"

"Aren't you ashamed of that?"

"No. Even though I did not know where my powers came from, I played according to my natural ability. There's nothing to be ashamed of."

"Can you tell us how you managed to capture someone who had the same telekinetic abilities as you do?"

"Well, it was a matter of surprise. I think the details were in the news."

"How do you plan to using your powers in the future?"

Steve hesitated. "I think I may run for president in the next election."

Some reporters started writing immediately into their notebooks. Others backed off, grabbed their cell phones, and spoke into them. One guy in the back said, "How can you be president? You have no experience whatever."

"I know that. I'll just have to bone up on the latest news. Anyway, I haven't made a final decision yet."

Then Steve noticed another big, ugly-looking guy in the crowd who didn't look like he belonged in the group. He barged his way up to the front of the group and said, "You're not going to run for anything, because you're going to be dead."

He pulled out a gun and pointed it Steve. It looked like one of those big guns that maybe Dirty Harry carried around. Steve reacted instinctively, pointed his finger at the gun, and pushed the force field up the barrel. The guy pulled the trigger, and the gun exploded in his hand. He fell on the ground, yelling. His hand was bleeding badly.

The cops showed up immediately. One cop pointed a gun at Steve and said, "Okay, drop your weapon!"

Steve raised his hands. "I don't have a weapon."

The cop looked confused. "Then how did you shoot him?"

"I didn't shoot him. He shot himself."

The cop's eyes widened as though he'd suddenly thought of something. "I understand it now. Just like Paris!"

"You're right!"

An ambulance showed up, and the guy was hauled away. The cameras were still rolling.

Carl Jenson said, "That was an amazing demonstration of your powers. When will you be making an announcement of your plans?"

"I don't really know. Maybe in a week or two."

He thanked Steve, and the group disbanded, walking off and shaking their heads at one another in amazement.

He knew he could not live in his condo any longer and decided to take up the CIA on the offer to live in a gated community. Then again, why not create his own gated community, a mansion in the countryside? He thought about looking around to see what was available. Then he remembered that the CIA had a place picked out for him. He decided to call Edwards to see what they had to offer.

He called and got Edwards's secretary. "Hello, this is Steven Thomas. May I speak to Richard?"

"Oh, hello. He is not available at the present time. May I take a message?"

"Yes, as you will soon find out, my identity is no longer a secret. At one point Richard offered me the opportunity to live in a gated community. In fact I would prefer a separate house away from everyone. I can pay any difference in cost. Please let Richard know of my needs."

She said, "Fine, I will give him the message."

He thought about his letter to the dean. The news would be out soon. At least he didn't have to come up with an excuse for why he wasn't returning to teaching. He jotted off a brief email to the dean. Then he decided to call Bert.

"Hello, Bert. The jig is up—the world will know soon who I am."

"What happened?"

"You'll see it on the news—about a half hour ago a guy by the name of Carl Jenson from the newspaper, a flock of other reporters, and several TV cameras showed up at my door. He said they knew who I was and asked me questions, including my plans for the future. What do you think I said?"

"Wait, let me think … You said you wanted to move into the White House."

"Hey, Bert, how did you get so smart! Actually I

said I may run for the president in the next election. They all seemed shocked. I really don't know what to do now."

"Go for it. Why not? Does Becky know yet?"

"No, I figured I'd just let her find out from the news. Also, I've decided my condo is no longer safe. I'm going to move to some kind of gated residence."

"Come on over tonight, and we can discuss the whole thing."

"I'm a little worried about traveling. I'll see Becky later. We can then both come over, probably in her car, around 7:30 as usual."

"Okay, see you later."

Steve hung up, called Becky, and left a message about going to Bert's place.

The phone rang almost as soon as he hung up.

"Hi, Steve, this is Richard. I got your message. I think we have the perfect place in Los Altos. The house is surrounded by a wall and has a remote-controlled gate. Peter Schwartz, a real estate agent we work with, can show you the place. He'll be expecting your call. Here's his phone number and the address of the place."

Steve jotted down the info. "Okay. I'll give it a look. Do you have a second choice?"

"No. We're convinced that you'll love this one."

"Okay, thanks."

Steve hung up. He was exhausted, so he lay down and took a nap. When he awoke, it was around six. He called Becky to make sure she'd got the message.

"Yes, I just got home and listened to it. I can make it to Bert's tonight. What are you doing for supper?"

"No plans yet."

"I'm cooking something. Come on over."

"Right. I'll see you soon."

Steve thought about the clothing the CIA had given him and thought it might be a good idea to use it now, so he dressed in the disguise. All dressed to hide, he got into his car and drove over to Becky's place. At the door he knocked, and Becky opened it.

"Hi, doll. Do you like that better than *babe*?"

"Not much. How about sweetie-pie—that's *sweet-e-pi* ... get it?"

"Oh, I see. Very mathematical."

"Come on in. How about a brew?"

"I'd love one. By the way, have you seen the news yet?"

"No, not yet. Something must be new, right?"

"Right, very new! My identity is, or will be, known to the world. TV cameras, newspaper reporters, the works showed up at my door today. I had no choice but give them an interview."

She turned on the TV, and they watched the news together. Her eyes widened when she saw the guy who pulled a gun. "Oh, God! That guy has a gun!" Then she saw the gun explode. "You're amazing. What am I going to see you do next?"

They finished watching the news, and she got out a couple of beers. "So, are you going to really run for president?"

"You know, I have no idea how to start. I guess there's

some organization I have to contact. I think both parties will want me to join them. Do you think I should join one?"

"I lean toward the Democrats, and I think you do too. Then again, you could just be independent."

"I'm concerned some people may know me by my car. Let's take yours."

"Okay. You can put yours in my garage."

They ate, cleaned up the kitchen, and headed over to Bert's place.

After they arrived Bert said, "I have news which you might consider bad. You have to be thirty-five to run for president."

Steve said, "Oh, I forgot about that restriction. Well, that's one decision I don't have to make. I guess I could insist on a constitutional amendment, but there's not much chance that that will pass. So what are my options?"

Bert said, "You could go for secretary of defense. That would fit in with your powers. You could essentially control all the armed forces."

"Not really. The president is commander in chief, so what would I control? Say, why don't I run for president anyway? At least I can make a statement about my desires for changing things. That might have an effect."

Bert commented, "That's a good idea. With your power, everyone will listen. We'll just wait for someone else to tell you about the age factor. You should do it soon, however. Maybe call a press conference."

"Okay, let's make a list. My top priorities are one, free health care for everyone; Two, raise the minimum wage.

In fact it should be proportional to the cost of living, and it should be reviewed by Congress every year; Three, free public education through community college." Bert and Becky nodded, so he continued. "Another thing wrong with the educational system is that the curriculum is the same for everyone regardless of mental ability. For example, everyone must pass some kind of algebra to graduate high school. There should be alternatives to a high school diploma, say certificates in specific fields. People can be good plumbers, electricians, nurses, construction workers, et cetera, without knowing any algebra. I think that the Germans have apprenticeship programs. And another thing, why should the states have so much say in things? There are lots of things that should be universal, not state controlled, education being one of them."

Bert said, "Hey, how about my calendar idea?"

Steve laughed. "That's low order priority, but I'll think about it."

After a rather long evening of conversation and some backgammon, Steve and Becky left. While driving back to her place Becky asked, "What was that about a calendar?"

After he explained Bert's idea, Becky said, "Hey, that's neat. But thirteen is considered unlucky by most people, so the public won't buy it."

"That's exactly what Bert said. By the way, I didn't tell you that I called Edwards and left him a message that I would like a secluded and gated house. He called back and said he had just the thing and gave me the address.

I'm going to look at it tomorrow if the real estate agent is available. Want to come?"

"No, I got a last-minute call from my boss, and I have to go to work tomorrow."

"Okay, I'll let you know what it looks like."

They arrived at her place and went in.

She said, "I'm ready for a nice shower. Care to join me?"

"Hey, we've never done that before. Sounds like fun."

They showered together and turned in. Between the sheets he said, "Not only do you look good, you feel good."

"You feel better. Wait, don't say it. Let's agree on fourteens."

They laughed, kissed, and soon forgot about numbers altogether.

When he awoke he found a note. "I'm off to work. See you later."

He drove home and fixed breakfast. The phone rang. "Hello. This is Carl Jenson from the *Mercury*. Do you remember me?"

"Yes. How could I forget?"

"Good. We'd like to talk to you about your plans regarding running for the presidency."

"Yes, I'm glad you called. I'd like to share my ideas. When's a good time?"

"Can you come to our office tomorrow around two p.m.?"

"Okay, I'll see you then."

He hung up and was glad for the call. It seemed they

hadn't yet discovered he didn't meet the age requirement. He then called the real estate agent and arranged to meet at the house Edwards had recommended. He met the agent at the front gate.

"Hello, Steve. My name is Peter Schwartz, Century 21 Realty. I read about you in the paper today. What an amazing story. Speaking of amazing, this house is just that."

They went in. Schwartz explained the features of the house in detail. Steve spent about fifteen minutes looking around. The house sat on two acres of land and had six large bedrooms, a den, a four-car garage, a separate workshop, a beautiful kitchen and family room, and, unlike most houses in the area, both an attic and a basement. On top of all that, it was furnished! The yard was just California native plants, with no lawn to mow, so he would save on water. Another way the property differed from a lot of high-end ones was that this one had no swimming pool. He didn't want a pool anyway, since it was just another source of work.

For security it was enclosed by an eight-foot-high wall on all sides with a remote-controlled front gate that had a video camera and microphone for visitors to announce themselves. Another video camera was installed over the front door, and several others had been placed around the house. It was too much. He really didn't need all the room, and he hoped he wouldn't need all the security. Then again, if he and Becky got married and had a family it would be ideal.

Steve said, "I'm surprised at all the video cameras, but I like it. How much?"

"The CIA already owns it, and I've been told they're giving it to you, so to you it's free. They said they owed you that much."

"Wow, they are very generous. When can we close the deal?"

"If you come over to my office, we can do it right now. You won't officially own it until all the paperwork is processed and filed, but I've been told you can move in immediately if you want."

Steve followed him to his office, signed all the papers, and got the keys, remote controls, and instructions on operating the cameras. The house was his.

He went back to his condo, picked up a some clothes, a few books, a six pack, a few snacks, and some other miscellaneous things. Then he headed over to his new house. He opened the gate with the remote, drove in, and parked in front of the house rather than using the garage. He opened the house and went in, carrying the stuff he'd brought.

The refrigerator was larger than the one at the condo. He turned it on and put the six pack in it. He checked the security monitors and replayed feeds from the cameras. He saw himself coming in and walking around inside. He was awed at the place. He'd never believed he'd actually own a house like this one. He couldn't wait to show it to Becky. He locked up and headed back to his condo.

C H A P T E R   3 0

THE NEW HOUSE

By the time he got back to the condo it was five thirty in the afternoon. He started to think about moving. He decided that many of his books, including dozens of math textbooks, didn't need to go into the new place.

Becky called. "Hi. I'm back. I'd like to see the new house."

"Well, it's new to me but not really new. Why don't you come over here to the condo, and we can go together."

"Okay, I'll see you shortly."

He hung up, got out some boxes he'd saved, and began packing up the books he no longer needed. He knew of a bookstore that took old books of any kind. He'd cleared one shelf by the time the doorbell rang.

"Hi, beautiful."

"I like that—it goes with *handsome*."

"Well, let's go. Let's take your car."

They walked out to her car. A few people stood around and stared at them. He'd forgot his disguise and realized he'd no longer have the privacy he was used to. Two of the guys stared at Becky up and down. He knew they felt what he felt the first time he met her. Doing their best to ignore the onlookers, he and Becky left for the new house.

On the way he said, "By the way, I got a call from this guy Jenson of the *San Jose Mercury*. He wants to do a story about my plans. I'm going to meet with him tomorrow. No mention of any age limitation on the presidency. I guess it'll be big news soon."

"That's interesting. You should take a list so you don't forget anything."

When they arrived at the front gate, he used the remote to open it. They drove in, and Becky said, "This looks like a mansion!"

He opened the door, and they went in.

"Let me show you around." He took her on a tour of the inside.

She said, "This is great. I love it! What are you going to do with six bedrooms?"

"Well, the master bedroom for us, an office for each of us, and one each for the three kids."

She frowned. "You're planning too far ahead. Maybe I don't want three, or two, or one."

"I'm just joking. I don't even know how many I want."

"So, Steve, when are you going to move in?"

"Probably in a week or so. Do you want to be my roommate?"

She smiled approvingly. "I thought you might ask. I have to worry about my house of course. I don't think I should sell it. I may get fed up living with God and move back."

His head moved back, and his eyebrows rose. "I hope you don't mean that. Besides, you could become God's wife. That reminds me, Bert told me once that, according to the Bible, God has lots of sons."

"Really? Where in the Bible does it say that?"

"I think he said it was Genesis 6 verse 2."

"That's interesting. I'll check that out. Who was their mother?"

"No mention of that. Furthermore, no mention of God's daughters. We agreed that the Bible was written by a male chauvinist."

"I believe it. Let me know when you get settled. In the meantime I'll contemplate moving in."

"Contemplate? You mean you're not sure?"

"I can live here on a part-time basis. I don't have to empty my house."

"Well, let's head back. I think it's time for dinner. How about the Bold Knight?"

"Good idea. Let's go."

After dinner they went back to the condo. More on-lookers watched them go in. One guy came up and said, "Hey how about a demo of your powers?" Six or seven other people were watching.

The guy had a pen in his shirt pocket. Steve said, "Hey that's a nice pen—let me have a look." With the force he slid the pen out of the guy's shirt pocket and floated over to his hand. He then let it go and left it floating in midair in front of him for a few seconds, raised it about ten feet in the air, and then moved it back to the guy's pocket.

"My God, how did you do that?"

"I wish I knew. Maybe some day I'll find out."

The onlookers looked at each other and shook their heads in amazement.

Steve said, "Bye for now," and they went in. "Do you think I should have done that or ignored him?"

"I think it was okay. If you're going to run for president, you should come across as a friendly person. It was the right decision. Have you decided what you're going to say to the newspaper? As I mentioned before, you should make a list."

"Okay, let's do it now."

They made a brief list of his plans for the presentation.

When that was done he said, "Care for a little chess?"

They played chess for the rest of the evening. They checked the eleven o'clock news, and there he was again talking about his plans.

Becky said, "There you are again. Somehow I really can't believe all this. Unfortunately I have to get up early and go to work tomorrow, so I'll see you later. Keep me informed about any important news."

He said, "Sorry to hear that. Why don't you quit?"

"I'm giving it serious consideration." She walked out to her car and left.

The next day, Steve drove to the Mercury office, went in, and asked for Jenson. He appeared and said, "I just want to confirm with you that this interview will be recorded and probably shown on the TV news."

"Yes, I understood that that would be the case."

He and showed Steve into a large room containing a TV camera, a photographer, and several other people.

Steve got out his notes and told them his ideas. He also mentioned Becky's idea about term limits for the Supreme Court. Then something not on his list suddenly occurred to him. "Say, why is the gasoline tax so much per gallon? It should be a fixed percent of the cost like every other sales tax. Why is gas different?"

Then he remembered Bert's calendar idea and described that to the reporters as well. "And another thing, why should religions not pay taxes? All income above what they contribute to charities should be taxed."

He paused. "I can't think of anything else, but I may in the future."

Jenson said, "I guess that ends the interview. Thank you very much for sharing your ideas. I know many people have asked you for a demonstration of your powers, but would you mind giving one for the cameras?"

Steve looked around and spotted a rather large container against the wall. "Is that where you put your trash?"

Jenson said, "Yes, we use a lot of paper, and the excess goes in there along with other trash."

Steve spotted two wastebaskets that were almost full. He picked them up with the force, floated them to the big container, and inverted them, dumping their contents into the big container. Then he returned them to their original places. The reporters and camera operator gasped. No one said a word; they just stared at him.

After about ten seconds Steve said, "Is that good enough?"

Jenson raised his eyebrows, nodded, and said, "More than enough. Thanks. It will be on the news tonight."

Steve remarked, "Okay. Thank you for the opportunity to speak my piece."

On his way out, people made it a point to get out of his way. He said polite hellos and good-byes. It was interesting that no one mentioned the age requirement for being president, he thought as he drove home.

CHAPTER 31

SKIP

Skip was charged with robbery and murder. He was tried, convicted, and sent to prison. The prison officials knew of his former powers and placed him in solitary confinement in a special cell. He tried often to use his powers but found that he no longer had them.

He thought about the bank robbery that failed. Who was that guy who seemed to have the same power he had? How could he find out?

While in prison he reflected often about his whole life. He remembered his father, a drunken idiot who liked to beat him up. The slob had also hit his mother on a regular basis. He'd thought about killing his father, but as a kid he'd been no match for the brute.

He remembered that he hadn't been able to concentrate on schoolwork. Instead he'd think about his father, whom he hated. He took up basketball and found that he was pretty good at it so he just continued to play. At least he had friends on the team, which took his mind off his father. Then one day he found that he could control the ball mentally. He was shocked but used it to shoot basket after basket from practically anywhere on the court.

Then a few mathematicians found that the number of baskets he made was highly unlikely, so he decided to decrease them. He found that a believable number was around sixty percent so he tried for that, unless his team was losing, in which case he had to increase his percentage. Then he was approached by a pro team, so he quit high school to play pro ball full time. He was flunking just about everything anyway.

Then one night at a local bar he was approached by group who wanted to make money gambling on his shots at basketball. They would bet he'd make a certain number of baskets. Since he knew he could control exactly how many baskets he made, he agreed to their plan. They gave him a percentage of the winnings, and he became friendly with them. Then one day he was amazed to find that he could control things other than the basketball. Unfortunately he talked about his ability to the gang he hung out with, and they convinced him to help them rob banks. He didn't want to lose their friendship, so he complied.

Sitting in his prison cell, he realized it was all a big mistake. What would he do now? He decided to cooperate as much as possible with the prison system. Maybe he could get out on parole early. After a month or so it was decided that since he was a well-behaved prisoner, he'd be allowed to take classes. He decided to study for his high school diploma, his GED. He liked the teacher, studied religiously, and eventually got it. He enjoyed the sciences most of all.

He had been sentenced to life in prison for his criminal acts. He thought, *Life in this place?* He was depressed, but since he was enjoying learning he just decided to keep studying. Maybe they would decrease his time in prison if he cooperated.

But then one day he went to put his shoes on and he discovered he could pick them up with the force. Wow, he had the power back. How powerful was it? He tried bending one of the bars in his jail and found that it was easy. He put it back to normal to avoid any detection. He had stashed lots of money in a bank account under an alias. If he could get out he would be in great financial shape. He could start his life all over again.

He gradually learned the prison layout and began planning his escape. After a few weeks he finally made the decision to do it. He waited for a new moon, and then at 2:00 a.m. he used the force to break the jail lock and walked out to the main prison lobby, where a guard was sitting. The guard looked at him in shock and pulled out a gun, but Skip was quick to disarm him and hit him with the force, knocking him unconscious. He left the building. It was very dark out, so he was able to walk to the main gate undetected. It was easy to sever the lock, and he walked out. He placed a conical force field pointed back at the prison gate behind him to deflect any bullets, and started to run. He heard shots, but nothing hit him. He was out!

SKIP IS OUT!

teve's new place was furnished, so he decided to leave the condo furnished as well. Nonetheless, he felt he should get rid of a lot of stuff and clean it up in general. He resumed going through his old textbooks and decided to keep about forty; the rest he put in boxes for the used bookstore in Saratoga. He packed up a few boxes of his clothes and other stuff. He got rid of a lot of class notes, old math tests, and other paperwork. Then it was time for the news, so he put the TV on.

There he was at the Mercury office. He was impressed with himself. He watched his power demonstration and wondered what effect it would have on the government, especially the president. The CIA and FBI already knew about him, but now the government would realize that everyone would know about his powers. Only time would tell.

The phone rang; it was Becky. "I saw you on the news.

You were great! I liked your demo. You can take my garbage out any time."

Steve said sarcastically, "Very funny. Actually not funny at all. I'm worried about what could happen next. The government people will see it of course. What do you think they might do? Do you think they might consider me a threat?"

"Who knows? I can pay you a visit later in the day, or should I wait until tomorrow?"

"Tomorrow is better. By the way, I don't have a phone there yet. I do have a cell, though, which I hardly ever use. Let me give you the number. Say, do you have a cell phone?"

"Except for my job, I basically have it for emergencies. I hardly ever use it."

"I guess we both live in the past." They traded cell phone numbers, and he told her he'd call her the next day.

He hung up and decided to go to bed early. He liked to read in bed before going to sleep, and he was almost done with *Walden Two*. He decided to finish it in bed. He turned in.

The next day he loaded up his car with boxes and drove to his new place.

After he arrived, he unloaded stuff and then spent a few hours arranging things and putting things away.

At three o'clock he plugged in one of the phones he'd brought from his condo and checked for a dial tone. No service yet. He decided to go back to the condo and pack a few more things. When he arrived, there was a message on his answering machine. "Hello, Steve. This is Richard

Edwards from the CIA. I have some very bad news. Please call me back."

Steve thought, *What could be bad?* If it was *very* bad he knew what it was: Skip was out. He returned the call. Once he was connected to Edwards, the CIA official got straight to the point.

"Hello, Steve. I'm really sorry to bug you, but it's an emergency. Hodges has broken out of prison. He's on the loose again."

"I suspected that from your call. How did he do it?"

"Very early this morning he broke the lock to his cell and attacked a guard, who is now in the hospital. He was knocked unconscious but is okay. Hodges managed to get to the main gate unnoticed and broke the lock to it, opened it, and walked out. The guards on the tower saw him running away and fired at him, but the bullets didn't stop him, like they all missed. Later on we heard that a men's clothing store was broken into. The cops found a prison outfit in the store, which we identified as his, so we know it was definitely he who broke in and got some new clothes. He also broke into two cash registers and got a few hundred dollars.

"You were right about killing him, but we couldn't do that. Since the circumstances are now highly unusual, we are going to try to get permission to kill him, that is if we ever catch him again."

"I'd like to help, but we have to find him first. He'll probably be more careful this time. My guess is that he'll shy away from banks, but you never know. What else would he do? Maybe drugs, in which case he'll just join the crowd of drug pushers!"

"You may be right. That wouldn't be as bad as banks. Anyway we'll keep you posted."

Richard hung up. Steve wondered what Skip would do now. Right now it wasn't his problem. He hoped Skip wouldn't show up for awhile.

He called Bert and gave him the news of Skip's escape. He then called Becky at work. "Hi, Beck. I have some bad news—in fact, *very* bad."

"*Very* bad? That only means one thing. Skip is out free."

"You guessed it. How did you get so smart? I got a call from Edwards." He told her the details of what Edwards had said.

"There's nothing *you* can you about it, right?"

"Right, I told Edwards we would have to know where he is if he wanted me to do anything. He said he just wanted me to know about the escape and would keep me informed. Anyway, I'm moved into my new house. Actually I'm cleaning up the condo a little right now. How about I call you tomorrow?"

"That's good, since I have a friend who's getting over a divorce and I promised I would meet with her tonight."

"Oh, that's too bad. I hope you can cheer her up a little."

"I think she'll be all right. Call me tomorrow."

Steve worked on cleaning up the condo and getting the last of his personal stuff out. On his way out he bumped into a couple of neighbors.

One said, "Hey, I saw you on the news. You have some great ideas. I'm voting for you for president." His friend nodded and said, "Yes, me too."

"Thank you. I think this country is in need of some change."

Steve said his good-byes and drove off. He stopped for groceries on the way to the new place. When he got there, he unloaded the car and then looked around. *My God, this place is way too big for me,* he thought. *It will take getting used to.* He'd noted before that the house had a fair number of bookshelves around, so he unpacked some books and shelved them. Then he prepared and ate supper. He wondered about the news, checked his TV, and found that Comcast had not set him up yet. *I guess no news is good news.* He decided to explore the house and property and did a little survey. Too much room, he decided, inside and out! He turned in.

Saturday morning he woke around 9:30, put a pot of coffee on, and thought about breakfast. Then he got a call on his cell phone. It was from Becky.

"Hi, handsome. How's the new house?"

"Oh, it's beautiful, just like you. No, actually you're better."

"Flattery will get you everywhere. Are you ready for a visitor?"

"Of course—come on over."

She arrived at the front gate and rang the bell. He saw her on his gate camera and let her in with the remote. He opened the front door, and she walked in.

She said, "What a place! It's like something out of a beautiful dream. What are you going to do with all this space?"

"Live in about twenty percent of it, I guess. It's going to get some getting used to. I haven't eaten breakfast yet. Have you?"

"Yes, but I could do with a cup of coffee."

"I just have happened to have put a pot on."

He poured the coffee and started to make breakfast. Then he thought, what about a vacation?

While eating he said, "I've never taken a cruise. Have you?"

"No, never, but I'd like to. Do you have any in mind?"

"I've heard the Panama Canal is a nice one. We fly to San Diego and take the cruise through the canal. And it's a new canal! I think it stops a few places along the way like Costa Rica and Aruba and ends up in Florida somewhere. Then we fly back. What do you think?"

"That sounds great! When can we leave?"

"It'll probably take a while to book it. I'll check around and let you know. In the meantime, how about a little tennis? I don't know if I ever mentioned that I'm a member of the local racket club. We can play there."

She paused and then said thoughtfully, "You know of course that you're now the most famous person in the United States. Have you been to your club lately?"

"Actually, no, I haven't. You're right. I have no idea how I'll be greeted. Let's just go and see."

"Okay. I have to go back to my place and change. We can take my car."

At her place she said, with raised eyebrows, "I think I'll bring a change of clothes for later, unless you consider that too presumptuous."

"Yes, I think you're stepping out of line. I'll forgive you this time, but only if you go to bed with me tonight."

"It seems like you give me no choice, but just this once."

They laughed together, and he said, "You're really a lot of fun. Where did you get your sense of humor?"

"I have no idea. I really didn't know I had one until I met you."

"That's hard to believe. Anyway, let's go."

They eventually arrived at the club, got out of the car, and walked in. He saw two of his buddies—Paul Kist and Mike Gipson—and the club president, Kevin.

He said, "Hi, fellows. I'd like to you meet my friend Becky. What's going on?"

No one said a word. They all just stared.

Then finally Kevin said, "Hi, Steve. Long time no see. You know, around here no one knows what to think of you. First you win the French Open, and then we find that you had a secret weapon. There are differences of opinion as to whether you deserve it or not. You're almost a god. Do you think God should be allowed to play in the French?"

"God? No, I don't. I guess maybe I should give the money back, but no one from Paris has contacted me, so I thought they didn't really care. I was not a rich person before the French, and at the time I just wanted to make money. What would you have done in my place?"

Kevin paused and then said, "You know, I'm not sure

what I would have done." He then turned to Paul and Mike. "What about you guys? If you had that kind of power, would you have played for the money?"

They looked at one another and hesitated for a few seconds. Then Paul finally said, "Yeah, I guess I would have."

Mike said, "I guess I would have too."

Kevin put his hand out for a shake and said, "Okay, we forgive you. On the other hand, if you can afford it, it would be a nice gesture to give the money back. At least make an offer."

Steve shook hands with all three of them and said, "I'm not sure if they want it back. What would they do with it? I played according to my natural ability, but I think I'll call them and see what's up. I'll let you know."

Then Kevin said, "It's nice meeting you, Becky. Do you really want to play tennis with God?"

She stared at him for a few seconds but finally said, "Only if he lets me win and forgives me my sins."

They all laughed. Steve wondered again about her great sense of humor. He was glad that they all appeared to be on friendly terms.

Then Kevin said, "I'm sure you've been asked many times for a demonstration of your telekinetic powers, but could you give us one?"

"Sure, why not?"

He looked around and saw a racket leaning against the wall of the clubhouse and a couple of balls next to it.

"Check out that racket over there."

They watched while he used the force to float the racket

through the air over to Kevin and a ball each to Paul and Mike.

They all shook their heads in amazement.

Paul said, "How in hell can you do that?"

"I have no idea. Maybe God is trying to tell me something. If I ever find out, I'll let you know. Well, time for a little tennis. By the way, all of my games from now on will be telekinetic free."

They laughed again.

Paul smiled and said, "In that case I'm up for a set or two."

"You're on. See you later."

On the way to the court Becky said, "You handled that very well. I think I'll marry you after all."

"Before I meet with the president?"

"No, after."

"That's what I thought."

Even though it was a very old joke, they both snickered. They enjoyed three sets of tennis and headed back to his new place.

Then Steve said, "You know I'm really tired of giving demonstrations of my power. I think that will be the last one."

"I'm a bit tired of seeing them too. I'm glad for that decision."

SKIP GOES STRAIGHT?

They got back to his new place and opened up a beer each. Steve said, "With this power I'm starting to feel like I'm sort of an outcast from the human race. I am literally no longer human. I was actually surprised that the guys in the club accepted me back."

He glanced down at his phone. "Looks like my phone now works, and I have a message. Let me see who called."

"Hello, my name is Robert Hanson. I, and lots of others, heard your speech on TV, and we are very much in favor of your views. We are in the process of forming a political action committee to push for your run for the presidency. When we get more organized, we would like you to come to a meeting with us to talk more about your ideas. Please call back. Thank you."

"Wow, maybe I'll make the presidency. I'll call him back tomorrow. My list of changes from that meeting was basically sketchy. It should be complete and contain ironclad arguments. We could work on it right now, if that's okay with you."

"Good idea. Let's do it."

Steve got out his old notes. "I added a few things already. Here's my list so far."

1) Free health care for everyone.

2) Free tuition for everyone through community colleges. Of course colleges would still have entrance tests as they do now. Students would have to keep a certain grade point average.

3). There will be a minimum wage, adjusted every year based on changes to the consumer price index.

4) All drugs should be legal, with warning labels of course, regulated and taxed like cigarettes and alcohol.

5) Term limits for the Supreme Court.

6) Get rid of the penny.

7) Legalize all gambling. Why limit it to the Indians?

8) Legalize prostitution. Nevada has it. Why not every state?

9) Usury. Banks, via credit cards, charge too much interest. There should be a maximum, and it should be regulated.

10) Religions pay taxes.

He said, "I think we've talked about most of these things. What do you think?"

"Wow, that's an interesting list. I've thought of most of them before. I've always wondered why banks, via credit cards, were allowed to charge such high rates. I think I'm in favor of them all, but the last one will never pass. Most people are too religious to penalize the churches."

"You may be right. I won't press it."

"What if the government refuses to make any changes? How are you going to react?"

"I guess I could knock down a few walls of the White House. Just joking of course. I don't know what I could do. I'm in the embarrassing position of having lots of power but being morally unable to use it. I think we should try just using some logic. Most of these ideas are just common sense."

"Yes, but common sense is an oxymoron since it isn't common at all."

"I thought about that myself using that exact word, *oxymoron*. What's the expression, 'Great minds think alike,' or something like that. Maybe you're able to read my mind. What's it called, telepathy?"

"It does seem like we think alike. Hey, I'm hungry— let's eat."

"Okay. How about the City Diner?"

"Fine with me, but we may have a small problem. I don't know how many people saw you on TV, but you may be mobbed by the crowd. I think you should put on your disguise."

"Good idea." Steve got out a hooded sweatshirt, hat, and dark glasses. "What do you think?"

"It looks good. I think you'll be hard to recognize. We'll take my car since some people may recognize yours."

They drove to the diner. Before getting out of the car Steve said, "Let's get a table in the corner. I'll sit with my back to the inside of the diner so few people can see me."

"Okay, let's go."

They went inside, found a nice table, and ordered. They managed to eat unnoticed, paid, and left.

After they got back, he said, "Well, that worked out okay. I wonder how other famous people handle situations like this."

"I don't know. Maybe they join very exclusive clubs, eat in very exclusive restaurants, and in addition have their own personal kitchen staff. Maybe you should hire a live-in cook."

He gave her a puzzled look. "I don't want a live-in cook unless you want to volunteer."

"I like to cook, and I guess I'll be 'live-in' part of the time. You know, your neighborhood is high class. Maybe you should try to meet a few of your neighbors and find out where they socialize."

"Interesting idea. I'll take a few neighborhood walks to see if I can bump into anyone. But wait, I can't do that because I don't want anyone to know where I live. I got this place for seclusion in the first place."

"Right, I forgot about that. Actually, I don't think you'll be bothered in most places. People might even be a little afraid to approach you. Just stay away from low-class dives, which you do already."

"We have the rest of the evening to blow. What shall we do?"

"Why don't we refine the list? You said before we should make are points *ironclad*."

He said, "Good idea! Let's type them up for future reference. You be the typist." Becky agreed, and Steve set up his computer for her to type the items.

"Let's see, the first item was *Free health care for all.* I don't know how anybody can oppose it. I suppose the Republicans would say it's too expensive or socialistic. My argument is that *it is* both expensive and socialistic but, as Bert said, so is free public education. I think that K–12 education is the most expensive item on all state budgets. Say, I just thought of something. If you remember the Preamble to the Constitution, the fifth item is 'promote the general welfare.' Free health care does just that, as does free public education. I think that takes care of that one, don't you?"

"Yes, the 'promote the general welfare' point covers a lot of things, including the minimum wage. That's great!"

They went down the list, writing supporting arguments for each item. Becky finished typing and then printed the list. She said, "We've accomplished a lot, and it's almost eleven, so how about if we call it an evening."

"Okay. Let me check to see if I have cable TV yet so we can check the news."

He checked, and he had reception, so he turned on the news.

"We are here at the White House meeting with Press Secretary William Harris. Mr. Harris, Steven Thomas has said he will be running for president next year and has provided a list of things he would like changed. What is the reaction of the government to these changes?"

"Well, first, to run for president one must be thirty-five years old or older. We do not believe Mr. Thomas is old enough to run. As far as a reaction to his list of changes, it is strictly up to Congress and the president to pass such laws. The president is somewhat alarmed over the list of changes given the fact that Mr. Thomas has such telekinetic powers. It is hoped that he will not consider using those powers to make changes above and beyond the normal democratic methods of change."

"The other telekinetic person, Daniel Hodges, has broken out of prison. What is being done to find him?"

"Yes, we are very alarmed over that. Both the CIA and FBI are working to find him. It is hoped that Mr. Thomas will help in this matter, as he has in the past."

"Thank you, Mr. Harris, for talking to us."

Steve turned off the TV and said, "Well, the news is out that I'm too young to run for president. But at least I may get the public thinking about those changes. I'm still going to meet with the PAC group and see if I can have an effect."

"I guess the age issue was bound to come out. Yes, you should continue pressing for change."

Steve leaned back and stretched. "One of the most underestimated things in the world is a good stretch!"

"I agree one hundred percent. By the way, would you like to go to bed with me?"

Steve smiled. "Of course. As I recall you promised, *just this once.*"

"Yes, it will be once at least."

They laughed and went to bed.

The next morning they awoke and ate breakfast. Steve decided to call the PAC guy Robert Hanson. He telephoned and got a recorded message: "Hello, this is the phone of Robert Hanson, chair of the Steven Thomas Political Action Committee. Please leave your message and phone number after the beep."

Steve spoke. "Hello, this is Steven Thomas returning your call of yesterday. You probably know by now that I am too young to run for president. I am still willing to meet with you and your group. Please call and let me know the time and location."

Steve then said to Becky, "Say, I wonder if there is an age requirement for vice president. Let's check the web." They checked and found that it was the same, thirty-five years.

Steve thought for a few seconds and finally said, "How about if we eat here tonight? I have a nice steak and salad stuff."

"Good idea. I'm against eating out too often, especially since you're now famous. It's a good idea to avoid public appearances."

"Say, I know what we can do today. I have several

boxes of books at the condo that I want to get rid of. There's a Friends of the Library bookstore over in Saratoga that takes all books. And near there is a place called Villa Montalvo, which has nice hiking trails. We can go over there, drop off the books, browse for any books you might like, and then take a hike."

"Sounds like a great idea. Let's do it."

They drove to the condo, parked, went in, got the books, and then headed over to Saratoga. They entered the store and dropped the two boxes of books on the main counter. The two older women behind the counter stared at him, obviously recognizing him. One said, "I really liked your list of changes. Too bad you can't run for president. Is there a chance for a demo of your powers?"

Steve remembered that these ladies usually often had to carry boxes of books to the back room so he said, "Those boxes are quite heavy. Here, let me help you."

He used the force to pick up the boxes and float them ahead of himself as he walked to the back room. Their eyes opened in amazement, and they shook their heads.

One of the ladies said, "You have to see it to believe it! Thank you very much. We'll give you each a free book."

He said, "Thank you! We'll take a look and see what we can find."

They browsed around. Becky found a Dean Koontz novel, and Steve noticed the sixth edition of *Advanced Engineering Mathematics*. He had only the first edition at home, so he decided to get the later one. They got the two books, thanked the ladies, and left.

When they were outside, Becky said, "I thought you going to stop giving demos."

"Well, maybe that will be my last. I kind of know these sweet old ladies and made an exception for them."

"That was very nice of you. My reasons for falling in love with you keep increasing."

They headed over to Villa Montalvo and started the hike.

Becky said, "I love this place, especially the redwood trees. I like the hike to the top and the great view of the valley from there."

"Yes, I agree. I always make it to the top."

They hiked for a few hours and then returned to the car and drove back to his new place. He checked his email and saw a message from Bert. Becky looked over his shoulder while he read.

"Hi, Steve. So now everyone knows you can't run for president. I think you should still press for your ideas. Come on over, and we can chat and play backgammon."

Steve said, "Do you want to visit Bert this evening?"

"Sure, I'm in the mood for a little backgammon. Maybe I'll win a little money."

He had another email but didn't recognize the sender.

"Hello, Steve, this is Dan Hodges. I bet you're surprised to hear from me. I am writing to you because I have decided to go straight and give up crime. I know I am wanted by just about everyone but I thought you might help me to avoid going back to prison. I was smart enough earlier, with the help of the Mafia, to have created an alias and I was able to open a bank account to deposit money. My new first name is John. Anyway, I hope we can meet sometime, perhaps at a local coffee shop. Please respond and let me know."

Steve and Becky just stared at each other.

He shook his head and said, "Holy cow! I can't believe it, can you?"

"No, absolutely not! Are you going to trust him?"

He thought for a few seconds. "What are the choices? If I don't he may end up back in crime."

"Right, and there is hardly any way to trap him, since the prisons can't hold him anyway. If you want him out of the way you would have to kill him, which may be very hard indeed!"

"Yes, you're right. If he's really sincere that would solve the government's problem. I think I should meet with him. I can use my force field as a guard."

Steve hit *Reply*. "Hi, John: I'm very surprised at your decision but very glad to hear that you made the decision to go straight. I am willing to meet with you. I am curious as to the reason for your decision. Please explain." He hit *Send*.

They just sat there staring at each other. Steve thought about what coffee shop to use for the meeting. Then his computer beeped to announce a new email. Becky watched as he read it.

"Hello, Steve. Thanks for your reply and thanks for agreeing to meet with me. In answer to your question I got involved in robbing banks because I got to be friends with the wrong people. The power I had went to my head. I thought I might be able to actually become a dictator and take over the government. I know now that it was a stupid decision. I think that in addition to the government the crime syndicate would like to see me dead. Fortunately my powers can protect me and hopefully they both realize that if they try anything I might kill them instead. The coffee shop I have in mind is Ed's Coffee Shop on Market St. Let me know the best time for you."

Becky said, "He seems very sincere. I remember hearing a statistic once that about half of criminals who get out of prison go straight, so it's not uncommon."

"Yes, I remember something like that. Ed's Coffee Shop. I've never heard of it, but I'll look it up."

He immediately emailed Skip back, and they agreed on a date and time.

He then said, "In the meantime let me call Bert. He'll be interested in the news."

He phoned Bert, accepting the invitation to visit and play backgammon, and said they had some important news to tell him in person. They arranged to meet at their usual time.

Steve and Becky popped open a beer each and worked together to prepare their home-cooked meal. They ate and then headed over to Bert's place.

"Hi, gang. Come on in and have a seat. How about a beer? Tell me the news."

They accepted their second beer, and Steve said, "You won't believe this, but we got an email from Skip Hodges.

He said he wants to go straight and give up crime. He asked for my help in getting him off the hook."

"What? That's amazing! It's hard to believe. What are you going to do?"

"He proposed getting together at a coffee shop downtown, and I've decided to accept."

"But he's still wanted by the federal government."

"Yes, we know, and he knows that too. By the way, he changed his name to John but didn't give a last name. He said the Mafia helped him get an alias, and they helped him create a separate bank account to hold his money, so he's probably well off. I don't know how much he has but probably a lot."

"Boy, you guys are full of news. I have a bit of interesting news myself. I wondered about the age requirements for running for office in other countries and was surprised at what I found. It turns out to be the same in France, Germany, and England. You want to take a guess at what it is?"

Steve looked at Becky. "What do you think?"

"They're a bit more liberal, so I would guess thirty."

"Yeah, I would guess about the same."

Bert said, "You're way off—it's eighteen!"

Steve frowned. "Really? That low? It's hard to believe."

Bert nodded. "Yeah, surprising, isn't it? Maybe it's because the voting age is eighteen, so why not have the same age for running for office? I don't think anyone would actually vote for an eighteen-year-old, but maybe they would for a twenty-five-year-old. You can make that fact known to your PAC group and maybe the press. If the public hears about it, they may press for a constitutional amendment."

"Yes, that's a great idea. We should make it known."

They all had a good time playing backgammon for the evening. Then Steve and Becky said good-bye and left.

They got back around 11:30 to find another message from Hanson, the PAC guy. Hanson said the PAC would be ready to meet with Steve on the following Wednesday, gave the address of the meeting, and asked Steve to call if he couldn't make it.

Steve said, "I guess I'll meet with these guys. I can give them a copy of the list of our main points and tell them many of the items fit in with the 'promote the general welfare' part of the preamble. That should go over big. I can also tell them the age for running for office in Europe."

"Good idea. I'd like to be there. Do you mind if I come?"

"No, I don't mind, but then again do you want to be known as the girlfriend of God?"

She smiled and then frowned. "That's a good point. We have been seen together by quite a few people, but I don't think anyone knows my complete name so far. Maybe we should try to keep *that* a secret."

She yawned and stretched her arms out. "I'm going to leave you now since I have to go to work tomorrow. It's been an exciting week!"

They kissed good-bye, and she left for her place. He thought about the fact that they had been spending so much time together. It was fun, but maybe too much of a good thing was not the best. He wondered what it was like to be married. If they had kids, they could both stay home to take care of them. That would be nice.

He thought briefly about whether he should tell the CIA about Skip going straight. How would they react? He decided against it since, given Skip's powers, even if they knew where he was they wouldn't be able to apprehend him, much less kill him. Steve realized he had been lucky to knock Skip out the first time.

Anyway, as Becky had said, it had been an exciting week. He felt sure the future was going to be even more exciting. He hit the sack and fell asleep immediately.

CHAPTER 34

MEETING WITH THE PAC AND SKIP

On Wednesday Steve printed thirty copies of the notes that Becky had typed up, stuck them in a large manila envelope, and left to meet the PAC group.

He arrived at Victorian style house with quite a few cars nearby, including a truck with *San Jose Mercury News* emblazoned it its side panels. He knocked, and the door was opened by a well-dressed gentleman who said, "Hello, Steve, I'm Bob Hanson. We spoke on the phone. Come in."

Inside he found group of about fifteen people, including reporters and people with TV cameras. He didn't like the fact that he was going to be on TV again.

"I didn't realize we were going to be on TV."

"Oh, I'm sorry. I should have told you. But if we're going to have some effect, we have to be known to the public. You realize that, right?"

"Yes, I suppose so."

"I'd like to introduce you and have you give us a talk on your views. Is that acceptable?"

"That's what I came here for, so of course."

Hanson introduced him and thanked him for coming to speak to the group. Steve spoke for about a half hour about his ideas. He then handed out copies of his list.

He concluded with, "In addition, I would like to remind you of the Preamble to the Constitution of the United States of America, which starts 'In order to form a more perfect union.' The important thing for us it item five—promote the general welfare. Free health care, free education, and a higher minimum wage are all things the government can do to promote the general welfare. I think our forefathers would agree. It is our job to insist that they do that!

"Finally I would like to tell you what the age for running for office is in Europe. In all of France, Germany, and England it is eighteen! Maybe it's time for a constitutional amendment!"

With that finish, he got a loud and long round of applause.

Bob Hanson got up and said, "Thank you, Steve. That was a great speech. Those last two points are memorable and ones I've never thought about. Now, if anyone has a question, I'm sure Steve can answer it."

One woman asked, "Mr. Thomas, how can we get our message out to Congress and the president?"

Steve answered, "Well, this meeting will be on TV, so they will get the message. Another way is to write to your congressperson and senator. Send them a copy of the list I gave you. Large companies have lobbyists, so why not us? Put pressure on the government in every way possible."

A gentleman asked, "You have this tremendous tele-kinetic power. How can it be used to pursue our cause?"

"I have thought a lot about that. I really do not want to use force in any way to influence the government. I think we should do as much as possible without thinking about force."

Another man asked, "You are in favor of raising the minimum wage. Big companies are job creators. Forcing a higher minimum wage on them will put people out of work. What do you say about that?"

"I have heard that argument before, but I have never read or heard any proof or seen evidence that supports that claim. Do you have any proof?"

"No, not really."

Steve continued, "Here are some facts. The current wage, corrected for inflation, is now the lowest it has been since 1952. If we raise the average wage we will save 4.6 billion dollars on food stamps. The average wage has dropped significantly since the 1970s. A healthy economy is measured by how much money people spend. If people don't have money, they can't spend it. That seems to me to be an argument for the minimum wage."

A woman said, "Some of my friends say you're a so-cialist since you want health care to be free. What should I say to them?"

Steve thought of Bert's statement. "You should ask them if they believe in free public education. If they do, tell then they are socialists!"

The woman said, "That's a good response! I'll use it."

Steve said, "We have socialistic institutions now—Social Security, Medicare, and of course free public education. That doesn't mean we are socialists. We still have capitalism. Most developed countries have free health care."

No one else seemed to have any questions, and he got another round of applause. Hanson got up and said, "Thank you, Steve. It has been enlightening. I hope we will all write or call our congresspersons and press for these changes. This concludes the formal part of our meeting, but we have coffee, tea, and other goodies here, so feel free to help yourself and socialize."

Steve tried to mix in with the group, but very few people spoke to him further. He suspected it was because of his power. At least no one asked for a demo; they'd probably all seen his demos on television.

Steve left for home, feeling very good about the meeting. He wondered what would come of it. Since the meeting ended around nine, he figured there'd be some coverage of it on the eleven o'clock news. He watched it and was pleased with his appearance.

At 11:30 Becky called. "I saw you on the news. You were great! Marry me soon!"

"Right after I meet with the president."

"Not funny anymore. It was good that we typed up the list and you handed out copies. It should make the newspapers. The question is how will the government react?"

"Only time will tell. By the way, I'm meeting with Skip,

alias John, tomorrow at noon. I'm going down earlier, around 11:30 to check out the scene."

"I guess I don't have to say be careful, since I know you will. Remember, he has the force as well as you do."

"Yes, I am well aware of that. I'll keep you posted. How was your day at work?"

"Oh, the usual, nothing exciting. Nobody connects me with you yet, which is good."

"Good. I'll call you tomorrow night to give you the latest news."

"Okay, talk to you then, Bye."

He got a short email from Bert: "I saw your meeting on TV. Great job!"

He hit *Reply*. "Thanks, Bert. After seeing it myself, I liked it too. Tomorrow I am meeting with Skip, alias John, downtown at Ed's coffee shop. I'll keep you informed."

Thursday, August 29

Steve headed downtown to Ed's Coffee Shop around 11:30 a.m. He parked about a block away and approached cautiously. He walked up and down on the opposite side of the street. Finally, around 11:45, he entered the shop and checked out the menu.

He remembered Skip to be tall, lean, and clean shaven, with a crew cut, but no one matching that appearance seemed to be in the coffee shop. He left, crossed the street, and waited outside a clothing store, pretending he was looking into the store window. Several people came and went. Eventually he saw a tall, lean man with a short beard who was carrying a briefcase. The guy looked around suspiciously. He was wearing dark glasses and a hooded sweatshirt with the hood up. He entered the coffee shop and seemed to be looking for someone. He then disappeared into the shop. Steve thought that he might be Skip. He reminded himself that he must call him John. Steve surrounded himself with a two-inch force field and entered the coffee shop. He spotted the man he believed to be John sitting in a corner booth with a cup of coffee.

He walked over and stood next to the man's table. "Hello," he said casually. "Do I know you?"

"Is your name Steve?"

"Yes. Are you John?"

"Yes, have a seat."

Steve mentally congratulated himself on his success, sat down, and said, "Hello. We finally meet. How are you?"

"Not too bad, but it could be better. How about you?"

"I am doing well also. I notice that you've grown your hair longer and have a beard."

"Yes. I'm trying to change my appearance as much as I can. I think with the dark glasses and short beard I'll be pretty hard to recognize."

"I agree. So you'd like my help. What would you like me to do?"

"I know you're friendly with the CIA and FBI, and I thought you might be able to call off the hounds. You have a good argument—they'll probably never find me, and even if they could they'll never be able to hold me. They'd have to kill me, and unless they catch me off guard, they'll never be able to do that. If you tell them I'm going straight, they might decide to quit the chase."

"That's true, but how do I know you *are* going straight?"

"I brought along something which will help convince you."

John picked up the briefcase and put it in front of Steve. Steve wondered if it was be a bomb.

John said, "The briefcase contains one hundred thousand in cash. I have lots of money and can afford it. If it's a bomb, we're both dead. There's no one behind you, so open it and take a look."

Steve opened it slightly, looked in, and saw packages of hundred-dollar bills. He closed it.

John said, "I know that it's not a guarantee, but I can't think of any other way to convince you. I have several million dollars from my basketball winnings and bank robberies. Does this present help convince you?"

Steve was beginning to believe he was telling the truth. John appeared smarter than he'd thought before the meeting, and he seemed to be a very honest guy.

"You know, John, I had the impression that you were a loser based on how you earned the nickname Skip. You seem to be a very different person now. You seem more intelligent than I'd thought before today."

"My father was a drunk and beat me on a regular basis. My mother tried to help me, but she was essentially powerless. I hated school, and basketball was my only outlet. I feel I have finally woken up to the truth about life. I think I may eventually go to college. You may find it hard to believe, but it's the truth. I think you and I are the only two people with the powers we have. We should become friends. What do you say?"

Steve was amazed at the turn of events. "I'm very surprised to hear you say all that. Yes, I am willing to be your friend. By the way, how did the telekinetic power come to you?"

"While playing basketball I found that I was suddenly able to control the ball with my mind. I think I was about sixteen at the time. I didn't use it for anything except to shoot baskets for quite some time. Then eventually I became aware that I could use it in other ways. I then fell in with bad company and got into robbing banks."

Steve listened intently and nodded.

John continued, "Let me ask you, what are you doing now? Are you doing anything with your power?"

"I'm not doing anything with the power, but I have some ideas to improve the life of the average person here in America. I recently joined a Political Action Group to make some changes."

Steve explained the list of changes he'd proposed to the PAC. "I suppose if the government refuses to cooperate, I can threaten them with my force field."

"Force field—that's an interesting term for it. I've never thought of it that way. Also that's an interesting list. I would consider joining your group, but I think I should remain as anonymous as possible for now."

"Yes, I understand. Where are you staying now?"

"I'd rather not say. We can communicate via email

and cell phone. Here's my number. I trust you won't give it to the FBI." He gave Steve a card containing his phone number, email address, and last name—Davis. Steve gave him his card.

Steve said, "I trust you, and you can trust me. You know, I really don't need this money. You should keep it."

"No, take it. You never know when you'll need some cash."

"Okay, if you insist. Well, it's been an enlightening meeting. I'm very happy to have talked to you. I don't know how the government will react, but I will try to convince them to give up the search for you. I'll be in touch."

CHAPTER 35

ED'S BAR AND GRILL

Once he was home, Steve decided to call Edwards and explain the situation to him.

"Hello, Richard. I'm glad I found you in. I have an interesting piece of news. Hodges emailed me saying he was giving up crime and wanted to meet with me. He sounded very convincing. We emailed back and forth a few times, and I finally agreed to meet with him, which I did. He wants me to plead with you to stop the search. I trust his sincerity. Since we both have the power, he wants us to be friends."

"Wow, that's interesting, but he is a criminal, and we can't just stop searching for him. I have to admit that he was well behaved in prison. The guards said he was always reading and studying, and he even passed his GED."

"That's interesting. That confirms my suspicion of his sincerity. I know that under normal circumstances you'd have to keep trying to find him, but obviously the situation is not normal. Hodges has a power that would make it very difficult for you, or I, to catch him even if we found him. I think we were lucky the first time. Under these circumstances, it is logical to just stop looking."

"You have a point. Let us consider it and get back to you."

"Okay, thank you. I appreciate it."

Then, for the hell of it, Steve decided to count the money in the briefcase. There were twenty packages of hundred-dollar bills, and each one contained fifty bills. It was indeed one hundred thousand dollars.

A week later, Edwards called back. "Hello, Steve. We've considered your arguments and agree that the situation is not normal so have decided to call off the search. However, we would like to keep in contact with you and, since you may become friends with him, for you to let us know of any changes."

"I'm very glad to hear that. I think it was the right decision. I think I'll be seeing him fairly often and can call you if necessary."

Steve called Becky at work on her cell phone. "Hi, love. Are you too busy to talk?"

"No, I'm on a coffee break. What's up?"

"I met with Skip, and he seems very sincere. As so-called proof of his sincerity he offered me a briefcase full of money."

"Really? How much?"

"He said one hundred thousand, but I didn't count it

there. It looked like a lot. I told him I didn't really need it, but he insisted, so I accepted it. Just for the fun of it, when I got home I counted it, and it was indeed one hundred thousand dollars. He wants to be my friend. Anyway, he urged me to call the CIA and plead his case so I called Edwards and explained the situation. Edwards was reluctant but finally said he would get back to me. He just called back. He agreed to stop the search but asked me to keep tabs on Skip, if possible, and report any changes. By the way, let's call Skip John from now on, since that's his new name."

"Okay, John it is. Wow, that's great news! So that problem is solved!"

"I'm going to call John and tell him the news. He'll be very happy. Maybe I should propose getting together, since he wants to be my friend. I don't know what we can talk about or do together, though. It seems the only thing we have in common is the force. Maybe he has some ideas."

"Yes, you should call him. Let's see, today is Thursday. Would you like to spend the weekend with me?"

"You needn't ask. Your place or mine?"

"Come over here for dinner tomorrow. I'll try and cook up a pleasant surprise."

"Okay, see you tomorrow around five."

He hung up and called John. When he told him that the CIA was calling off the search, John said, "Wow, that's great news! That's a great burden lifted from my head. I owe you a lot. How about getting together and celebrating over a drink?"

"Sure, why not. Where shall we meet?"

"Ed, from Ed's Coffee Shop, also has a place called Ed's Bar and Grill. It's about two shops north of his coffee shop."

"Okay, what time do want to get together?"

"How about five?"

Steve checked his watch; it was 4:35. "That's fine. I'll see you there."

Before leaving, he sent a quick email to Bert to tell him the latest news. Steve was still a little suspicious of John. He also wondered what they would talk about besides their telekinetic power.

Steve found Ed's Bar and Grill and went in a little before five. John was sitting at a table toward the rear, again wearing his hooded sweatshirt, hat, and dark glasses.

Steve went to his table and sat down. "Hi, John. How are you?"

"After your good news, I'm great." A waitress came over and asked about drinks. They each ordered a beer.

Steve said, "So what are your plans for the future?"

"Well, before today, just surviving. In prison I got a chance to get my GED. I studied the usual subjects—history, English, and math. I feel like I learned a lot. I also learned how to play chess."

"Hey, that's great. You've come a long way. You also made a good impression on the CIA. I play chess, too. We'll have to get together and play sometime."

"I'm just a beginner, so don't expect any competition."

Steve said, "Have you ever wondered how the two of us ended up with this telekinetic power?"

"I thought about it in prison but couldn't figure out anything. How about you?"

"I considered it too and, as did you, came to no conclusion. I think there must be some purpose behind it, but as yet I can't imagine what it might be. Have you thought about what you might do with it?"

"One possibility is to become sort of a superhero and fight crime like Superman or Captain America. Another option is to join the military and use it to solve some of the problems of the world. I have no idea how I would get started actually doing it though. I think I want to continue to remain anonymous."

"I thought of those things also, but if we were meant to do something significant I don't think it was those kinds of things. Maybe something will happen in the future to tell us."

"I think you're right. Let's wait and see."

"It's been an interesting get-together. We should meet up sometime for some chess. I'll call you."

"That'd be great!"

Just then four guys came barging into the bar brandishing guns. One guy went to the bartender and said, "Hey, you, let's have the cash in the register."

Another guy said, "Okay, gang, everybody take out your wallet and put it on the table in front of you."

Steve and John stared at each other. Steve whispered, "Have you ever disarmed anyone in this type of situation?"

"Not quite, but I think I can handle it."

"You take the two on the left, and I'll do the right two.

Grab their guns and toss them behind us. Then knock their feet out from under them. Then, to keep your identity a secret, let me take over. Do it when I say *three*."

Steve counted, "One, two, *three!*" They simultaneously reached out with the forces, grabbed the guns, sent them clattering toward the back of the room, and knocked each man down. Steve then got up and walked over to them. "If you don't want to get hurt, just stay on the floor." He turned to the bartender and said, "Call the cops!"

One of the would-be robbers got up and rushed at Steve, but with a swish of his arm Steve knocked his feet out from under him again. The man collapsed did not try it again.

The ten or so other customers in the bar all stared at Steve in amazement.

One guy said, "You're Steve Thomas, the telekinetic guy."

Steve said, "Yes, you're right."

Most of the customers just continued to stare, though several came over to shake his hand and thank him.

In about ten minutes three policemen arrived. The bartender said, "These guys tried to rob us, including the customers."

One cop said, "How did you subdue them?"

The bartender pointed at Steve. "He's the magic guy!"

The cop looked at Steve for a few seconds. "You must be Steve Thomas. Great job! We need people like you on the police force. Why don't you join?"

Steve smiled. "I'll think about it."

The police took a few statements from the bartender and others, handcuffed the gangsters, and walked them out.

The bartender said, "Would you and your friend care for a little supper? It's on the house. In fact, all your meals here in the future are on the house!" They accepted the offer.

After they'd ordered, Steve said to John, "Well, that was a bit of excitement. You did pretty well. I don't think anyone noticed your movements since they were all looking at the gangsters."

John said, "You seem to be good at this kind of thing."

"Well, I had a little experience in Europe."

Over supper they talked about chess, and John showed some knowledge of the chess openings. Steve said, "Say, why don't you come over to my place for a game of chess after we're done here?"

"I'd really like that. What's your address?"

Steve gave John his condo address, and once they'd finished their meals they left Ed's Bar and Grill and headed out.

At the condo Steve said, "Care for a drink?"

"I'll have another beer."

Steve opened two bottles, and they sat down and played several games. Steve won each game but thought that John had promise.

John said, "I guess I'm not very good at chess."

"You're not bad. You just made a few mistakes. The way to win at chess is to play very carefully and wait for your opponent to make a mistake. If you think of attacking the other guy right away, there's a tendency to overreach and make a mistake. Wait for him to screw up."

"Good advice. I'll be more careful next time."

"Well, it's a bit late. Time to call it a day. Let's stay in touch."

When John had left, Steve called Becky with the news even though it was almost eleven. "Hi, love, I hope I'm not calling too late."

"No, I was just checking the news."

"You'll never guess what just happened." He explained the incident to her.

She said, "Wow, the force came in handy again!"

He then told her about his chess get-together with John afterward.

"It's good that you're becoming friends. You definitely have something in common! I'll see you here tomorrow night for dinner."

"Right, see you then."

C H A P T E R   3 6

BECKY'S PROBLEM

Since Steve was coming over the following night, Becky thought about what to make for dinner. She decided to prepare her favorite lasagna dish. It was after 11:00 p.m., a bit late to go food shopping, but she had to go to work tomorrow and didn't want to have to deal with the Friday afternoon rush of people stocking up for the weekend. She drove to Safeway, parked, and had started walking toward the store when a large van pulled up next to her. Two guys wearing masks jumped out, grabbed her, and dragged her into the van. She tried to scream, but they muzzled her and taped her mouth shut. Then they blindfolded her and tied her hands and feet.

"Okay, Nick, let's go!"

"You got it, Jake!"

Then Jake said, "You're going to make us a lot of money. Your boyfriend Steve is going to pay for your return to the tune of two million bucks."

She tried to keep track of where they were going. It didn't seem like they used a freeway; instead they took quite a few left and right turns. Eventually they came to a stop and took her out. Once they were inside a building, they ungagged her and removed the blindfold. One of the guys—they were all wearing masks, but she thought the voice sounded like the driver, the one they'd called Nick—said, "Now you're going to call your boyfriend on your cell phone and explain the situation." He took her cell out of her purse and gave it to her. She was able to hold it even though her hands were tied. "Now call!"

She hesitated and thought about not calling but decided her only hope was for Steve to free her. Nick slapped her across the face. "Quit stalling and get on the phone."

"Hey, Nick, take it easy on her. We want her in prime condition!"

"Right, Vic, but she has to call."

She finally called Steve on his cell.

Steve was watching the eleven o'clock news when his cell phone rang. He was a bit surprised and wondered who would call at this hour, maybe John Davis? He answered it.

"Hello, Steve, this is Becky. I've been kidnapped."

"What? *What*?"

Becky didn't answer; instead a male voice said, "Hello, professor. We have your little darling here, and she is for sale. For only two million bucks you can have her back in good condition."

Steve's eyes widened, and he could feel the sweat beading on his forehead. "Kidnapped? Who are you?"

"That's obviously none of your business. We want you to get the cash ready in a briefcase or two or three. We will call you back Monday night. That will give you plenty of time to get the money. We'll then tell you how to deliver it. If you don't deliver she gets hurt."

Steve finally said, "Okay, I'll have it."

He then gave the phone to Becky. "Tell him he better get it or else."

She took the phone. "Hi, Steve. I guess you heard him. I had no choice."

"Don't worry—I'll get the money, and you'll be free Monday."

Jake grabbed the phone and hung up.

They took her to a back bedroom and laid her on a bed.

Nick said, "Boy would I like to get at this babe!"

Jake said, "Forget it. This is strictly a business proposition. We don't want the merchandise damaged."

She heard a click and knew they'd locked the door. Her forehead started to sweat. Tears filled her eyes. Here she was, hands and feet tied, locked in a room. She thought briefly about the possibility that if she could untie her bonds she might be able to escape through a window but then noticed that the single window in the room had bars on the outside. There was no hope. She winced and cried again.

Tears came to Steve's eyes. What could he do? Was there any hope of saving her? The only hope was the money. He had to pay them off. How could he get a huge amount of money out of the bank without arousing suspicion? Maybe he should call the CIA or FBI. He knew Edwards wouldn't be in his office at this hour but remembered that Tony's card had listed a hotline number, so he found the card and called it.

"Hello, this is Steven Thomas. My girlfriend has just been kidnapped. I've worked with Richard Edwards in the past. Please call me back." He left his landline and cell phone numbers.

After about thirty minutes his phone rang.

"Hello, Steve, this is Richard Edwards. We're sorry about the kidnapping. Under the circumstances this is an FBI problem, but we can handle it. What are their conditions?"

"They want me to have two million dollars ready by Monday night. They'll call then and tell me what to do. I have the money, but I really want to catch the bastards."

"We can come to your place on Monday. When they call back we can trace the phone to find out where they are."

"They called from my girlfriend's cell phone."

"That may be hard to trace. We'll just have to wait and see what they want you to do. I guess if you're willing to pay you should get the money. We can contact your bank tomorrow and let them know that the withdrawal is legitimate. You can get the money on Monday morning. We'll show up at your place Monday evening so we can be there when they call.

"And here's my cell phone number just in case you need to contact me. We'll see you Monday."

Steve was very glad the CIA was going to help.

Becky eventually dozed off to sleep. It was a very uncomfortable night with her hands and feet tied. She awoke Friday morning and stared at the cord tying her hands. It would not be easy untying it, even with her teeth. She wondered what Steve could do to save her.

After about an hour Jake came in. "Hello, Becky, did you have a nice night's sleep?"

She pouted, and tears came to her eyes. "It was horrible with these ropes on my hands and feet."

"I'm sorry about that, but we can't take any chances about you getting away."

She yelled in fear, "How am I going to get away, with bars on the windows and the door locked?"

Jake ignored her. "Here, we have some breakfast for you and even some coffee. Let me untie you so you can eat. This room has an adjoining bathroom if you need it."

He untied Becky's hands and feet and left, relocking the door. There was a small table and folding chair in the room so she could sit and eat. Breakfast was scrambled eggs, white toast, and coffee. She wasn't particularly hungry but figured she'd better eat since she didn't know how often they would offer her food. Then Jake came back, picked up the plate and silverware and said, "We won't tie you up this time. We you know you're not going anywhere." He then left, relocking the door.

She cried often and thought about how much she hated those bastards. She imagined having a gun to shoot them. She suffered through Friday, Friday night, and Saturday, getting not much to eat.

On Saturday evening, after giving her some supper, Jake left, relocking the door. After a little while she heard the outer door open, close, and lock. It seemed that they'd left, since she heard no conversation from the other room. She lay on the bed staring at the ceiling and dozed off. She then woke up suddenly to purring in her brain. She listened for awhile and then was surprised that she could turn it off. She could turn it on and off repeatedly. She remembered how Steve had told her about turning his buzzing on and off and wondered about the power. She was hopeful.

She looked around the room to see what she could move. On the table were a place mat and a salt shaker. She concentrated on the shaker, and it moved! She picked it up and moved it around. She picked the place mat up and turned it over. Then she picked up the chair, turned it upside down and moved it around. Wow, she had the power! She couldn't believe that she actually had it.

She experimented moving items around in the room. She was surprised again at how adept she was with the force. She thought, *Is the force strong enough to defend myself?* Steve had used his power to defend them very well. If she had the same force, she was confident she'd be able to use it to defend herself.

What next?

How was she going to get through the door? She looked

at the lock. The door was flimsy, having a space between the door and the frame, and she could see the lock. It was a deadbolt. Could the force saw the lock in half? She tried pushing the force field through the crack in the door and pushed it against the lock. Then she realized that *saw* was the wrong word. Instead of using a back-and-forth motion with the force, she used it like a knife cutting vegetables, and it sliced through the lock with ease. She was very surprised about the power of the force and happy that it worked so well. She opened the door. The outside room was dark. She turned the light on and saw her cell phone on the kitchen table. She wondered just how powerful the force could be. She saw a full bottle of wine on the counter. She grabbed it with the force and lifted it in the air. She moved it around quickly and found that she could accelerate to a high speed if necessary. It took no effort at all. There were other bottles of wine and booze around. They would be good weapons. She put several bottle on the table in front of her.

She could call Steve, and he could come and get her. But, wait, she didn't even know where she was. The front door was locked. She checked the back door and found that it was unlocked. She thought about running away but had this feeling of power and wanted revenge. She grabbed her phone and went out, walked around to the front, and looked at the house number, 916. She walked out to the street, looked up and down and found that the house was fairly near the corner. She walked to the corner and looked at the street sign: Park Place. She immediately dialed Steve from her cell phone. He answered.

"Hi, handsome, this is Becky."

"What? You sound happy—what's going on?"

"I'm free. The address of this place is 916 Park Place. The gang's not here right now. If you get over here right away, though, we can catch them."

"Maybe you should leave before they get back."

"I don't think I need to."

"What? Why not?"

"I'll let you guess, but just in case you should get here fast."

"Guess? How can I guess? Anyway, I'll be there as fast as I can make it."

Steve thought, *Becky sounded happy, and she asked me to guess?* There was only one reason: she had the power!

She went back in the house, found her purse, and wondered if Nick, Vic, and Jake had stolen her money. Yes, the cash was gone, but everything else was still there. While she waited she wondered how she would handle things if they came back. She had the bottles, but if they had guns, then what? She then realized that killing her would deprive them of their ransom, so they would just try to grab her again. She picked up a bottle of whiskey with the force and threw it against the wall for practice. She was surprised at how fast she could make it move.

She noticed a clock on the kitchen wall, which showed the time as 12:15. She sat down at the kitchen table and poured herself a glass of wine. It was cheap wine, but it

tasted good. Then she thought about how she would surprise them. She thought, *I'll just sit here with the table
between me and them. It will take them time to get to me,
plenty of time for me to throw bottles.* She turned off the
kitchen light. The streetlight outside was bright enough for
her to see her wine glass.

Steve looked up the address in online maps. He found it,
went out, and jumped in his car. He hoped he was right
about the force. Why else would she act like she didn't need
him? There could only be one answer.

After about another ten minutes she heard the door lock
click. The three guys came in and turned the light on.
When they saw her sitting at the table drinking wine they
gasped in surprise.

Jake said, "How did you get loose? How did you get
out of the room?"

She leaned back confidently and smiled. "Oh, I'm a
magician—didn't I tell you? Oh, I guess I forgot."

Nick said, "Well, you're going right back in there."

"You mean you don't want to join me in a glass of
wine?"

Jake said, "I don't know how you got free, but we're
going to tie you up right this time."

Nick and Jake approached her, and she said, "Here have
a whole bottle." She threw the wine bottle at Nick and with
the force accelerated it. It hit Nick squarely in the forehead.
She heard a loud crunch sound, and he fell. Vic pulled out

a gun and approached her. She knew he wasn't going to use it, but she used the force to grab it, yank it out of his hand, and move it to her hand. She then pointed it at him.

He backed up. "H-h-how did you do that?" He stood there in awe, staring at her.

She said, "You have to be careful with guns. They are dangerous. Now why don't you just sit down until the police arrive." Vic started to back up toward the door. She looked at him and thought about grabbing him with the force, but at the same time Jake charged at her. Instinctively she turned to face him and pulled the trigger. Jake grabbed his chest and fell. Vic opened the door and started to rush out, only to run into Steve, who pushed Vic back into the house and knocked him to the floor.

Steve looked at Nick and Jake, lying on the floor, and smiled. "It looks like you got the power at just the right time."

"You can say that again. Now we are finally equals!"

"Are these guys dead?"

Instead of answering, Becky shouted, "Behind you!"

Vic had gotten up and with a switchblade was about to attack Steve from behind. Steve turned around and punched him hard in the head with the force at the end of his fist. There was a loud crack, and Vic went down.

Steve and Becky grabbed each other and hugged. "So did they beat you or molest you?"

"No, I'm okay. That guy Nick wanted to rape me, but the leader, who I think was Jake, the guy I shot, prevented him from touching me. He just wanted the money."

They checked the bodies of the three hoodlums and found that they were all dead.

"I guess I hit him pretty hard with that bottle of wine and must have shot Jake dead center in the heart. You must have hit that guy, Vic, pretty hard also."

"Yeah, I was pretty mad. I actually wanted to kill him, and I guess I did."

"What the hell do we do now?"

"Call the cops I guess. The trouble is they might convict us of the crime of murder. I say we just vacate the premises and call the cops later."

CHAPTER 37

CELEBRATION

While he drove them back home, she called the police from her cell phone and gave them the address where they would find three dead gangsters. She emphasized the word *gangsters*.

They arrived back at his new place. They sat at the kitchen table and stared at each other.

She said, "Well, it happened. I got the power as we suspected I might. Boy, I can't believe the timing."

"Yes, it happened as I thought it might, and at the perfect time. It seemed to take a while, and I really wasn't sure if would occur. The question is whether some godlike power planned it that way."

"I thought the same thing. I believe there is a godlike force operating."

"This calls for a celebration stronger than beer. I just happen to have a bottle of cold champagne. How about a glass?"

"I'd love it!"

He uncorked a bottle and poured two glasses. "Here's to the both of us and the power!"

She nodded, and then they tipped their glasses and drank.

She said, "Boy, that's delicious. I feel like a brand new person, but what am I going to do with such power?"

"Become a tennis pro and play Wimbledon!"

She laughed hysterically. "Your sense of humor exceeds mine by a mile. You're ahead by four points."

They had a second glass of champagne.

He said, "Hey, I just thought of something we can do. We can play tennis, and both of us use our powers. It will be a fascinating match."

"Yes, but no fair yanking the racket out of the other guy's hand."

He roared with laughter. "You just got five points on the sense of humor score. Now you're ahead."

"Hey, another thing we can do is give tennis exhibitions, like the Globetrotters in basketball."

"Yeah, we could rally with twenty balls at the same time. If four or five balls came to me at once I could just pause them in mid air and hit them back one at a time."

She really laughed. "You just picked up five points."

"Let's call it even at fourteen." They laughed again.

They kept drinking and laughing. They eventually finished the bottle, got up, and kissed. He slid his hands down to her butt. "You know, you've got a great ass."

She grabbed his. "Yours isn't bad either."

"I'd like to give yours a serious inspection."

"And I yours, not to mention that stuff hanging between your legs."

They both laughed. They checked the time; it was 2:20 a.m. They went to bed.

The next morning when Steve opened his eyes, he had a little headache. He checked the clock; it was 11:15. Becky continued to sleep. He got up, went into the kitchen, and put on a pot of coffee. He thought about yesterday—what a day! *Becky has the power!* He wondered whose power, if either, was the strongest. If they had an argument, he thought, it could get dangerous. He laughed.

Becky entered the kitchen. "I heard that laugh. What's so funny?"

"I was just thinking with the power we both have, if we had a fight things could get a little dangerous."

She frowned. "And you think that's funny?"

"Right now I think everything is funny."

She paused and then said, "Maybe you're right. Everything is funny, not to mention unbelievable. But we have to get serious. There must be a way to find out why we have this power."

"I've thought a lot about that and have come up with nothing. I think the reason will eventually become apparent. I have a slight headache. Do you?"

"Just a little one. Nothing a cup of coffee won't cure."

He poured two cups of coffee and said, "Hey, what's today? Sunday? I have to contact Edwards."

"Why?"

"When I got your call about the two million I decided

to pay it. I called Edwards, told him what happened, and then we decided we were going to try and catch them somehow, but I should have the money ready just in case."

She smiled. "So you think I'm worth two million dollars?"

"At that price you're a bargain!"

She leaned over and kissed him. "You're beautiful, and you're mine!"

"Yes, and you're mine! Should I call him or email him?"

"Email. Then you can carefully choose your words."

"Good thinking, but I have to come up with an explanation that keeps the fact that you got the force a secret. How about saying the gang went out on Saturday night, you got free, and you got hold of your cell phone, called me, and I came over to free you."

"But what about the fact that one guy was shot?"

"Hmm, that's a problem. We can say that during the struggle the gun got knocked loose, you picked it up, and shot one of the guys."

"That's good, but there's one more problem."

"Really, what's that?"

"The bedroom I was in was locked with a deadbolt. The way I got out of it was that I used the force to cut the deadbolt in half. If they have any brains they will wonder how in the hell I did that."

"I see, that is a problem. On the other hand it's cops who are going to see the room, not the CIA. Maybe they aren't smart enough to notice, or maybe they'll just think the lock was broken. Are there other bedrooms in the house?"

"Yes, I think there are two others, but they might not have deadbolt locks."

"I guess we should just keep our fingers crossed and hope for the best."

He typed the email saying that Becky was free, explaining the situation in detail, and giving him the address of the incident.

Steve said, "That takes care of that. Well, it's Sunday afternoon. What shall we do?"

After thinking a minute she said, "Why not just show me around your property? I haven't really seen the entire two acres."

"Good idea." They took a little tour. They even climbed up on the wall and walked around to see the surrounding territory. After the tour they went back into the house.

She said, "This is a neat place. If you want seclusion, you got it!"

Steve checked his email and saw one from Hanson. They both read the email, which said the Democratic Party would like him to attend a meeting next Saturday at 7:30 pm. He was given the address.

Steve said, "God, I'm getting more and more political. Should I go? Should we go?"

"Why not? It sounds like fun. We can go separately and make believe we don't know each other."

"All right, let's do it."

"Hey, you were going to teach me how to play the game of Go."

"Yeah, I remember. It's normally played on a

nineteen-by-nineteen board, which, I think, is way too big. Another size is thirteen by thirteen, which is much better, but for learning a normal chessboard of nine by nine is good."

"What? A chessboard is eight by eight, not nine by nine."

"Go is played on the intersections of the lines, not the spaces."

She thought for a few seconds. "Lines? Oh, I see. That's interesting."

He got some checkers out to serve as go stones. He taught her the rules, and they spent the rest of the day studying and playing Go.

"Wow, that was fun. It's an interesting game. Do you have any books on it?"

"Yes, I have a few. I can give you a beginners' book. Hey, it's around 5 o'clock, let's check the news."

He turned on the TV news.

"Scientists from Near Earth Asteroid Tracking, NEAT, have noticed a large object, apparently an asteroid, that seems to be heading toward Earth. It is still a long way off and will continue to be studied.

"In local news, police received an anonymous tip about a house containing three dead men. When they entered, police found the bodies of gangsters Jake and Vic Ford and Nick Anderson. The three men were wanted for kidnapping, robbery, and murder, and the FBI had offered rewards of two hundred thousand dollars each for information leading to the arrest of the men. One was shot, and the other two were bludgeoned to death. Police have no suspects for the three killings and are investigating ties to gang warfare."

Becky said, "Wow, *gangsters* was the right word! Do you think the CIA will tell the FBI that they should give us the reward?"

"I hope not. Maybe I should contact Edwards again and tell him to keep it quiet."

"It's interesting that my boyfriend has so much money he can turn down six hundred thousand dollars."

He just stared straight ahead without looking at her. Then he shook his head and said, "We don't need any more money, and we don't need any more notoriety. We have too much of both already."

She nodded in agreement and then said, "By the way, I need to go shopping for some clothes and food."

"Do you need any money?"

"Yes. Those guys took my money but luckily left everything else."

"I guess you didn't think about getting it back, which is understandable. How much did they get?"

"I think it was around eighty dollars."

"Small change." He picked up the briefcase he'd received from John and opened it. "Please don't spend any more than what's in this briefcase."

She laughed and pulled out two hundred-dollar bills. "Okay, I promise. Say, do you have an extra remote so I don't have to ring the bell to get into this place?"

"Oh, sure. I forgot all about that." He opened a desk drawer and took out a remote and a key.

"Here's a key to the house. The remote works for the garage door as well as the gate. The left button is the gate, and the right button is the garage. The key works on all the doors in the house, inside and out."

She accepted the remote and key and said, "My car is over at Safeway where the gangsters grabbed me. I'll need a ride there."

"All right, let's go."

He drove her to the Safeway lot.

"Thanks. I still have to go to work tomorrow. Let's have our dinner next Friday. I'll see you then if not sooner."

"Okay, bye."

As he left the lot he thought briefly about her safety but then remembered she had the power now. He laughed and shook his head; she could always maintain her own safety.

Over the next few weeks Steve was flooded with emails. Some people loved his ideas, some wanted him to be president, some Christians asked if God had sent him, some others asked if Satan had sent him. He wondered how his email address had got out. Perhaps people from the newspaper had let it be known. He thought maybe he should get a new one.

Over the next few months Steve's ideas becomes more and more popular. All blue states and many red states implemented free health care and free education through community college, and most considered modifying their minimum wage. Almost all states legalized the recreational use of marijuana. Many legalized other formerly illegal drugs. Steve wondered if the reason for it was that state politicians felt threatened by his power. Surveys indicated that most people considered him sent by God or some superpower. A minority considered him an agent of Satan.

January 7, 2020

The federal government, pressured by the states, passed new laws. Congress passed free health care for all citizens. The Department of Education lobbied to make all education free. Congress agreed, and a bill for free education through community college was approved by both houses. A more progressive tax system was instituted, with the rich paying a higher share.

The recreational use of marijuana was no longer a federal crime. Other drugs were also made legal and taxed in a manner similar to alcohol and cigarettes. The red states who resisted were forced by federal law to comply. Taxes were raised. The majority of the people seemed to be happy to trade money for security and free education. Steve and Becky were surprised but very pleased. Pressure was also being put on the government to change the age requirement for becoming president to twenty-five.

CHAPTER 38

FLIGHT?

9:00 a.m., Wednesday, March 4, 2020.

Steve thought about the strength of his power. How could he measure it? While he was pondering that, his phone rang.

"Hi, Steve. This is Bert."

"Hi, Bert. Nice to hear your voice. How are you?"

"I'm fine, but something suddenly occurred to me. Have you ever tried to use the force to lift yourself up?"

"Lift myself up? No, I'd never even thought of it. I guess I can try it right now. Wait a minute, and I'll try it."

Steve put the phone down, moved into a clear space in his living room, and applied the force to himself. He moved himself a foot off the floor. His eyes widened, and he shook his head in shocked disbelief.

He got back on the phone. "I can't believe it, Bert—I actually lifted myself up about a foot."

"Wow, that's amazing! The next question is how far can you lift yourself, and can you move yourself around. Try moving yourself around the house."

"Okay, let me experiment and call you back."

Steve hung up and tried moving himself around. He raised himself about a foot again and moved himself from room to room. He experimented with speed and found that he could speed up and slow down. He decided to go outside and continue experimenting.

Outside he lifted himself up above the roof of his house and looked around. He then lowered himself immediately to about three feet and moved himself around the property. He was surprised at how fast he could go. He decided to check his speed. He paced off a distance and estimated it at about four hundred feet. Then, using a stopwatch, he timed himself and found that he made it across in six seconds. That was about sixty-seven feet per second. He went inside and got out his calculator. He'd traveled at forty-five miles per hour, but that was an average. He must have gone at least sixty miles per hour in the middle of the yard, and he could probably go faster than that. He could actually fly!

He sat down and stared at the wall. He got up, went to the kitchen, opened the fridge, got out a beer, and took a few swallows, then a few more.

He called Bert. "Bert, I can't believe it. I can fly!"

"Holy smoke, or should I say *holy hell!* You're like Superman. In fact, you're better. Superman didn't have telekinetic powers as you do. How high can you lift yourself?"

"I lifted myself above my rooftop, but I came down as soon as I could since I didn't want any neighbors to see me. Then I did an experiment."

"Really? What did you do?"

Steve told him what he had done and calculated.

"Wow! I wonder what your top speed is."

"I have no idea. How the hell am I going use flying to do anything? I have to think about all this."

Steve hung up. He couldn't believe the state of affairs. *What the hell will happen next?*

Becky decided she had to check her powers. She went out to Grant Ranch, a large area where she had hiked in the past. She hiked to a desolate area and experimented. She picked out a large boulder three feet in diameter, and to her surprise she could lift it. She could move things about one mile away. She could pick up the boulder from about a quarter of a mile away, but it was harder.

Suddenly she wondered if she could pick herself up. She tried, and she lifted herself. She shook her head in amazement. She found a secluded field and experimented some more, moving herself around at various speeds. Wow—she could actually fly! She really couldn't believe it. She wondered if Steve had discovered he could fly. If he had, he might not tell her, but perhaps he'd realize that she might discover it on her own. How would she bring the subject up? She decided to just wait and see.

She went home, opened a beer, and sat down to think. How was all this possible? *If there is a godlike power behind it all, why would I need to be able to fly? Is it some kind of joke?* She shrugged and decided to check the news.

She learned that demand for Steve to be president was very high. She also heard about the asteroid.

Steve checked the news. "Scientists from Near Earth Asteroid Tracking, NEAT, continue to study the asteroid. It is quite large. It seems to be in Earth's orbit around the sun but moving in the opposite direction as Earth. It's possible that it's not an asteroid but some kind of satellite."

Steve frowned and wondered what it could be. The news continued.

"We reported recently about a week-long demonstration by a large group of people gathered in Washington DC to protest the decision not to change the age requirement for holding the office of president. Nationwide opinion polls show that a wide majority of voters want Steve Thomas to be president. Today, Congress held the required constitutional convention and passed a constitutional amendment to lower the age to twenty-five. The president signed it into law."

Steve realized he was getting more and more support to run for president. He had to make a decision: should he run? The social pressure was strong and couldn't be ignored. What should he do?

The phone rang; it was Becky.

"Hello, handsome, how are you?"

"I'm good. Have you checked the news lately?"

"Yes. They want you for president. What are you going to do?"

"I don't know. Let's talk about it. Come on over."

Becky arrived, and they hugged.

Neither said a word for a few moments. Steve thought about the fact that he could fly. If she could too, would she bring it up?

Finally she said, "Have you discovered anything new lately?"

He looked at her suspiciously and said, "How come you used the word *discovered*? It seems like you think there might be something unusual."

Her eyes widened briefly, and then she looked down, blushing slightly. Finally she said, "Maybe that was a poor choice of words. I used it because *I* have discovered something. Do you want to guess what it is?"

Steve stared at her. "Is it something very significant?"

"Yes, it is, *very!*"

Then he knew. "You can fly!"

She grinned. "You know that because you can do it too, right?"

"Yes, I was worried about whether I should tell you, but now that problem is solved."

"How did you discover it?"

"I'm ashamed to admit that it was Bert's idea to see if I could lift myself up. How about you—how did you discover it?"

"I went out to Grant Ranch so I could be alone in a

big space to experiment with my powers. It just suddenly occurred to me to try and pick myself up."

"Congratulations—you have a better imagination than I."

"Thanks, but that's neither here nor there. What the hell do we do now? How do we use it?"

"I say we just leave it to providence, like the force itself. It's just part of the puzzle. One thing I wonder about is whether John can do it. I think I should call him. We should also tell him that you have the power."

Becky nodded and said, "I'd like to meet him. Why not call him and invite him over?"

"All right, but not here. Let's meet at the condo." He called John and invited him over to the condo. Steve and Becky went there, and they met.

John and Becky greeted each other rather formally. They opened three cans of beer.

They told John about the kidnapping and that Becky had the telekinetic power as well. He seemed very surprised but pleased.

Steve finally said, "John, have you discovered anything new lately?"

John stared at him. "The way you ask that suggests *you* may have discovered something. Did you?"

"Yes. Did you?"

"Let's cut the nonsense. Yes, I discovered I can fly. Can you?"

"Yes. It looks like we each discovered it independently."

John smiled. "I'm glad that's out in the open. What the hell do we do now? Go flying together?"

They all laughed. "Becky and I agree that it's all part of the plan of providence. We do nothing. Keep it quiet until necessary."

John said, "I agree."

They sat there sipping their beer, each in their own thoughts.

John finally said, "Steve, the public wants you to run for president. Are you going to go for it?"

"I don't know what I should do. What do you think?"

"I think God, or whoever is up there, wants you to do it." Pointing to Becky, he said, "You can put us two on your cabinet."

Steve smiled and shook his head. "I don't know about that. But I think you're right. What do you think, Beck?"

"Yes, go for it!"

"Okay, the decision is made! It must be part of the great plan."

Becky said, "*The Great Plan*, I like that. The great plan of providence."

C H A P T E R   3 9

THE ASTEROID?

Thursday, September 10

Scientists at NEAT, who had been studying the approaching object for months, announced that it was not an asteroid. It was cylindrical, with a diameter of about four hundred meters and a length of about fifteen hundred meters. They believed it was actually a spaceship. It was headed directly toward Earth.

Governments around the world reacted with worry, and the developed countries, led by the United States and Russia, started to increase their military readiness for possible conflict.

Thursday, October 15

Scientists now definitely called it a spaceship, and it was orbiting Earth and slowing down. It appeared to be seeking a geo-stationary orbit. People were alarmed, and some people called for the military to shoot it down. The leaders of the world said absolutely not, as it might be peaceful.

Tuesday, October 20

The spaceship parked itself over Washington, DC. Congress and the president agreed to postpone the coming presidential election. The military was on full alert. Many residents of Washington began leaving out of fear of an invasion by aliens. Many aspects of the economy had already come to a halt over the past week. People were no longer buying houses, cars, appliances, or any other large items, just food and essentials.

It occurred to Steve that he might be needed and would probably be asked to go to Washington. He called Becky and John, and John came over to the condo.

Steve said, "My god, aliens from outer space. What are those old movies about aliens—*E.T., Close Encounters,* what else?"

John said, "*2001: A Space Odyssey, Alien.* I saw those while I was in prison."

Becky arrived and said, "My god, visitors from outer space. What's the latest news?"

"The ship is just sitting there high up over the White House. They must know a lot about us, like we're the most powerful country. And they must have known the location of the capital. I'm willing to bet that the government will ask me to come to Washington. If so, I think we should all go."

John said, "I'm still essentially a wanted criminal. Maybe I shouldn't go."

"You've grown a beard, and the longer hair makes a difference, too. With dark glasses and a hat, they probably won't recognize you. Besides, with your power, not to mention ours, what the hell can they do? Even if they did recognize you, they'd probably conclude that you are more valuable free than in prison."

"Okay, you're right. I guess I'll tag along if they call."

Nothing happened for the next two days except that the military had trained its large guns on the alien ship.

Government leaders, alarmed at the potential for disaster, decided to have Steve Thomas come to Washington. Since Vice President Andrew Charles had dealt with him in the past, he was asked to contact Thomas.

Thursday, October 22

Steve was at home relaxing over a cup of coffee when the telephone rang.

"Hello, is this Steven Thomas?"

"Yes, it is."

"Steven, this is Vice President Andrew Charles."

"Yes, sir. I thought you might call. How are you?"

"I'm fine right now. Have you been keeping up with the news?"

"Yes, and it is alarming. What's going on?"

"Well, the visitors seem peaceful, but one never knows. The president would like you to come to Washington in case you are needed."

Steve remembered the last time he'd been needed. This

one was obviously much more important. "Yes, I can come. Can I bring my girlfriend and another friend?"

"Certainly. If it is not too short a notice, Anthony Wallace can pick you up as before. He can come by tomorrow around nine a.m. He'll call you first."

"Yes, I remember Tony. We'll be ready."

Steve hung up.

Steve immediately called John and Becky and asked them if they could pack a bag and come over the next day at nine. They agreed.

Steve packed a bag. Becky and John appeared the next day before nine. At 9:30 the phone rang.

"Hello, Steve. This is Tony. Are you ready to go?"

"Yes. You know that there are three of us, right?"

"Yes, I do. I'll be there in about thirty minutes."

Tony arrived, and Steve introduced Becky and John. He drove them to the airport in an SUV, and they boarded a plane and took off.

Steve said, "Tony, it's been a while. How are you?"

"I'm good. I've been promoted to second in command on the west coast."

"Hey, that's great! Congratulations."

They discussed old times. Tony mentioned the kidnapping of Becky. "It was amazing that she got loose and was able to call you. I guess those guys were not too good at tying knots."

Steve hesitated, thinking about what had really happened. Finally he said, "Yes, they were a little sloppy."

9:00 a.m., Saturday, October 24

A smaller ship left the large mother vessel. As it neared the city one could see a large sign on the front. It said PEACE. People hugged one another and shook hands in happiness. The ship was about the size of a large bus, with four cylinders, one on each corner, that seemed to be forcing air downward in helicopter fashion. It floated down to land on the center of the south lawn of the White House. No one got out.

The police and the marines cordoned off a large circle around the entire lawn. The press was busy taking pictures and capturing video.

After an hour went by with no activity, the president decided to use the public address system to talk to the vehicle.

"Hello. Welcome to the United States of America. We are very happy that you come in peace and are pleased that you know something of our language. My name is Gerald Brown. I am the president of this country, and we would like to meet you and find out more about you. We believe you would like to do the same with us. Please let us know who you are and from where you come. We will be happy to provide for any needs that you have. Please make yourself known to us. Thank you."

After about fifteen minutes a voice from the ship boomed out, "Thank you for your peaceful reception. We have been studying your radio signals for some time and have learned your language. We look very similar to you except that we are quite a bit taller. Our average height is 7.2 of your feet, or 2.2 meters, so please do not be alarmed when you see us. We would like to meet with you and your leaders. Perhaps you can provide a vehicle to take us into your building."

The president thought, *Wow, seven feet tall!* He got back on the loudspeaker system. "We can certainly do that. Please allow us a little time to make preparations. How many individuals will be visiting, and by what name or title would you like to be addressed?"

The voice responded, "There will be five of us. You can call me Omar."

The historic conversation between the US president and the visiting aliens was captured by all the TV and radio crews crowded around the White House and broadcast live around the world.

Knowing that he was speaking not only to his own citizens but to virtually everyone on the planet, the president then said, "This is probably the most important event in the history of the world. We have the opportunity to learn about life in other parts of the universe and to perhaps increase our knowledge of science and technology. The aliens come in peace, and we should give them a friendly reception. Let us all be friendly toward them."

THE ALIENS COME

The welcoming committee sat in a large room. In the front were five large chairs facing the committee for the visitors. The group consisted of the president, vice president, several cabinet members, including the Secretaries of State and Defense, and a few high-ranking members of Congress. Richard Edwards of the CIA and Frank Dillon of the FBI were also present, as were several Secret Service agents. In the back of the room, well behind the committee, were about twenty marines. They wore bulletproof vests and were well armed, having their weapons hidden at their feet. The president, Tony had told them on the flight over, had been reluctant to have the aliens come to the White House without Steve being present and felt more comfortable knowing that Steve was there.

A large limo approached the shuttle, and five aliens emerged from the ship and walked up to it. They wore rather bulky coats that could possibly conceal weapons and hats that looked a little like helmets. The hats had a strange peak that looked like it could be pulled down to cover the eyes. Other than being indeed tall, the aliens looked like humans, except they had only four fingers on each hand. They boarded the limo and were taken to the entrance of the White House.

Within minutes, the five aliens had entered the meeting room. They introduced themselves and thanked the audience profusely. They were given seats in front of the hall.

Finally the president said, "Can you tell us who you are and why you came here?"

Omar got up and said, "We are from a planetary system in your galaxy, which of course is also our galaxy. We estimate that our civilization and technological progress is about two thousand years ahead of yours. We have been exploring space for a long time, say five hundred of your years. We came here on a self-sufficient vehicle that you might call a *planetoid*. It provides all the food, including protein, we need. It also provides fuel. Our vehicle is currently parked in essentially the same orbit as Earth on the other side of the sun. The planetoid's gravitational effects on the movement of objects in your solar system are too small to be detected. We have been there for about thirty years and during that time have been monitoring your radio waves. We are pleased with your fairly recent technological progress but not pleased with your political problems. We have chosen your country to visit because we found that you are the most powerful country on your planet. We can help you solve your problems. In exchange, we would like you to provide a space for us to live."

Steve, Becky, and John listened carefully to his speech. They also noticed the aliens' hands, which had three fingers and a thumb.

Steve whispered to Becky and John, "I wonder if their number system is of base eight."

Becky whispered back, "There's absolutely no reason why it would be ten, that's for sure."

John nodded. "Oh, I see. Ours is ten because of our hands, right?"

Steve looked at John, thinking of his naïveté, and suspected Becky was probably doing the same. He finally said, "Yes. I guess you have to be a math or computer type to realize that."

"Well, sorry for my ignorance. You're way ahead of me education-wise, but I'm going to try and catch up."

Steve smiled at him. "We have confidence that you'll make it."

Then John said, "Don't you think we should formulate some kind of plan in case of trouble from the aliens?"

Steve looked at him and then Becky. "I think you're right. The worst case is if they pull out weapons. If that happens we can try to disarm them. Let's call that phase one. If that fails, in phase two we should use the force directly to attack, punching them in their heads and bodies with it. Hopefully, though, they are peaceful, and none of that will be necessary."

The president gasped in surprise at Omar's request for space. He turned and whispered to the small group around him and then turned back and said, "It seems you are planning to move into this country. Is that right?"

At that comment Omar frowned and appeared angry, but he quickly smiled and said, "Yes, your planet is very plentiful, and we would like to live here."

Just then Richard Edwards from the CIA spoke up. "How many people are we talking about?"

Omar again frowned, appearing even more irritated. "About one thousand to start."

Edwards continued, "How many are on your planetoid ship?"

Omar squinted, acting like the question annoyed him. "Let us say twenty thousand."

Becky said to Steve, "He doesn't seem very friendly, does he?"

"No, I detect trouble!"

The president continued, "And you want that many to come to Earth?"

"Well, not quite all. We will keep about one thousand in our planetoid and other ships."

"So how large a space do you think you will need?"

"We are thinking of maybe eight or ten square miles. Maybe a small island or space in a remote spot in your country."

At that point the president whispered again with his small group, which included Edwards. Finally he said, "Thank you for your questions, Richard. Omar, it will take us some time for us to consider your request. At this time we ask that you return to your ship."

Omar said, "Can't you provide us with a place to stay while you decide?"

The president glanced at the others in the group, most of whom shook their heads. "I'm afraid not. The decision is an important one and will take time. We prefer that you leave."

Omar rose, signaling for the others in his group to do the same. They stood up, pulled down the peaks from their caps and simultaneously pulled out weapons that looked like guns. Their hats were definitely helmets. Members of the government hit the floor. It was clear they had been briefed on this possible situation and were getting out of the way so the marines in the rear could shoot if necessary. Secret service agents immediately moved in front of the president and vice president and drew guns.

"I'm afraid you have no choice. We are staying, and you should consider yourselves hostages."

The marines pulled out their weapons, and both sides opened fire, the alien weapons appearing to shoot some kind of laser rather than bullets. Several marines were hit; the remainder ducked behind protection in the back and continued to fire. Bullets appeared to have no effect on the aliens, however. The marines, obviously realizing this, stopped shooting.

"As you can see we are not affected by your weapons."

Omar then pulled out a device resembling a cell phone and made a call. People watching the large mother ship observed two other small ships leaving, and at the same time more aliens emerged from the ship on the ground.

Steve's head jerked back in surprise. Becky grabbed his arm, and John said, "This is it! We act!" Steve glanced at Tony, who signaled the go-ahead.

Steve said, "Looks like we're needed! John, remember Ed's place, when we disarmed those guys?"

"Yes, we repeat that here—phase one!"

"Right, what we do is grab their weapons. Becky, from what you told me about your kidnapping you seem to know how to grab a gun."

"Yes, it was easy. I can handle it."

"I don't know if our force field can stop laser fire, but if we act fast we can disarm them before they fire. We proceed slowly from three sides. Becky, you take the right, John, you the left, I'll take the center. If it works, bring the weapons that you grab to yourself. We may be able to use them later. We enter slowly so as not to make them suspicious. When I raise my left hand, do it immediately! Disarm the ones nearest you. Ready? Good luck, though I hope we don't need it. Let's go!"

Omar said, "We have reinforcements arriving, so you have no hope."

The telekinetic group entered the room simultaneously and slowly. Steve quickly raised his left hand, and in the next instant the alien weapons all flew out of their owners' hands. Steve, Becky, and John each caught one, and the other two weapons landed on the floor in front of them. Omar and his group looked shocked.

Edwards stood up. "You see, Omar, we are not as backward as you may think. We have learned the power of telekinesis, mind over matter, and we order you to leave."

Just then several new aliens entered the room with guns drawn. With one of the laser weapons, Steve pulled the trigger and fired, hitting an alien, who fell. Becky shot at another one, who also fell. The third one, obviously realizing they were defeated, rushed out.

Omar pulled out his phone and seemed to be giving an order. He then said to the group of government officials on the floor, "We are beaten. We will return to our ship. We apologize for our action, but we were desperate." Then the five of them filed out of the room, taking their dead and wounded comrades with them. They walked to their small ship, got aboard, and left. The small ship took off and headed back to the main one. The two other small ships that had been headed for Earth turned around and returned to the mother ship. The main spaceship remained over Washington for about fifteen minutes but then left.

Many of the committee members present shouted for joy, shaking Steve's hand and hugging him.

Steve looked at Becky and John. "It's now clear why we have this power—to save Earth from an alien attack!"

Becky replied, "Yes, it seems so. It seems we didn't need to fly. That unsolved problem still exists."

C H A P T E R 4 1

PEACE

There was some worry that the aliens might return, and there was talk about sending a ship to the other side of the sun to see if they were still there. It was decided to wait a few months. Steve, however, was sure that the shock of humans having telekinesis has rocked the aliens' confidence.

Steve and Becky decided to marry. They did it quietly in the Unitarian Church in San Francisco. Bert and John were their witnesses. After several months the presidential election proceeded, and Steve Thomas was elected president.

Becky became pregnant.

Steve said, "We have to think of a name for him or her."

She said, "I'm against naming boys after the father. How about you?"

"I agree. It's too egotistical. I like Susan for a girl."

"I like Michael for a boy."

"Okay, that settles that."

About nine months later a son was born. The economy was booming. Then, a year later, a daughter was born. About two years went by, and Steve was elected president for a second term. They found that their son was very bright and their daughter was not far behind.

Then one day little Mike said, "Mommy, look what I can do. See that teddy bear over there on the couch?"

Becky watched as the teddy bear rose and floated across the room into his hand.